Lullaby for Leo

A NOVEL OF DISCOVERY AND FORGIVENESS

By Michael March

HELLGATE PRESS

ASHLAND, OR

Lullaby for Leo
2021 MICHAEL MARCH
Published by Hellgate Press
(An imprint of L&R Publishing, LLC)

Hellgate Press
PO Box 3531
Ashland, OR 97520
www.hellgatepress.com
Interior design: Sasha Kincaid
Cover design: George Deyo
ISBN: 978-1-954163-22-5
Printed and bound in the United States
10 9 8 7 6 5 4 3 2 1

IV LULLABY FOR LEO

1

November 12, 1971, 8:08 A.M.
Outskirts of An Khe, South Vietnam.

Tuning out the musical mating calls of the white-cheeked gibbons and the shrill warbles of the Asian barbets, Leo runs his hand over the sweat oozing from his brow and scans the jungle's dense greenery. The fireteam leader cradles his M-16 and, adjusting the straps on his rucksack, hops over a pool of water below the stand of mangroves and hustles the twenty meters to join his point man. The NCO drops to one knee behind a clump of thick brush and smacks at the mosquitos buzzing around his ear. "Okay, Rip. What you got?" His voice is a hoarse whisper.

"Dinks, sarge." Corporal Ripton aims an index finger at the hut, half a football field north of their position. "I saw Victor Charlies. Three of them cut across the field and ran inside the school."

Leo's facial muscles tighten. "Any sign there might be more?"

"I didn't see any, but you know Charlie. Where there's one, there might be a regiment of those sneaky bastards."

"Yeah. Well, let's hope not. Listen. Follow me. We'll stay under cover and check out the trail on the right flank. Let's see what we're dealing with."

His plan becomes moot as a spatter of automatic weapons fire erupts from the front window. The rounds kick up dirt around Leo and Rip's position. Both men flop on their bellies. Each aims their M-16 and fires off a short burst at the muzzle flashes.

"Come on. Let's pull back," Leo orders. "Follow me. Stay low."

Rip reloads a magazine and raises to one knee. "Gotcha, sarge."

The two men race toward the tree line, zigzagging as they run.

The squad members drop to the ground and lay down cover fire. Carter unfolds the M-60's bipod feet and falls on his belly. Flipping the machine gun's safety into the "F" position, he squeezes the trigger and replies with accuracy.

Blake lifts the M79 launcher. He adjusts his rangefinder and fires a high-explosive round. The thump of "Big Ed" is a reassuring sound to him and his fellow grunts. The grenade sails toward its target and explodes at the base of the schoolhouse wall, blowing out large pieces of straw, wood, and dried mud. The grenadier digs into a front pocket on his nylon vest, loads another round, aims, and fires. The rocket arcs skyward and impacts below the window, ripping away another section. The enemy fire stops.

"Fire off some Goddam smoke," Leo shouts, unhitching his rucksack. "Ripton, Caswell, drop your packs. You're with me."

Blake flips open the breach of his weapon, loads another 40mm projectile, and fires. The missile lands a few feet short of the school. The white smoke wafts in the gentle breeze and obscures the view of the one-story hut.

Leo throws out a hand. "Carter, cover us with the sixty. The rest of you spread out. Watch your interval and lay down support." He leaps up. "Come on, let's move."

Rip and Caswell take off and follow in a crouch. After a dozen steps, the three men leave the shelter of the jungle canopy and sprint across the open field.

Leo plucks a fragmentation grenade from his vest and pops the pin. "Watch it. Stay back." He lobs the explosive through the large cutout in the damaged wall. "Fire in the hole," he barks, forcing Rip and Caswell back a couple of steps with his outstretched arm.

The explosive discharge blows out another section of mud and straw bricks. Leo throws up a hand signal as the smoke disperses and leads Rip and Caswell to the building's edge. He crouches and peers around the corner. Two black pajama-clad VC are busy scrambling out of the side window. One's dripping blood from a shoulder wound.

Leo fires a burst from his M-16. His men empty their magazines.

••• ••• •••

Wednesday, March 17, 1972
Oakland, California. On-Time Transport Bus Terminal

The loud blast from the airhorn startles the uniformed veteran. His breaths come in short spurts as his deep-set brown eyes dart from side to side. He's searching for the elusive enemy, one he's left far behind in the jungles of Southeast Asia. He shudders and arches his back against the plastic chair. The older couple seated across from him avert their eyes when they catch him staring. Leo adjusts his gaze and focuses on counting the cracks in the slate grey wall around their heads. His eyes lock on the circular clock hanging above the chalkboard bus schedule. The time shows it's ten minutes short of noon.

Pinned to the left side of the oversized green jacket dangle Silver and Bronze Stars, a Purple Heart with oak leaf cluster, and an assortment of decorative military ribbons. Short a Good Conduct Medal, he's confused about too many things beyond his control. A civilian once again, the former combat soldier prays the constant ache in his forehead will fade with time, and the memories of what he's done in the name of God and country will cease haunting him.

Leo's pledged to stay positive. And why shouldn't he? Inside his jacket pocket sits a ticket to the San Francisco bus station. From there, he'll take the shuttle to the airport, grab a sandwich, and board the three o'clock flight home to Atlanta. Feeling somewhat better, he closes his eyes and tries to relax.

"Hey, you, Sergeant Dumbass."

Leo's muscles tense. His eyes spring open. A pimple-faced long-hair, his eyes hidden behind a dark pair of shades, stands over him.

"You proud of yourself, asshole?" says the buttinsky, pulling off his sunglasses. "Did you have a good time killing people? Any water buffalo?"

Leo clenches his jaw. "Screw off, turd." He scrambles to his feet and takes a step forward. "I ain't in any mood. I don't need your crap."

The barbershop reject slips on his glasses. "Oh, yeah. Right. I almost forgot. Your type loves violence."

The soldier balls his hands into fists. "I don't care what you think. Get the hell away from me, or I'll give you a beating you won't soon forget."

Caught off-guard, his adversary skips off in the direction of the soda machine with the "OUT OF ORDER" sign taped over the money slot.

Leo drops back into his seat and narrows his eyes. "Stupid idiot!" The veteran's survival instincts kick in as the peal of a bus horn shocks his senses. He rolls off the chair and straddles his duffle bag, fighting to gather his wits.

The pest hasn't taken the hint. "What's with you, psycho? Paranoid?"

"I'll show you who should be paranoid." Leaping forward, Leo presses his palm against the troublemaker's Adam's apple and forces him back two steps. "I've had enough of you. Get out of my face!"

Without a word, his tormentor turns tail and dashes past the newsstand and through the exit door.

"That's right, moron," Leo shouts. "Scram! Di di mau!"

A male voice rumbles through the box speaker hanging above the ticket counter: "The twelve-thirty to the San Francisco terminal will begin boarding in two minutes. Please proceed to Line C and have your ticket ready. Thank you for using On-Time Transportation."

••• ••• •••

They're fifteen minutes into the bus ride, and as far as Leo's concerned, the trip's already fourteen-and-a-half minutes too long. *Thank God it's only a forty-five-minute ride. These seat cushions smell like dog farts. I can't believe this damn driver has managed to find every pothole in the road, and bridge traffic sucks a big one.*

The chubby black woman in the aisle seat pokes him as she lifts her Baby Ruth and takes a bite. He tries to ignore her probing elbow, keeping his eyes riveted on the window.

An elbow jabs him again. “Hey, will ya stay on your side of the seat, please?” Leo grumbles, avoiding eye contact. “You keep poking me.”

The woman gives him the once over. “Hmm. Sorry, soldier boy. Didn’t mean to hassle you.” Her eyes settle on his military decorations. “You some kinda war hero or something?” she says, gobbling down the rest of her candy bar and serenading all within earshot with a short series of staccato belches. Her seat cushion moans in protest as she swivels her heavy bottom and digs a hand into her bag.

Leo detects the sound of air escaping from between her butt-cheeks and wrinkles his nose as she rips apart the wrapper of a York Peppermint Patty and swallows the circular piece of chocolate in one bite.

He turns toward the window and catches a squad of Hell’s Angels heading in the opposite direction, rumble past. The Harleys shoot by too quickly for him to get a good look.

The olive drab of the military convoy following behind the choppers sends chills through his body. The sight rekindles painful memories. Leo leans back in his seat and shuts his eyes, but there’s no escape. The vivid imagery of that day with the 196th Light Infantry Brigade takes control once again. He tries to block out the day at the schoolhouse, but there’s no escaping the past. As he falls asleep, he finds himself back in the jungles of the Central Highlands.

••• ••• •••

A pain in his right calf gives Leo a reprieve from the unrelenting nightmare. The thanks this time belong to the oversized passenger next to him.

He glares at her. “What the hell’s wrong with you? You kicked me. Stay on *your* side. I don’t need any hassles.”

“Sorry, general. I didn’t know you were so touchy. You ever hear of an accident?” She slides a cherry Lifesaver into her mouth and breaks it apart with her molars.

It takes extra effort for Leo to corral his emotions. "Jeez. You need to get it together. Didn't your mother teach you manners?" He shoves both his trembling hands beneath his thighs and grits his teeth.

"I don't need the likes of you teaching me anything," she huffs and turns away.

The bus slows, turns right, and inches forward. A baritone voice overrides the hiss of the airbrakes. "Ladies and gentlemen, this is your driver. We're about to arrive at the San Francisco, On-Time terminal. Please, collect all your belongings and prepare to exit. Thank you for letting us get you to your destination on time."

Leo lets out a sigh as his attention shifts to grabbing the shuttle and then boarding the long flight home.

2

Friday, August 17, 2012, 6:39 P.M.
The Rectory, Birmingham, Alabama

The pert brunette smacks her lips as the icy-cold blend of crimson liquid, spiced with Texas Tequila, hits the roof of her mouth and burbles into her stomach. Lisa winces and places her glass on the table. Brain freeze has found another victim. She presses a thumb and forefinger over her left eye and rocks back and forth. Slowly, the painful sensation recedes.

The young woman lifts her drink and runs the tip of her tongue around the rim. Her lips pucker as the salt rolls across her taste buds. "Ah. That's more like it," she says, blowing a tuft of out-of-place brown hair from in front of her eye. The slightly intoxicated bar patron points at her half-empty glass and throttles back against the black upholstery. "This drink is mighty tasty, Mags. Now I can relax a little."

Her friend takes a long gulp of her frozen Daiquiri and lifts out the lone strawberry floating at the top of her glass. The cone-shaped fruit disappears between her bright red lips.

Lisa licks the edge of her glass. "It's been a rough week at the paper, don't you think?"

Maggie wiggles an eyebrow and plucks the strawberry stem from her mouth. "Feels like any other week to me. I'm happy anytime that automatic deposit shows up in my checking account."

"You're crazy, girl. My feature article on corruption within the city council took me way longer to finish than I originally imagined. Thank God, it's done and awaits my editor's approval."

Her companion's oblivious to Lisa's comments. She's enthralled with the action on one of the Plasma televisions hanging over the bar. On-screen, a large man with a bright red beard, horses a fat blue finned tuna into his boat. Blood splashes on the fisherman's legs as the enormous fish rolls around on the deck and fights for survival. Maggie loses interest when two male patrons stroll into the restaurant. She keeps an eye on them as they find a table.

"Are you paying attention to me, Maggie?" Lisa asks.

Her girlfriend gives her a quick wink. "I'm a bit distracted. Go ahead."

"I know I should be happy. I have a plum assignment with the city desk, but I don't know if I can keep this up. I'm tired of trying to find dirt on city officials and spitting out articles exposing crooked food inspectors."

Maggie drains the rest of her drink and pats her sternum with the tips of her red-tipped fingernails. "Don't be so touchy. The conspiracy theorists pay your bills." The slender blonde leans back and plays with her straw. "What about me? For six years, three days a week, I put out my Magical Maggie column. Don't you think I'm tired of the grind?" She giggles. "My readers would abandon me if they knew I've been through three marriages."

"You can count on me to keep your secret."

Maggie waves to the waitress. "Let's order something to eat. This rum makes me light-headed."

"Good idea." Lisa wraps her lips around the straw and slurps the crushed ice from the bottom of her glass. She pulls the slender piece of plastic from her mouth and licks the end. "What plans do you have this weekend?"

"I hope to work on some extracurriculars with Corey. I've got a couple of hours' worth of investigative journalism planned. With any luck, I'll get a couple of helpful tips for my column."

Lisa rubs her lobe and plays with her hoop earring. "Whoa. Sounds perverted when you put it like that."

"I hope so. I can use the exercise."

Lisa's face turns red. "You're so bad. Please, no more. You conjure up images I would prefer not to explore."

Maggie chuckles. "You're such a prude. I bet I know what you have planned." She sighs and plays with her straw. "You'll stay at home with your cat and watch television like you do every weekend. Right?"

"What's wrong with being a homebody? Molly loves me, and she's amazing company."

"If you say so, sweetie. I guess you forgot how good a guy is for relieving stress."

"I beg to differ, Mags. Men have a talent for injecting unwanted drama into your life. I know from experience." She sighs. "I've never gotten over my first and only love."

"From what you told me, you messed it up with Travis. Besides, you're looking at it all wrong. Certain types of drama can be highly romantic."

••• ••• •••

Lisa cradles her Smart Phone and listens as her mom's answering machine clicks on. "Hello. You've reached Enya. Sorry, I'm not home right now. Please leave your name, number, and a short message. I'll call you back as soon as I can."

"Hmm, strange," she announces as she checks the time on her Seiko. *Where would mom be at this hour on a Friday night?*

Lisa has her mom's routine down pat. The senior Partainian should have her hair in rollers and relaxing on the couch, curled up with Patrick Jane, and a rerun of *The Mentalist.* The last time they spoke, her mom said she'd added *Silver Linings Playbook* to her to-do list. That must be it. Mystery solved.

Molly purrs as her mistress strokes the underside of her furry belly.

"She's gone to see a movie. Right, girl?" Lisa pushes the sizable grey and white cat from her lap and gets to her feet. "Come with me into the kitchen. I'll give you a treat."

The graceful feline chases after her owner, and catching up, bounces off Lisa's leg. Her slightly inebriated mistress, thrown off balance, manages to collect herself. "No, no, girl. You mustn't trip me."

She collects a small bag from the cupboard's center shelf and drops three Temptations Catnip treats on the cream-colored kitchen tiles. "Here you go. Enjoy them, you big hairy fur-ball."

The cat sniffs around and examines the small olive squares. Satisfied, Molly uses her sandpaper-like tongue to direct one into her mouth, then rolls onto her stomach and swats at the air.

Her mistress bends to check the water level in the shiny silver bowl. The melodic tones of her phone stop her short. Dropping the bag of treats on the kitchen counter, she strolls to the mahogany coffee table in the living room. Retrieving her cordless phone, she reads her brother's name and number on the display screen.

She wraps her fingers around the handset. "Hi, Jared. How are you, little brother?"

"Lisa, I left you a voicemail. Why didn't you call me back?"

"I must have missed it. Why? What's up?"

Jared doesn't say anything. Lisa can hear him crying.

"I have awful news, Sis. Please, sit down."

She tenses her body but remains standing. "Go ahead. Tell me. What's wrong?"

"It's Mom. There was a car crash. She's dead."

A tidal wave of panic washes over Lisa. "What? Impossible."

"I'm so sorry," he whimpers. "I wouldn't joke about such a thing. It's true. Mom's dead."

The phone falls from her hand. Lisa reaches for the box of tissues and collapses on the couch. She wipes her eyes and finds the phone between the cushions while Molly meows and trots to the corner of the room.

"Oh, my goodness. Sorry, Jared. I lost the phone for a minute. How did this happen?"

"Hit and run on Georgia 400 yesterday evening. Mom's body is at the morgue in North Fulton Hospital. Denise identified her remains and called me. That's all I know."

Lisa wipes her nose. "What do we do first?"

"I have the phone number for the funeral home we used for dad."

"Oh, my God. Oh, my God. Oh, my God..."

Her brother interrupts. "Lissie, get a grip. Can you take off a few days? There's plenty we'll need to straighten out. Would you meet me at the house?"

"Of course. I'll leave in the morning. Uh. I should be there around noon. I love you, Jared."

"I love you too, Sis. See you then."

Lisa reaches down and rubs Molly's neck. Her cat's eyelids flutter, then close.

3

Saturday, August 18
Alpharetta, GA.

She pilots her blue Prius along Windward Parkway. Molly relaxes on all fours in the passenger seat. A leather harness with a leash looped around the headrest restricts her movements.

"We're almost there, girl, another half mile."

The cat stands and laps at the water dispenser's spout that Lisa's taped to the inside of the door.

"Don't worry, baby, almost there."

The car turns left at Cogburn Road and takes another turn at Bethany Bend. Lisa's stomach churns. Her flow of tears gains in intensity. "I can't believe mom's dead, girl. It doesn't seem real."

The Norwegian Forest cat trills twice and tries to walk across the center console, but the leash won't allow her.

Her owner tickles the kitty's neck. "I know, I know. I love you too."

She makes a right and rolls into the driveway, parking next to the white SUV with Georgia plates. Her brother rushes from the house, his eyes red and puffy.

Lisa pushes open the car door and hops out. "Oh, Jared, how could this happen?" She yanks a tissue from her purse and blows her nose.

He throws his arms around her. "I know. It's hard to believe."

She points to her Toyota. "Please help me with Molly's stuff. They're on the floor in front."

"Sure, Lissie. Whatever you want."

Jared opens the passenger door as his sister climbs onto the driver's seat. She reaches across the center console and unhooks the cat's leash. "Come on, girl. Let's go inside."

Molly leaps onto the seat and rubs against her owner's face. Lisa cuddles her and backs out of the car. She walks to the side door of the house and throws down a black hair-tie—the gray and white feline dives for it.

••• ••• •••

Jared lifts his cell. "Hello, is this Barton's Mortuary?"

"Yes, it is." The baritone male voice has a distinctive Southern twang. "This is Beau Reddick. I'm the funeral director. How can I help you?"

"I'd like to arrange for my mother's cremation." Jared chokes up momentarily. "She's at the North Fulton Hospital morgue. We'd also like a memorial service."

"You have my deepest condolences. May I have the name of your loved one?"

"Yes, of course. My mom's name is Enya Partainian. My family has used your services before, for my dad, Malik, about three years ago."

Jared can hear the tap, tap, tap of fingers on a computer keyboard.

"Ah, yes, Malik Partainian. I found him in our database, September 12th, 2009. His wife bought the platinum package at the time. We can discuss the commemorative options when you come in. Meanwhile, I'll have her transported from the hospital. North Fulton, you said. Right?"

"Yes, North Fulton." Jared places his hand over the phone. "Lissie, we need to drive over to the funeral home. What time should I tell him?"

His sister wipes her eyes. "Whenever." She crumples the Kleenex and drops it into the plastic wastebasket. "We should head over there right now and take care of it. Don't you think?"

"Yes. I agree."

Jared lifts his hand from the receiver. "My sister and I will see you in about twenty minutes, Mister Reddick."

••• ••• •••

Monday, 12:30 P.M.

With the curtains tied back, the oversized stain-glass windows filter in the sunlight and cast colorful rainbow swirls on the far walls of the chapel. Rows of straight-back wooden chairs are arranged on either side of the red-carpeted center aisle and stand watch over the dozen floral arrangements surrounding a small circular table at the front of the chamber. A brass urn, with a mother of pearl band around its center, sits at the center of a white tablecloth. Within that molded container rest a few pounds of ashes, the remnants of Enya Partainian's earthly existence.

A framed eight-by-ten color picture of their mom, together with their dad, rests on the right side of the table. On the far left hangs an assortment of photos. They're pinned to a white background and organized chronologically. At the top left corner, there's Enya as a little girl. Next to it, an image of her as a teenager, then another taken at her wedding. The pictorial history continues with candid shots of Enya in various stages of adult life. Above the array, in black ink, appears scripted lettering: *To Live Your Life is to Accept and Cherish Love,* a phrase created by her daughter this morning.

Denise dabs at her tears as she reads the maxim. She gives Lisa a peck on the cheek. "Enya would have loved your sentiment. I think it's wonderful."

Lisa sniffles. "Thank you. I know how close you and mom were."

"For sure, friends since grade school. Both of us pledged for the Alpha Gamma sorority at Lassiter, and together, we attended Georgia State. We were each other's maids of honor." Denise bursts into tears. She wipes her eyes and falls into a chair beside her husband.

Lisa joins her brother amid the mass of bouquets and wreaths, semi-circling the table. The aromatic scent of lilies, orchids, and roses is unmistakable.

She takes another look at the photo collage. “Can you believe mom’s gone?”

“It’s rough.” Jared finishes examining the condolence cards included with the floral arrangements. He steps back and reaches for his sister’s hand. “I know how you feel. This never-ending nightmare is real for me too.”

“It’s much worse,” she sobs. “I feel like someone ripped out my heart. Mom was my best friend.” Lisa reaches for Jared’s shoulder.

He casts an arm around her waist. “We’ll get through this, Sis. Come on. Sit with me.”

“I’m okay. Yes, let's sit. We have a few minutes before the service.”

A middle-aged woman, flanked by a pair of men, signs the registry at the chapel entrance. When she finishes, they parade down the center aisle.

She takes Lisa’s hand. “Hi. I'm Alice Federstone. So sorry about your mom. I was in her Mahjong group. I’d like you to meet my husband, Alfred. This is our son, Teddy.”

The older man takes a step forward. “So sorry for your loss.”

Lisa nods. “Thank you for your kind wishes.”

Alfred offers a quick head bob in return. “Your welcome.”

Their son wears a solemn expression as he shakes Jared’s hand.

The Federstones turn and take seats in the third row.

“You know, Jared, we have virtually no family here in America. I think there are distant cousins in Armenia, but I'm not sure. Mom never talked much about it.” She twists around and surveys the half-filled rows of seats behind her. “Nice turnout.”

Lisa’s startled by a familiar voice.

“I’m so sorry to hear about your mother.”

She looks up to find a high school classmate and two other women standing in front of her. She bolts upright and embraces the speaker, a long-haired blonde wearing a grey checkered pantsuit. “Suzie, thank you for coming. How are you?”

Her friend flashes her wedding ring. “I’m fine. You know, I’ve married again, going on two years now. I hitched up with John Noyes. Do you remember him? Everyone called him Buzz in high school. His parents owned the pastry café on Shallowford. He’s expanded the business with his brother, and they’re doing quite well.”

"That's terrific. I'm so happy for you."

"Thanks." Suzie narrows her eyes. "Did you know Travis is back in town? I saw him last week at a charity event."

"Err…no. I didn't." She takes a deep breath and sighs. "Listen. We should meet for lunch once my mom's affairs straighten out. I miss you."

"I'd love that. I miss you too." Suzie pulls out her phone. "Give me your number, and I'll stick it in my cell."

"Great. It's 204-365-7091."

Lisa's friend taps the buttons on her keypad. "Check. I'll call you in the middle of the week, say Wednesday."

"Please. You better."

Suzie brings a hand to her forehead. "Oh, sorry. These are my cousins? They're visiting from Cincinnati." She extends a hand. "This is Mary and her twin, Janice. They're fraternal. Mary's older by twelve minutes. No one ever believes they're related."

Lisa makes a quick comparison. "No. I can see the resemblance." She hugs Janice, then her sister. "Thank you all for coming."

"You're welcome. I'll call you Wednesday morning," Suzie says, guiding her cousins toward the seats.

Beau, the funeral director, raps his knuckles on the wooden pedestal in the right corner of the room. A younger man with short brown hair and dressed in a black pinstriped suit stands next to him. "Ladies and gentlemen, may I please have your attention. Allow me to introduce you to Pastor Robert Goodman from the Church of the Universal Spirit." Beau shuffles to his right and surrenders his spot.

The crowd settles down.

Pastor Goodman steps to the podium. "Thank you, Director Reddick." He clears his throat. "My deepest condolences to Enya's children, Lisa and Jared. I've been friends with their mother for more than ten years. I knew Enya as a fine person who, without question, believed in the will of God and always put her friends and family before herself. She was a woman always ready to offer a helping hand. We're here today, not to mourn her loss, but to celebrate her life…"

Lisa's mind wanders. She's preoccupied with concerns regarding her mother's financial affairs. There's a bunch of paperwork and legal issues still to resolve. *Let's see now. I've contacted Social Security and canceled her insurance this morning. The duplicate key to the safe deposit box is in my bag, and I have joint access to mom's bank accounts. I'll call her attorney, Larry Dresden, this afternoon. What should Jared and I do with mom's belongings, and what about the house? I must think logically and work this all out.*

••• ••• •••

03: 27 P.M.

Lisa's rump rests at the corner of her mother's king-size bed. Two piles of letters sit on the comforter next to her. Her head jerks back involuntarily as she reads. "Oh, my God!" She drops the yellowed paper on the bed and seizes another. An excess of adrenaline pumps through her body. "Jared, get in here. You've got to look at these."

Footsteps echo throughout the hallway.

"Hurry up," she shouts. "You're not gonna believe this."

Her brother rushes into the room. "What's so important? I was stacking the extra set of dishes. The thrift shop's truck is coming by at five to pick them up."

Lisa holds out a paper. "Look at this. It's from a soldier in Vietnam."

Jared takes the letter from her and skims the first few lines. "No way. Sis, this is an old love note."

"I know. Right? There are dozens." She gestures at the papers on the bed. "They're from someone named Leo Miller. They date back to 1971 and 72. Who the hell is Leo Miller?"

Jared passes a hand through his long black hair. "I have no clue."

Lisa lifts her cell. "I'm going to call Denise. I'm sure she'll know."

4

5:45 P.M.

Denise's beige Dodge Caravan sits in front of the Partainian's green and white, two-story house. She adds a teaspoon of honey to her Juniper tea and stirs as Lisa pushes her chair away from the kitchen table and allows Molly to leap into her lap. The cat purrs as her mistress caresses her neck.

Jared points to the two stacks of papers on the table. "You were our mom's closest friend. Tell us about Leo. What went on between them?"

"It's no big mystery. Leo was a grade ahead of us in Lassiter."

The cat hops down as Lisa stands and lays her cup in the sink. "Why haven't we ever heard his name before? What happened to him?"

Denise plays with her spoon. "The Vietnam War happened. He and your mom were sweethearts during her sophomore and junior years. They cared a lot for each other." She takes a sip of tea. "Leo joined the Army after graduation. These are the letters he sent to your mom from overseas."

Jared sits up. "What happened between them?"

Lisa raises an eyebrow. "Something's weird here. I get the impression there's a lot more going on than meets the eye."

Denise tucks her elbows in toward her sides. "No, there's not. The story's quite simple. Leo spent three years in the Army. When he came home, he was all messed up." She shakes her head. "You're both too young. Back then, no one had any appreciation for the vets. The war in Vietnam ripped this society apart. It was a confusing time."

Lisa sits back down. “Come on now. I didn’t live through those times, but I’ve watched documentaries and learned about the war in history class.”

“Okay. Then you can imagine how the poor guy must have been.” Denise’s eyes widen. “His parents sent him to a counselor, but his problems only grew worse. Your mom finally couldn’t take it anymore. Their relationship hit a wall. He moved away. Florida, from what I recall.”

Lisa frowns. “Don’t you think it’s strange she saved his letters? Why didn’t she throw them out? I would have.”

“I don’t know. Your mom never talked much about him. She met your father right after that.”

Jared rubs his sister’s shoulder. “See, no big deal.”

Lisa loops her hand around and grips his. “I guess you’re right. No big deal.”

Denise checks her watch. “I have to go. Gotta get dinner ready.”

••• ••• •••

Tuesday, August 21, 8:53 A.M.

Lisa guides her Prius into the Bank of North Georgia’s parking lot and finds a spot in front of the entrance. She shuts off the car’s engine. “I’m nervous about this. What do you think we’ll find?”

“Stocks, bonds, probably jewelry.” Jared peeks at his watch. “We’ll know soon enough.”

She removes the key from the ignition. “It’s odd. I feel like I’m invading mom’s privacy. Still can’t believe she’s gone.”

“I know. I’m hurting too.”

The glass door to the bank opens. A young woman shuffles outside and presses her shoe against the door stopper. She smiles and waves politely.

Jared smiles back and opens his car door. “Let’s take care of this, Sis.”

Lisa sniffles. “Yeah, let's.”

••• ••• •••

Joyce Ritter meets Lisa and Jared outside her office door. "I'm so sorry for your loss. I was shocked when I heard the news." She reaches out and squeezes each of their hands. "I'm friends with someone in your mother's Mahjong circle. It's horrible. I heard it was a hit and run. Did they catch the other driver?"

Lisa grips her brother's arm. "You seem to know more about this than we do, Mrs. Ritter. We have an appointment with our family attorney later this morning. Hope he can fill us in on the details."

"Ooh, I'm so embarrassed. I thought you knew. And please, call me Joyce."

Lisa's face is expressionless. "No harm done, Joyce."

The banker points toward the teller cage. "Right this way. The safe deposit boxes are downstairs."

Jared offers Lisa his hand. "Holy Moses. A hit and run? How messed up?"

"Sure is. I hope we'll find out more from Mr. Dresden this afternoon."

••• ••• •••

The vault is well lit. From floor to ceiling, dozens of grey double-key lockboxes fill three walls of the small rectangular-shaped room. A door marked 321 hangs open. Its payload sits on the table at the center of the room.

Joyce slips the key into her jacket pocket. "I have some work to finish. I'll give you your privacy." She taps the outside of her hip and turns away.

"Thank you for your help." Lisa lifts the lid of her mom's box.

Jared squeezes next to his sister. "Buncha stuff in there."

"Yeah, I see." She lifts the clear Ziplock bag from the top of the stack. A stream of pearls and several other pieces of jewelry are visible inside. She lays it on the table and removes a manila envelope marked: "IMPORTANT PAPERS." Lisa opens the clasp and empties the contents on the table.

Jared digs into the box and finds a small leather pouch holding several gold coins. Next to it, there's a letter-sized packet of papers. He gasps, stunned by the printing across the front of the envelope. It reads: "LEO MILLER."

Lisa sorts through her documents. She finds the deed to the house, car title, a copy of her mom's will, U.S. Treasury bonds, and a portfolio of stock certificates. At the bottom are copies of their family's birth certificates, her dad's death record, and her parents' marital agreement.

She gawks at her parent's legal documents. "Jared! Look at the date on this."

Her brother's discovered a treasure trove of his own. "Sis, wait until you see what I've found."

Lisa ignores him. She thrusts the paper in his face and points to the lower right section of the State of Georgia, Fulton County marriage license. "Please, Jared. You've got to see this. The date is February 11th, 1974. I was born on September 11th of 73. It doesn't make sense."

"Yes, it does." He lays two papers on the table side by side. "Mom was married to Leo. Here's their marriage license and, look, the annulment form." He points to the dissolution agreement. "March 13th, 1973, less than six months after the wedding date."

Lisa inspects the official certificates. "I can't believe it. If this is factual, it means Leo's my biological dad." She leans forward against the table. "Mom lied to me my whole life."

Jared hands her another form. "This is your adoption papers. The date on it is March 15th, 1974."

She takes the form and dry heaves. "Why didn't Denise tell us the truth? She knew we would find these." Lisa collects the records and slips them inside the manila envelope. She places the bag of jewelry back in the box. "Let's put this away and get a cup of coffee. I need to think this over. This whole scenario is blowing my mind."

••• ••• •••

10:48 A.M.
Law Office of Attorney Larry Dresden,

Lisa and Jared have a ten-thirty. They sit in leather armchairs facing a huge desk piled high with dozens of manila folders surrounding a trio of glass-encased family portraits. Beyond the wooden monstrosity, a glass showcase buffers the wall. The shelves bulge with signed baseballs, a pair of symmetrically placed NFL pigskins, a Georgia basketball jersey, and a variety of Atlanta Braves memorabilia.

Hanging above the sports collectibles are an assortment of photographs featuring Attorney Dresden rubbing shoulders with national and local politicians and an array of professional athletes. Displayed a few inches to their right, the wall holds a vertically arranged record of his achievement: A University of Georgia diploma, Duke University Law Degree, and State of Georgia Bar Admissions Certificate.

The sound of the front door swinging open, and the receptionist's greeting triggers the impatient clients to shift in their seats.

Clothed in a black pinstriped suit, Larry Dresden bounds through his office door and slaps his brown leather briefcase on the desk. He drops into his black leather chair. "Listen. I know I'm late. Sorry. Had a nine o'clock downtown, and traffic was a bear getting back."

"Not a problem," Lisa crosses her arms. "We want to know about our mother's death. The bank manager told us it was a hit and run."

The attorney hardly flinches. "The police have your mother's death listed as suspicious. It's under investigation. An eyewitness to the crash stated a red pickup swerved across two lanes and sideswiped your mom's car, knocking her over the guardrail. Okay? Now you know what I know."

"That's insane," Lisa barks. "Why would anyone do such a thing?"

Jared pats his sister's hand. "Please calm down. Don't take it out on Mr. Dresden."

"Thank you." The lawyer tugs on his shirtsleeve and clears his throat. "I understand how you feel. Your mom's death is a shock to the entire community."

Lisa's chin trembles. "Believe me, my brother and I are devastated. Who can we speak to about it?"

The lawyer reaches into his suit jacket and retrieves a small piece of paper. "Here's the cell number for the lead detective. He can give you more information."

"I hope so." She takes the note and drops the paper into her bag. "Our mother was such a kind and generous person. Why would anyone want to kill her?"

"I have no idea." Larry slides open his top desk drawer and produces a beige folder. "Before we discuss your mother's final wishes, there's a sizable life insurance policy." He flips open the file and drops it on his desk. "It's for half-a-million, and to be shared equally by her children. I'll forward the paperwork to Prudential once you provide a copy of the death certificate."

"We'll take care of it," Jared says. "Lisa and I knew our mom had a policy but no idea of the amount. That number's substantial."

"I'd say so." The lawyer examines the sheaf of papers in the file. "Enya left the bulk of her estate to you both. Aside from a contribution to her church, she's instructed the assets be divided equally between you." He drops two copies of the will at the far end of the desk. "Here are the updated copies of Enya's will. She had me add an addendum. Please read the paragraph at the top of the last page."

"My mom and I speak... " Lisa catches herself. "I should say we spoke on the phone two or three times a week. I never heard a word about an addendum." She removes a tissue from her bag and blows her nose. "It's so hard to accept the fact I'll never see her again."

"I understand." The lawyer flips to the last page. "Please, look at your copies. Two weeks ago, I added the stipulation regarding your biological dad." He wrestles a letter-sized envelope from his desk and hands it to Lisa. "Here. Please, read this."

She tilts her head back. "There's no need. Jared and I have read the documents in my mother's safe deposit box. My adoption comes as a complete shock, but I'm aware of the details."

The lawyer hands her a letter opener. "I don't think you are. There's much more. Please, open it."

Lisa slices open the envelope. She passes a hand along the back of her neck as she focuses on the legal document. "What? An irrevocable trust?"

Jared leans over and rubs his sister's shoulder. "What's it say?"

She hands her brother the document. His eyes bulge as he reads down the page. "Two hundred and eighty-three thousand?" He taps the paper with the back of his hand. "Mr. Dresden, this is true?"

"Of course." Larry leans back in his chair. "Yep, from my mouth to God's ears. Your sister is the only child of Leo Miller. Mr. Miller set up a trust for your mother more than twenty years ago. Enya asked me to include the clause that, in the event of her death, his daughter would be the sole beneficiary of the funds."

Lisa gasps. "My God. This is surreal."

"Sounds about right to me," Jared hands her the letter. "He's your flesh and blood, not mine."

Lisa falls back in her seat. "Let me get this straight. My mother dies in a car crash that may or may not be intentional. Next, I learn I have a biological father I never knew existed, and now I learn he's set aside a truckload of money for me. Don't you think this sounds like a contrived script for a straight-to-video movie? Why would my mother have you add the stipulation two weeks ago? And what about Leo? Where is he?"

Her brother opens his mouth to speak, but the attorney beats him to it. "She never gave me that information." Mr. Dresden rolls his tongue over his teeth. "There isn't always an explanation for the twists and turns on the roadway of life. Could your mom have had a premonition? I don't know. I can't explain her actions. At the time, her request didn't seem unreasonable."

Streaks of mascara stain Lisa's cheeks. "Whatever the reason, what do you think I should do?"

"I know this all comes at you like a downhill speed skater on steroids." Larry's hand fumbles inside his top drawer again. "You need to accept facts and use the money to enjoy your life. That's what Enya would want." He digs out a business card and reaches across the desk. "This is my accountant, Marty Crawford. He's done work for your mother and is trustworthy and resourceful. There are financial considerations that need clarification. His office is ten minutes away. I can call and schedule an appointment."

Lisa raises an open hand. "Wait. I don't know. Let me think this through. I need a little time."

"Sure. I understand. I'm just trying to be helpful. You both have my deepest condolences and good wishes. I'll call you once the judge grants probate."

Jared drops his papers into his attaché case. "Thank you, Mr. Dresden. Lisa and I appreciate all your help."

5

Wednesday, 2:45 P.M.
Alpharetta Police Station, Criminal Investigations Division

The crewcut detective pulls a pad from his jacket, lays it on the desk, and looks up. "Firstly, let me give you both my sincere condolences. I'm glad to say we have new developments in your mother's case."

Both Partainians lean forward in their chairs.

"What do you mean by new?" Jared asks.

"We've unearthed important evidence. Your mom's death was not accidental."

Lisa clutches her brother's hand. "Her attorney informed us of that possibility. We don't understand. Why would anyone do such a thing?"

Detective Collins's pupils enlarge. "Don't know yet. We've found the other vehicle involved in the incident. The owner reported it stolen earlier the same day." He yanks a pen from the cup on his desk and examines the "Braves" logo printed on the front of it. "Do you know if there's anyone who had a problem with her?"

"No," Lisa replies. "She never mentioned anything to me. We were close and spoke frequently."

"Me either," Jared adds. "Our mother lived a good life. She did her part at the church and made friends, not enemies."

Collins taps the point of the pen against the desk. "Did either of you ever hear of Clarkson Research Group?"

Jared shrugs. "Never heard of it."

"No," Lisa echoes. "What is it?"

The Detective squiggles on his pad. "The company's in Cumming. They run taste tests, mock juries, surveys, that type of thing."

"So? What does this have to do with our mom?" Lisa's eyes wander around the office and spy a small refrigerator. "Could I have water, please? I feel lightheaded."

"Sure. Take a deep breath and relax." Collins walks to the fridge and pulls out a Dasani water. He twists off the cap and hands her the bottle.

Lisa takes a long swallow. "Ah, much better. Please, continue."

"Sure. You're quite welcome. We're working on a solid lead right now. We've connected your mother's death to two others."

Collins reaches into a folder and lays a piece of paper on the desk. "Here's a duplicate of the original we found on the floor of the stolen pickup. It's the directions to Clarkson Research. We spoke to the people at the company. Your mom and fourteen other panelists took part in a taste test last Thursday."

Lisa scans the paper, then hands it to her brother.

Jared examines it. He pinches his lips together. "What does this have to do with our mother's death?"

Collins narrows his eyes. "Plenty. Two people who participated in the same focus group are also dead. We believe whoever killed them took part in the taste test."

"Two others?" Lisa accepts the paper from her brother and hands it back to the detective. "How did they die?"

"Each of the deaths is a homicide. Please keep what I will tell you to yourselves. One victim is an elderly male. He suffered fatal stab wounds to his chest outside the Walmart on Mansell. The second, a pregnant female, was pushed in front of a Marta train early Friday morning."

Jared sits up. "Three people out of fifteen? The numbers defy the odds."

"I know. I wish I had more to tell you, but, so far, that's all I have. We're checking the other participants. We have our theories but no actual motive yet. I'll call you when I have an update. Sorry again for your loss."

••• ••• •••

Thursday Morning, 8:48
Main Street, Alpharetta

Lisa takes a sip of her latte and settles back in her chair outside the downtown Starbucks. "We still need answers. These killings can't be random."

Jared's mouth falls open. "It's bizarre, to say the least."

"Yeah, poor mom. What about the other people who died? It's so sad."

"Lissie, we've got to buck up and keep on keeping on. We'll get past this."

"You're right. I know we will." His sister brings a finger to her chin. "I think I've had it with my job at the newspaper." She clasps her hands in front of her. "Yep. I've decided. I'm going to quit. If you don't mind, I'd like to move back to Atlanta."

Jared examines her face. "You don't need my permission."

"Well… yes, I do. I want to move back into the house."

"I think that's a terrific idea."

Lisa's face lights up. "You don't mind?"

"Mind? No, not at all."

She raises her coffee cup in a mock toast. "You're such a good brother and a faithful friend. This way, I'll have plenty of time to sort through mom's things. Don't worry. I'm not planning on making the arrangement permanent."

"Believe me, Sis. I'm not worried. You can stay for as long as you like."

Lisa rounds her shoulders. "I think I should pay you rent."

"There's no way. Stay in the house for as long as you want. Your happiness is important to me. I'm thrilled you're moving back home."

"I'm glad you feel that way. I don't think the change will create a problem. I'm subletting my apartment, and I don't have much stuff." She's speaking to herself as much as to her brother. "My lease is month-to-month."

"Sounds good."

She frowns. "Work will be more of an issue, though. I should head back tomorrow and talk to my boss."

"Let me come with you. I can borrow a van from work, make it easier for you. I'm sure I can get off. They owe me a ton of vacation time."

Lisa's eyes dance. "Fantastic. I could use your help."

6

To suggest Sterling Jernkowski has had it rough is a vast understatement. Funneled through a succession of temporary homes and force-fed the unpleasant facts of life, he's learned from experience there is no God.

For the last eighteen years, his father has called Rutledge State Prison home. Sentenced to twenty-five years to life for murdering a homeowner during a bungled push-in robbery attempt, he's ineligible for parole, and any time off for good behavior is beyond the realm of possibility.

His mom, a drug-addicted hooker, overdosed on heroin six days short of her twenty-sixth birthday, and her bones lie beneath an unmarked grave in a Fulton County cemetery.

Without a single blood relation to nurture the upstart eight-year-old, Sterling found himself another statistic in the Georgia Division of Family and Children's Services. Running away incessantly, he shuffled in and out of a succession of foster homes. He muddled his way through grade school and three years of high school before spending two years in state prison, convicted of burglary and simple battery.

With no technical or people skills to speak of, a job as a short-order cook at a twenty-four-hour Breakfast Nook became the pot of gold at the end of his discolored rainbow.

A night waitress introduced the red-headed social misfit to the world of paid focus groups, which led the nimble-fingered waffle-maker to Clarkson Research Group in Cumming this past Thursday, and into the bowels of the Alpharetta Police Station today.

••• ••• •••

A three-foot length of chain shackles Sterling to the tabletop eye bolt in interview room number two. He shivers and glares at the detective. "Hey. I'm cold. When are you assholes going to let me out of here? I don't even know why I'm locked up. I ain't done a damn thing."

Collins whips out a Ziplock bag. Enclosed within the plastic film is a stained sheet of paper. "Your prints are all over this, Brainiac, and all over the Ford pickup you dumped. Let's face facts. You are royally screwed. We have two eyewitnesses who identify you as the attacker outside the Walmart on Mansell."

Jernkowski digs at his unkempt beard. "I don't believe you. You don't have squat on me, pig-man. Cops always lie. I know. I watch *Law and Order* on TV. I know."

The detective's face brightens. "Oh, is that a fact, numbnuts?" He lifts a paper from inside a folder. "What about this list we found in your room? It has personal information for the people who took part in the Clarkson Research taste test with you. How'd you come by it? The company said someone took the contact list from the front desk. The victims' names are on it."

"Victims? I don't know any victims. I didn't kill anyone, and I didn't cop any list." Sterling squirms in his chair. I don't know a thing about any of it. You planted the list."

"Sure, we did; do it all the time. You must've seen that on television, too? You know you can help yourself here. Why not cooperate? I'm on your side. I want to help you."

The door cracks open partway. A head pokes in. "Here. Check these out. It's the witness statements, Chuck." An arm stretches through the opening. "I called Northside. They're prepping a room."

The detective takes the folder. "Thanks, Lieutenant."

"No problem."

Collins examines the papers. He stares at the suspect and whistles. "Oh, boy. We've got the goods on you. You know this is a death penalty case."

"Don't matter what you got. It wasn't me." A wicked grin crosses Sterling's face. "I plan on giving you the slip anyway. My partner, Zookeep, is an escape expert. He's got a plan."

"You're gonna have a tough time on the road in your leg irons." The detective rolls his eyes. "You are one sick puppy. Tell me about this Zookeep? It's too bad we need to hand you over to psych services for a forensic evaluation. I'd love to see you burn for this."

Jernkowski sits up and rocks his head from side to side. "No need to worry about Zookeep. He's my business. You don't know me. You may think I'm crazy, but I'm as sane as you. I didn't do any freaking murders. You got it all wrong. Ask the people I work with at the Breakfast Nook. They think I'm brilliant. Go ahead. Ask any of 'em."

"Don't worry. You can bet we will."

The prisoner's eyes light up. "Hey! You know I never lose at the triangle board game they got at Cracker Barrel. I'm fast. I'm sure I hold the record."

Collins sneers. "I know the game. I'm not any good at it." He takes a quick breath. "You must be a genius."

"You're correct. I told you I am." Sterling smacks the table and howls with laughter. His face turns bright red. He coughs and clears his throat. "Okay, I admit I was there when those people got killed." He examines the stress lines on Collins's face. "But it wasn't me who killed them. I'm innocent."

The detective raises both eyebrows. "Oh yeah, then who did?"

Jernkowski's posture stiffens. "You don't know?"

"No. I don't. Why don't you fill me in?"

Sterling inches closer to the table and beckons Collins with a finger. "All those people you're talking about were already dead. They just didn't know it." He reduces his voice to a whisper. "I'll be honest with you. Zookeep did them all a big favor, put them out of their misery. Besides, I don't need any sleepwalking assholes sticking their hands in *my* pockets." His volume increases. "My bud got rid of the competition for me. This life's a rat race. Having a friend who'll watch your back is worth more than a trainload of gold?"

Collins offers a bemused smile. "I see your point. Hang on. I want you to write all this down. Let everyone know why he did it. Show them you're as right as rain." He slides a legal pad and a pen across the table. "We want to know your story. You can explain it from your perspective. Tell everyone about the Zookeep. Take your time."

Jernkowski picks up the pen and plays with the retractor at the top. "I already told you why he did it."

The detective grimaces. "Would you stop doing that, please? It's annoying."

The prisoner drums his feet on the floor, thrilled at his accomplishment. He stops his ballpoint thumb exercise and prints his name at the top of the pad. "You shouldn't feel sorry for any of these people. All of them deserved what they got. They were ungrateful bloodsuckers, but no more. They were the problem. Don't you understand? Zookeep's the disinfector. He's the solution."

Sterling follows the outline of his hand on the yellow legal pad. Staring at his handiwork, he taps the pen on the table and admires his artistic achievement. "Handsome, huh? Don't you get it, Detective? The picture. Hand---some, get it?"

"Yeah, yeah. You're just full of funny stuff. You can tell more jokes later. Start writing."

The suspect's eyes grow cloudy. A menacing snarl replaces the grin. He grits his teeth and gapes at Collins. "It's always been Zookeep and me against the world. You can tell all the newspapers to print that." His bold claim echoes through the tiny room. He runs a boney hand through his scraggly growth of beard and points to the plate-glass window across from him. "They makin' a video?"

Collins crosses his arms. "Of course, standard operating procedure. Say cheese for the camera. You're about to become famous."

"What about Zookeep?"

"Oh, sure. Zookeep's the star. We couldn't leave him out."

Jernkowski rubs a finger across his front teeth. He sits up and blows a kiss at the one-way mirror. The corners of his lips curl as his steely-blue eyes narrow to slits. "I'd like to thank all the people who've made this day possible."

••• ••• •••

Saturday 10:27 A.M.

Traffic is light on I-20. Jared signals left, changes lanes, and speeds past a plodding box truck. His sister's eyes wander as she stares out of the window and works her tongue over a grape tootsie roll pop. The opening lines of "Whole Lotta Love" by Led Zeppelin echo through the van's passenger compartment.

Lisa seizes the Galaxy smartphone from the center console and peers at the screen. It's a 678 number, an Atlanta exchange. "Hello. Yes, this is Lisa. Oh, yes, Detective Collins. How are you?"

Her brother rolls his head in her direction, then shifts his attention back to the road.

Lisa taps his arm. "Yes, I understand. He's here with me. Hold on a sec. Let me put you on speaker." She rests the phone on top of the dashboard. "Okay. Go ahead."

"Yes. Thanks," Collins says. "I wanted to let you and your sister know we have a break in the case. We've arrested the man responsible for your mother's death."

Jared signals right. He steps on the brake and pulls off onto the shoulder. "Great work."

Lisa wipes her eyes with a Kleenex. "Please, tell me. I want to know. Who did this?"

"Yeah. Who?" Jared chimes in, his tenor insistent.

Collins's voice cuts through the sounds of the passing cars. "Why don't you come to see me this afternoon, say around three? I'll give you the details then. There's too much to discuss on the phone."

••• ••• •••

3:00 P.M.
Alpharetta Police Station, Interrogation Room One

Detective Collins stands and slaps a photograph on the table. "This is him. He's denied the killings, but the evidence doesn't lie. He's guilty."

Lisa's bottom lip quivers as she fights back the tears. Jared hands her his handkerchief. "Here, Sis. Try and relax."

The detective drops into a chair. "You okay?"

She nods. "Don't worry about me. I'll be fine."

Collins plays with his pinky ring. "As it turns out, there are additional victims, three deaths in Decatur last month. He claims he's an innocent bystander. A guy he calls Zookeep is responsible. It's obvious to me it's his alternate personality." The detective points to the suspect's picture. "Yep. That's him. Sterling Jernkowski in all his glory."

Lisa glowers at the photo. "He's got crazy eyes."

"That's for damn sure." Jared wrinkles his nose as if a rotten odor has strayed into the interrogation room. "Looks like a scuzzball."

"He certainly is." The detective yanks out a paper. "Jernkowski's a social misfit. He grew up without parents, and a screwed-up foster care system spat him out.

Collins drops a folder on the table and opens it. "I'll bet ten to one he'll stay inside the Milledgeville State Hospital for the rest of his days. The sicko has a definite criminal mindset. He feels no guilt and has no concept of what constitutes a crime. I don't think the shrinks will find him competent enough to stand trial."

Jared moves to the edge of the chair. "Did he say why he did it?"

The detective bounces a curled knuckle against his lower lip. "Yes, he has, but his reasons defy logic. He claims the Zookeep wanted to help him financially, cut down the focus group competition."

Lisa looks puzzled. "I don't get it."

"It's simple. Your mom and the other two victims belonged to the Clarkson Research database, as does the killer. Jernkowski thought if he knocked off a few of the members, he'd make more money."

"It's all over a few lousy bucks?" Her eyes telegraph her anger. "This is the reason why my mom died? How sick."

Collins swallows hard. "This guy's operating with half a deck and is whack-a-ding-ho for sure. The doctors have their hands full on this one. The lowlife thinks he's right as rain. I've been on the job for fourteen years and dealt with a bunch of bizarre people. This one heads my list."

Lisa wipes the corners of her eyes. "If this is supposed to be closure. It's not working,"

Jared pats her on the back. "Take it easy, Sis. At least we know the reason why."

"I don't care why. I wish we had mom back."

7

September 12, 9:18 A.M.
L.A. Fitness on Windward Parkway

With the treadmill's speed set at four, Lisa keeps pumping her legs. Growing winded, she presses the electronic control and reduces the elevation level. Her lung's need for oxygen takes a back seat to the images on the video monitors hanging above the free weight area.

The CNN on-screen graphic shows the U.S. Consulate in Benghazi, Libya, is under attack. Four Americans are dead, including the ambassador, all killed by an angry mob protesting a blasphemous anti-Islamic video.

"Oh, dear God." Lisa stabs at the controls and shuts down the treadmill. As the electronic monster reacts to her fingertip commands, she grabs the towel from the side rail and wipes the sweat from her face. She hops from her perch and snatches the water bottle from the machine's side compartment.

"How awful," announces an unseen male.

She's caught in mid-swallow and coughs as a few drops of water dribble down the wrong pipe. It's the deep tones and slight Southern inflection causing her anxiety.

Lisa spins around. The familiar bright blue eyes, the chiseled good looks, and the buffed frame are partially concealed by a shiny red tank top.

"Holy Moses. It's you," she says as a heatwave of emotional uncertainty washes over her.

"Yep. It's me. I was waiting for my chance to say hello." He fumbles with his workout gloves. "Still looking mighty good, Lisa."

"I'd say the same about you, Travis, but it wouldn't be quite true." She gives him a sidelong glance.

He furrows his brow in mock disappointment.

She smacks his hip with her towel. "I'm joking. You look terrific. Let's walk." She grabs his hand and pulls him away from the mirrored wall. He offers no resistance.

"Thanks. You know, I still eat my Wheaties. Childhood habits are hard to break. I'm still confused about what happened between us."

Lisa's face reddens. "Ancient history. Life goes on."

"I'm glad you feel that way. Hey, I heard you were living in Alabama and worked for a newspaper."

"That's true. I'm back now. After my mom died, I figured I'd come home to Atlanta. I'll have time to get over her death and plan my next move."

"Suzie told me about your mom. I'm so sorry. She was such a fine lady."

"Thanks. I know. Would you believe a demented moron murdered her?" Lisa's attempt at a smile fails. "My mom always cared for you and felt awful when we broke up. She expected us to get married."

"Your mother was great. She treated me like I was part of the family."

"You shouldn't be surprised? You almost were."

Travis fumbles with his towel as they pass the check-in desk. "Our breakup still hurts."

She averts her eyes. "Yeah, me too. It was all my fault. I was foolish."

"It's old news. So, what are you up to now?"

Lisa hesitates. *Should I tell him?* She decides to take the plunge. "This is going to sound crazy, but I found out my dad isn't my biological father. He adopted me. My mother was married before and already pregnant when she and my adopted father met. I was five months old when they tied the knot."

"What? Sound's insane."

"It is. I found mom's old love letters, and her safe deposit box held all the details. You can imagine how freaked I am, but let's change the subject for right now. I'm still digesting it all."

An awkward moment of silence follows.

"So, Travis," Lisa says, taking the initiative. "Suzie told me you moved back to Atlanta. No more baseball?"

"Yeah. That's it for me. I blew out my arm two years ago. I went through two operations, but my fastball never came back. I couldn't get anybody out. The Dodgers did me a favor, gave me my unconditional release. I'm officially retired."

"I'm so sorry. I know how much you loved the game."

Travis lifts his arms above his head and stretches out his six-foot-five-inch frame. "I still do. I'm thankful I was at the Big Show for twelve years. I'm in decent shape financially. My agent invested a chunk of my money in a chain of organic food restaurants, and the business is cooking." He chuckles.

Lisa laughs.

Their eyes meet as he flexes his bicep. "I guess Suzie told you I'm divorced. My ex lives in Los Angeles. No kids, thank God." A wistful expression crosses his face. "The marriage was a mistake. Without a prenup, I got dragged through a bonfire and raked over the coals. But that's a whole other story. What about you? Never married?"

His directness unnerves Lisa, but she bounces back. "Err… no. After you broke my heart, I decided I'd had it with men. I only date women now."

Travis stops at the entrance to the men's locker room, wearing a puzzled look. "What a waste." He gives her a wink. "You're still a fox. Don't forget. You were the one who didn't wanna wait for me."

"Look how wrong I was." Lisa pokes him playfully. "I'm not gay. I threw that in for shock value. I guess I never met the right guy. My career always came first."

"You almost got me with that one. I see you haven't lost your whacky sense of humor. How's your brother?"

"Jared's doing well. He's a sales manager for a medical equipment company and gets to travel all over the world. Right now, he's out of town. His company has opened a new division and sent him to South America."

"That's great. Your brother's good people." Travis clears his throat. "Are you interested in getting a coffee after we finish here?"

"Sure, but I need to shower first."

He gives her a nudge with his elbow. "Okay. Remember to put it back once you're done. I need to use the hot water too."

Travis's eyes stay focused on her as she disappears through the doorway of the woman's locker room.

••• ••• •••

Windward Parkway teems with traffic. The Prius follows behind the shiny black Mercedes as it turns into The Original Pancake House parking lot. Travis guides the sleek four-door into a spot beneath the gaudy circular clock sitting above the orange and white restaurant sign. Lisa parks her Toyota next to his.

For the first time in a month, her attitude is on the rise. The masculine scent of her former boyfriend's cologne and the sight of the sunny skies are contributing factors in her newfound sense of optimism. This chance meeting has given her a kick in the seat of her pants and unleashed the repressed sentiments she's buried away for too long. There's hope for the future.

Eighteen years ago, the connecting cord to the man who was the love of her life unraveled. Travis had been the one and only, up until the October morning when she awakened and declared her long-distance intentions. She still questions her motives. No explanation ever made sense. Was it the fear of commitment, a deep-seated sense of self-loathing, or an unhinged desire for self-sabotage that caused her to pull the plug?

Travis opens one of the double doors leading into the restaurant. "This is still my favorite breakfast place. How many times do you think you and I ate here?"

"Too many." She throws her head back. "You and your Dutch Baby German pancake."

"Still love it, but only after a workout. It tastes great, but it's at least fifteen hundred calories."

Lisa does a search on her phone. "Eight-hundred-and-forty. The powdered sugar, butter, and syrup are extra."

"Your ingenuity always set you apart. Nowadays, these smartphones make it easy to fact-check anything."

"If I'm so smart, please explain how I ever allowed our relationship to end?" Her head dips. "I don't have a rational explanation for what I did."

"Hmmm. Me, either."

Lisa slides into a booth across from Travis. She avoids his eyes and, instead, watches the cars in the parking lot.

He reaches across the dark wood tabletop and nudges her hand. "Hey. What's with you? I figured we'd get something to eat, spend some time together."

She's bemused by the family at the next table and smiles at the blonde girl playing with two Barbie dolls. "I'm enjoying myself. It's just that seeing you after so long has made me reexamine my life choices." She raises an eyebrow. "I'm okay, just mad at myself."

"Don't be. We were young and foolish. At the time, you said you couldn't deal with the long-distance thing any longer. It caught me off-guard. I thought our love was strong, and we would work through whatever got in our way."

Lisa sighs. "I know. I'm afraid I didn't know what I wanted back then. You were a couple of thousand miles away. I couldn't see how our relationship could continue."

A young blond waitress lays two menus on the table. "Hi. My name is Pattie. I'm your server. What would you like to drink?"

Travis jiggles a finger. "Coffee, Lisa?"

"Yes. Thank you. You're still such a gentleman." She looks up at the waitress. "May I have a glass of water too?"

He nods. "Yeah. Make it the same for me."

"Okay. Be right back." The waitress turns and hustles past a table filled with a quartet of young people.

Travis reaches out and taps Lisa on the hand. "Where were we?"

"Talking about how foolish I've been."

"How about an alternate explanation?" He pauses as the waitress places the coffees and water glasses on the table. "You shouldn't look at it that way. Let's say you miscalculated. Don't beat yourself up over it."

••• ••• •••

Friday, 7:00 P.M.

Lisa allows the warmth of her fingertips to dissolve the emollients in the Olay Anti-Aging Moisturizer. She applies the foundation and follows up with a lavender concealer to accent the high points of her cheekbones. Her artistic prowess is on display as she shapes her eyebrows with a Maybelline Define-A-Brow pencil. Next comes the purple shadow to augment her lids' depth and dimension and then the eyeliner. She adds black mascara to define and enhance the lashes' thickness, then swipes peach blush across her cheeks.

"You're looking sharp. Still got it, girl." She winks at her reflection, appreciative of her cosmetological expertise.

Molly bumps open the door, meows, and rubs against her owner's leg.

"What do you think, girl? Well, I think he won't be able to resist."

The cat trills twice.

Lisa outlines her lips with liner and fills them in with a new shade of Revlon Super Lustrous Lipstick. She reads the product name written on the bottom of the tube and recites it aloud. "Cupid's Arrow." She crosses herself and smiles. "I sure hope your aim is true."

Finessing her hairbrush, she stares into the mirror and adds the finishing touch. "Looks perfect. Guess that's why they pay me the big bucks."

Retrieving her atomizer, she sprays a few drops of perfume under her chin. Her fingertips spread the spicy floral scent as she fights off a tad of uncertainty. Lisa plays it off and checks her watch. She's excited. A little dancing and a light dinner at the 11th Bomber Squadron Restaurant on Johnson Ferry are on the menu tonight.

Jimmy Page's tasty guitar licks are right on time. Travis Gentry's name appears on the phone's display.

A wave of anticipation washes over her. "I feel like I'm back in high school and heading out on my first date."

The phone rings again. Lisa ignores it and finishes packing her bag. "Okay, I'm all done." She throws her cat a kiss. "See you later, girl. Wish me luck."

Molly forces herself between Lisa's legs and mews.

My furry friend must sense I'm acting out of character. She thinks I'm paying a bit too much attention to my appearance and wants a little more affection. "Silly girl. Tonight's important. I must look my best. Travis and I were once sweethearts. I'm hoping he'll want to pick up where we left off. Fingers crossed."

She tiptoes into the bedroom and slips into her new open-toed stiletto heels. Her red toenail polish glistens. Lisa lifts her keys from the counter and shoves them into her grey Michael Kors bag.

"All right, big boy. Ready or not, here I come."

8

11th Bomber Squadron Restaurant

Surrounded by thin metal railings on three sides, a dozen couples slow dance to "Smoke Gets in Your Eyes," a fifty-year-old classic made famous by the Platters.

As the music filters through the house speakers, Travis slides his hand onto the small of Lisa's back and eases her closer. He stares at her reflection in the mirrored wall next to the DJ's station. "You look beautiful tonight and smell so sweet," he says, his eyes gleaming.

"Thank you." She blushes. "Do you remember the nights we'd sneak into Island Ford and drop our blankets on the riverbank?"

He throws his head back. "Oh yeah. Along with a six-pack or a bottle of Moscato, how could I forget?"

A dreamy smile breaks across her face. "That was toward the end of my junior year."

"Yep. Those were the days when we thought our love would last forever."

"I haven't forgotten." Lisa sighs. "I guess we shouldn't live in the past. There's no time like the present."

There's no reply from her dance partner.

She looks up and finds him staring. "Travis. What are you gaping at?"

"I'm not certain." He shuffles his feet and turns her one-hundred-and-eighty degrees. "Check it out. Now, you can get a bird's eye view."

Lisa's posture stiffens. "Oh, my goodness."

"Yeah. You see what I'm saying?"

As if mesmerized, she's unable to take her eyes off the curious individual leaning forward against the rail, surveying the hardwood dance floor from behind an oversized pair of horn-rimmed glasses. Well over six feet tall and garbed in a slinky black dress, an ill-fitting blonde wig crowns the onlooker's head. Dusky fishnet stockings caress her thick thighs and bulging calves, leading down to a pair of open-toed black pumps surrounding her boat paddle-sized tootsies.

Travis spins his date across the parquet and away from the mysterious stranger's sightline.

Lisa lifts her head and stares at Travis. "Why do you think people cross-dress?"

"I'm not sure, but I had a psych professor tell us people who play dress-up are expressing their reverse sexuality as a form of social protest. Sounds weird, huh?"

"Sure does." She nibbles her lower lip. "I feel bad. There's no way anyone would ask her to dance. The whole situation strikes me as awkward."

"It's none of our business. Let's enjoy ourselves."

"Yeah, you're right." Lisa flashes a weak smile.

The song ends with a big finish—the DJ's brash voice booms through the P.A. system. "Thank you, everyone. I'm going on break. The bar has half-price drinks right now. Take advantage. Be back in ten."

Travis takes Lisa's hand. "Let's take his advice." He points toward a group of people milling around the bar. "Come on. I'll buy you a glass of wine."

They negotiate the short flight of steps and maneuver through the crowd.

He lays a twenty on the bar. "A glass of Moscato for the lady? I'll have a Blue Moon."

The grey-haired mixologist winks and reaches into a small refrigerator beneath the bar. "Coming right up." He cracks open the bottle cap on the edge of the counter and gives his customer the once-over. "Hey! I know you. You're Travis Gentry."

His customer takes the beer and smiles. "Yep. You got me. I'm guilty as charged."

"No, shit. My son, Charlie, went to Sprayberry High. He played against you at Lassiter. After you graduated from Arizona State, I followed your career with the Dodgers. Gotta root for a homie, right?" He reaches out his hand. "I'm Roger Cannon. Can't wait to tell my boy I bumped into you."

Travis shakes his hand. "Great meeting you. Tell your son hello for me."

"Yeah. I will." He nods at Lisa. "Your wife?"

Lisa blushes and waggles a finger at the bartender. "Oh, no. We're simply good friends."

The barkeep turns over a wine glass and pours from a half-filled bottle. "Oops, sorry. I just assumed."

"Didn't anyone ever teach you not to assume?" she teases. "It makes an ass out of you and me."

All three laugh.

She takes a sip of her wine. "Tastes tangy."

"I'm glad you like it." Travis lifts his beer. "Why don't we go sit outside? We can watch the planes land on the airfield."

The server offers a two-finger salute. "Thanks for the advice on my word choice. I'll make sure I only presume from now on." He swipes at the twenty and opens the cash register as the couple weave through the sea of people.

Travis guides Lisa to an outside table and pulls out her chair.

"You're such a gentleman. Thank you."

He takes a seat beside her. "I still can't believe we bumped into each other. I'm so glad we did. I've missed you."

"Yeah, me too."

Travis sips his beer. "Neither of us are kids anymore."

"You're right. We're not. That's why I want you to take me home. There's something important I need you to see."

Her date raises an eyebrow and grins. "Like what?"

"I found love letters written to my mom from a soldier in Vietnam."

His shoulders slump. "You got me excited there for a second, but whatever you say." He takes another hit on his beer. "Please don't think I'm acting creepy, but I believe fate brought us together again. I've kept a special place in my heart for you. When we were teenagers, I believed we were twin flames and destined for a life together. When we broke up, I was devastated."

The roar of a motor overpowers the soft background music radiating from the outdoor speakers. The single-engine prop touches down and rolls to a stop.

"Travis, you wanna get out of here?"

His eyes stay glued to the aircraft. "You know I have a license to fly those things."

"You do? Tell me about it on the way to my place."

"Sure. Let's go." He chugs the rest of his beer and takes a last look at the small orange plane taxiing down the runway. He reaches out and offers Lisa a hand. His flesh is warm to the touch.

A bit lightheaded, Lisa swoons and leans against him. "Gotta use the girl's room on the way out." She grabs his arm for support. A jumble of encouraging emotions runs through her head.

The couple circles the dance floor and maneuvers into a hallway filled with white stucco walls sporting an assortment of World War Two era black and white photographs hung at eye level.

Travis flops into the empty wingchair beneath a bulletin board with a calendar of events pinned to the corkboard. "I'll wait for you here."

"Thanks, but I'm nervous. What if a certain person comes in?"

He looks amused. "Don't worry. I'll protect you."

"What will you do if she shows up?"

"I don't know." He muses for a moment. "Hmm. Smile and say hello?"

"You're still my hero, Trav. I won't take long." She cracks open the door and lets it close behind her.

••• ••• •••

Lisa enjoys the ambiance of the bathroom's 1940s motif. She stares into the mirror and preens her hair. Tightening her bra straps, she overhears Dwight D. Eisenhower's voice piping through the in-ceiling speakers sharing his D-Day narrative. The flush of a commode overpowers his dulcet tones.

Her peripheral vision engages. A door to one of the stalls swings open. Lisa pays scant attention and tears off a length of paper towel from the modern-style wall dispenser. As she dries her hands, the exotic aroma of a strong perfume assails her.

A figure dressed in black slinks next to her. "Count your lucky stars, girl. I noticed your date. He's a doll."

Caught completely off-guard, Lisa wears an awkward smile as her eyes travel upward to the source of the baritone voice. "Err…thank you." Her knees wobble, and she stumbles over her words.

"I know a guy's good looks shouldn't be the basis of any relationship. Their inner strength and selfless generosity are the true measures of a man. Don't you agree?"

Dumbfounded, Lisa's aware of the nervous perspiration beading on her armpits and forehead. She gawks at the toilet philosophizer, who fumbles with her off-kilter wig.

"How's it look?" The pseudo-female leans forward and twists the knobs on the sink. She rinses her hands and grabs a sheet of paper towel. "I don't think I'll ever understand men." Reaching into her pocketbook, she removes a tube of mascara and opens it.

Lisa doesn't say another word. She flies out the door, still clutching her crumpled-up piece of towel, and quicksteps over to Travis. "Oh, boy. That was weird."

He drops the People magazine on the table. "What is?"

"I don't think you want to know." She tosses her paper towel into the trash bin.

"Oh, yes, I do. Tell me."

She plants her feet in front of him. "Okay. You know the interesting person we saw earlier?"

"You mean the people watcher in the black dress?"

"Yes. That's the one." She throws up both hands. "Well, I needn't have worried about her joining me in the bathroom."

Travis slowly rises, a bewildered expression on his face. "Why's that?"

Her sly smile runs ear to ear. "Because she was inside one of the stalls."

His jaw drops. "Holy crap!"

"I know. I better be careful. If I don't watch out, I might have some serious competition to fend off."

He kisses her on the cheek. "Huh? What do you mean?"

Lisa squeezes his arm. "Never mind. I'm kidding." She pecks him on the cheek. "Let's head to my house."

••• ••• •••

Travis angles back in the rocking chair. "Wow. I can't imagine what you thought when you found these." He lays the letter next to the two dozen or so clustered on the bed.

Lisa picks up the paper and waves it. "It was a shock. How would you feel in my position? My whole life is one big lie?"

"Not true at all. You're the same person. You've done nothing wrong. There's no need to be ashamed."

She taps her index finger against her cheek. "I know you're right. I guess it's time to grasp the reality of it and accept the fact. I don't know if Leo's alive, but I want to find out."

Travis wets his lips. "What do you know about him?"

I know he and my mom were sweethearts in high school. The Vietnam War messed him up. My mom's friend, Denise, told me he moved to Florida after their marriage blew up. She wasn't sure what city."

"Does he still have any family in Atlanta?"

"I tried to find out but couldn't get anywhere. Legacy.com had an obituary for his father. The entry said his wife died several years earlier, and there was a surviving son. I called the website, but they couldn't tell me anything more."

Travis takes her hand. "Uh, oh. I see that look in your eyes. I remember what it means?"

"No, you don't." Lisa's face brightens. "I want to write about him. I think his experience in Vietnam and my journey to find him would make for a terrific story. One of the letters had the name and hometown of one of the men in his squad. Dead or alive, I plan on finding my dad."

"As headstrong as ever, I see. I remember your junior year when you quit the high school soccer team because the coach wouldn't let you wear your lucky maroon scarf to practice."

Lisa gives Travis a playful poke. "That's not fair. You know I didn't have a good relationship with the coach, and at the time, you said you agreed with me." She chuckles. "Besides, I'm not impulsive. I've been thinking about this project since I first found out."

"You're a funny girl, but I understand where you're coming from."

"Did you know there are more than six hundred men named Leo Miller in Florida? I've worked through a quarter of the list, but so far, no luck."

"I have a suggestion," Travis says. "Why don't you hire a private investigator? They're good at finding people."

"No way. I want to do this my way. I looked up the phone number of the soldier mentioned in one of Leo's letters. I called him and explained who I am. He lives in Knoxville and willing to meet with me."

"You're kidding? When are you going?"

Lisa flutters her eyelashes. "All depends on you."

"On me? What do you mean?"

"Do you have any plans next week? You ready for a road trip?"

"You expect me to drop everything?" Travis rises from the rocking chair and spreads his arms.

Lisa glides to him.

He stares into her eyes. "When we were younger, you had my number. I guess time hasn't changed much. Your idea is crazy, but I'm game. Who else is going to keep you out of trouble?"

9

Monday, September 17, 1:35 P.M.
Muldoon's Barbeque on Neyland Drive, Knoxville

The old-timer sports a full white beard and wears his khaki Vietnam vet's hat slightly angled to one side. He frowns at the sight of the small digital device Lisa sets at the center of the table. "I ain't too comfortable with you using that thing."

"No problem." She clicks off her hand-held recorder. "You wouldn't mind if I take notes then, Mr. Caswell?" She removes a small notebook and pen from her bag.

He flicks cigarette ash on the floor and squints across the table. "I suppose it's okay. You see, I got this thing about electronic stuff. Puts out radiation, and ain't no good fer you. And you can call me Bobby, none of this mister crap."

"Okay. As I explained, I want to learn about my dad. Tell me, what kind of man was Leo Miller?"

"Why? Is sarge dead?" He takes a hit on his smoke.

"I don't know. That's what I want to find out."

Bobby sways back and forth. "Oh. I see. Well, I hope you do. The sergeant saved my life. I would've died if he hadn't stopped me from bleeding out."

She grabs her companion's arm. "Did you hear that? My dad's a hero."

Travis's eyes widen. "Yeah, I did. You should be proud."

"I am." She turns back to Bobby. "Do you ever hear anything from Leo?"

The old vet swipes at his whiskers and drops more ash on the floor. "No, never did, sweetie. After I got hit, they medivacked me out. I spent five months at Walter Reed and never stayed close with the guys, except for one. I brought a letter I got from him a while back, has an address on it. I was surprised as hell when you called and figured it might help."

The waitress drops a black plastic ashtray on the table. "Please use this, sir. I'm the one who sweeps up around here."

Bobby stubs out his smoke. "Sorry, miss. I wasn't thinking."

"It's no biggie. Your food's coming out soon. More sweet tea for you, miss?"

Lisa lays a hand over her glass. "No, thanks. I'll float away."

Travis raises a hand. "I'll have a coffee after all."

"Yeah, and how about a refill for me?" Bobby holds out his cup. "Could you brew us a fresh pot? This coffee tastes kinda stale."

Lisa waits for the waitress to leave. "Bobby, can you tell me about the day you were wounded?"

"Hey." He points across the table. "Is your girlfriend always this pushy?"

Travis grins. "Only when she's not asleep."

The old vet chuckles. "You're weird, boy. Tell her I don't like to talk about it, makes for some bad mojo?"

Lisa coats her words with maple syrup and Orange Blossom honey. "Come on, please. You can trust me. I promise to pay for lunch if you do." She puts on her sweetest Shirley Temple smile.

Bobby flicks his Zippo and lights another cigarette. "You already told me you were paying." He takes a deep drag and blows the smoke against the window. "Three packs a day ever since my wife threw me out. You can make a note if you want." He examines the tip of his smoke. "I'm ready to tell you about the day at the schoolhouse." As he twists the live end of his Lucky Strike into the bottom of the ashtray, Lisa notices the tremor in his hand.

She sucks in her cheeks but doesn't comment on it. "Yes, please. What do you recall about the day?"

Bobby fires ups another smoke. "I remember I got hit and thinking that's it. I ain't going to make it."

"Oh, you poor man. What else about that day."

"I'll tell you what I can. My memory's hazy." He unbuttons his plaid sports shirt. "Here. Look at this." The flesh of his right shoulder and chest attest to severe wounds and medical care. "Nasty, huh? Even after all these years. The gooks got me good. Two AK-47 rounds."

She shudders. "Oh, my God."

Travis rubs her shoulder. "Must've been rough for you, sir."

Lisa clears her throat and leans forward. "I'm so sorry for your suffering."

Bobby finishes rebuttoning his shirt. "Thanks. I appreciate that. I still ain't right, but life goes on."

"If it's not too much to ask," Lisa says. "Please, tell me whatever you can."

"Sure. Let me think for a minute." He examines his cigarette pack, then shoves it into his shirt pocket. "I remember the Hueys dropped us off just after sun-up. Rip took the point. We humped it about two klicks to the village. We got there at eight hundred hours. The sarge moved up to check on Rip. The rest of us stayed back behind the tree line. That's when the VC peppered us with small arms fire. The muzzle flashes came from the window of the schoolhouse." Bobby's eyes glaze over. "We gave cover fire while Leo and Rip hustled back to join us."

"You must have been terrified. You were all kids."

"I was twenty, didn't know anything back then. It seems like I know even less now."

Travis tilts his head back. "I know how that is."

Bobby glares at him. "What's that supposed to mean?"

"Wasn't meant for you. I was talking about myself. Your comment reminded me I still have a lot to learn."

"Ahh, I understand. Sorry." Bobby's smile reveals the missing teeth on the upper right side of his mouth. "I get pissed off easy. Shrink says it's from PTSD."

Lisa elbows Travis. "He didn't mean to offend you. What happened next?"

"Yeah. Okay. Let's see. Uh, your dad orders me and Rip to follow him. The plan is to outflank Charlie. We set our toasters on high and dropped those bastards right in. They popped out the window like chickens late for a feeding. We wasted them. The ones hidden in the jungle gave us big trouble. Those were the bastards who ripped open Pandusa's box and sucked us inside."

Lisa's pen stops moving. "I think you mean Pandora, don't you?"

Travis covers his mouth and coughs, trying to conceal a smile.

Bobby doesn't notice. He waves his hands around his head. "The one with the snakes in her hair. What's she called. Aw, it doesn't matter. The dinks were our problem. They laid a load of automatic weapon's fire on our butts."

"Is that when you got hit?" Lisa asks.

Bobby turns away. "Yup." He looks out the window and wipes his eyes with his napkin. "Not easy to talk about."

"I see how difficult this is. War's tough to talk about."

"For sure. The memory of that day haunts me. My life went sideways because of it. Group therapy at the V.A. doesn't do anything for me. The shrinks all stink. None of the medicines they gave me took the pain away. Gave up taking them after a while."

"I'm sorry for the agony the war caused you."

"There ain't no need for you to apologize, girlie. You're an innocent party. You weren't even born yet. Besides, your pop was with me."

Lisa bobs her head. "I appreciate all you've done for America. You're a hero. It's so unfair you still suffer."

"Thank you. Most people don't care. They don't want to understand."

She taps her fingers over her heart. "Well, I understand. I'd like to tell my dad how much I realize he sacrificed once I find him. Can you tell me anything you remember about him?"

Bobby lights another cigarette. "What do ya want to know?"

"What kind of man was he?"

"The best kind. Sarge had his shit wired tight and took care of his people. He was on his second tour when I came in-country. I don't remember who told me, but they said Leo came back cause his boys needed him. He got that right. Sucker knew how to keep us alive, most of us, anyway."

The aroma of savory spices and southern barbeque swirls around them as the waitress lugs a circular tray to the table and dishes out their food.

Bobby's nostrils expand as he takes in a big whiff and smiles. "Smells sassy."

The server slides a cup and saucer in front of Travis, lifts the carafe, and pours.

Bobby points to his coffee. "Hey. You didn't forget about me, did you?"

"No, sir." The waitress takes away his half-empty cup from the table and fills a new one with fresh coffee. "I'll leave the pot." She pushes aside Lisa's plate of pulled pork and sweet potato casserole to make room and points to a rectangular plate stacked with half a dozen squeeze bottles. "Barbeque sauces are right there. Anyone need hot sauce?"

"Got any ghost pepper?" Travis asks.

Bobby shakes his head. "You sure like playing with fire, don't you? Ghost peppers are serious down-home zingers. They'll pucker you up in no time." He points to one of the plastic bottles. "Try the sweet and spicy one instead."

Travis tilts his head. "Thanks for the tip, but I like the peppery flavor. I grew used to it when I was living in L.A."

Bobby smirks. "Suit yourself. It's your funeral."

Lisa glances at the tall blonde waitress. "I'm sorry. Do you see what I have to deal with?"

The woman in the white apron wears a grin. "I'll be right back." She steps away.

"You're a funny girl," Bobby hoots. "Your dad's sense of humor was sharp as a bayonet, but he played it dead serious most of the time. Had to."

"I appreciate whatever you can tell me about him. How about his hair color, his height, the look in his eyes?"

"Sure." Bobby raises his head and examines the ceiling tiles while he's thinking. "Let's see…regular looking guy, average height, maybe five-ten, brown hair. I think brown eyes; he had the thousand-yard stare. That's about it."

Lisa's eyes widen. "Thousand-yard stare? What's that?"

"It's the look a soldier wears when he's lived with too much war for too long. You don't feel human anymore. You're like an animal on the prowl. You need to destroy the enemy before he gets to you. Living another day's all that's important. You have no choice. It's either you kill Charlie, or he's going to kill you."

Lisa struggles with the explanation. She feels as if a thousand-pound weight is dangling from her neck. "It doesn't seem fair, Bobby. Hard to believe how tough it was for all you veterans."

The waitress sets a small red bottle on the table. "Here you go, cowboy."

Travis takes the ghost pepper concoction and pops open the top. "Thank you, ma'am. I'm much obliged,"

He sprinkles several drops of the tart-smelling liquid on his bun and sinks his teeth into the sandwich. "Oh, shit!" His face turns a bright shade of crimson. He spits out the barbequed beef and drops his food on the table.

Bobby pays no mind to the younger man's trouble. He keeps chewing and shoves a couple of French fries into his mouth. "Good stuff." He takes another bite of his pork. "Food's always tasty here."

Travis waves at the waitress. "Help. I'm burning up. A glass of water. Make it quick." He flaps a hand in front of his mouth as globules of perspiration break out on his forehead and cheeks.

"Didn't I warn ya?" Bobby quips.

The ghost pepper underestimator snatches the water glass from the waitress and guzzles the palate-saving liquid. Ice cubes tumble from the glass and scatter across the table.

He takes in a large gulp of air and wipes his face. "Whew. Stuff's way stronger than I imagined."

Lisa swallows a forkful of her sweet potato treat. "Don't you remember what Dirty Harry said?"

Travis raises an eyebrow. "No. Tell me."

She stares at her fork and tries her best Clint Eastwood impression. "A man's gotta know his limitations. Souffle's delicious, by the way. Let's eat up. Bobby and I need to finish our conversation."

••• ••• •••

Thursday, September 18, 9:30 A.M.
Partainian Home

Lisa's fingers tap on her laptop's keys as she adds the finishing touch to what will become the third chapter of her work of narrative non-fiction, as yet untitled.

"Travis, would you describe Bobby's demeanor as withdrawn?" she shouts through the doorway into the living room, trying to get his attention.

He presses the mute button on the TV remote. "What d'ya say?"

She gives up and marches inside. "I said, would you say Bobby seemed withdrawn when we spoke with him?"

"I'm no shrink, but I think there's a lot more wrong than that. He's a tortured soul." The volume of Travis's voice intensifies as he walks with Lisa into the kitchen. "The old guy's a trip, kinda cranky and unpredictable. I think he has a big dose of Post-Traumatic Stress Disorder. He said so himself."

"Give him a break. He's had a tough life and never gotten over the horrors of war. A lot of our soldiers have the same problem. My mom's friend said my dad had major mental challenges. Back then, when the Vietnam vets came home, no one knew what they had. I've done the research. In World War Two, they called it shell shock."

"I heard the term before, Lisa. I would think a minute of combat is too much."

"I agree. By the way, I have an appointment with Denise at Panera Bread in an hour. You want to come along with me?"

He waves two fingers. "Uh, I think I'll pass. I'm better off staying away. I didn't do you any good with Bobby in Knoxville. I thought he might lose his temper and punch me in the mouth."

"He has PTSD issues. Denise doesn't have any such problem."

Travis lays a hand on her shoulder. "You know, I'm so proud of you. I admire the way you stick to your guns. You're superambitious, and I know your book will be great."

"Thanks, butterbean. You're my main inspiration."

"I've got to get downtown anyway. I need to see my buddy at the mayor's office. You want an interview with your mom's murderer. Right? Randy thinks he might be able to arrange it, but no promises."

She kisses him on the cheek. "Thanks so much. I couldn't do this if it weren't for you."

"Glad you feel that way. I'm not fooling around when I say I admire your courage and ambition. You're talented, tenacious, and…" Travis stares into her eyes. "I'm in love with you."

Lisa blinks several times. “My head is spinning. I can’t believe how crazy this is. I’m in love with you too.” She waves a small piece of paper. “I don’t mean to change the subject, but I found the phone number of the Nam buddy who wrote to Bobby. It’s too early. I’m going to call him later. I need to finish getting ready. I’ve got to get to Panera.”

“Good. I’ll go see if I can arrange an appointment for us in Milledgeville.” Travis picks up his keys from the coffee table. “I’ll call you later.”

••• ••• •••

Denise drops an envelope on the square tabletop. “I brought along a bunch of pictures.”

Lisa thumbs through them and lays the photos on the table. “These are so good. I’m thrilled.”

“Least I can do. I wish I had more. Most are from a party at my house during the summer of our junior year.” She turns one over and points to the date, July 12, 1969. “Leo was set to leave for boot camp that Monday.”

Lisa plays with her ponytail holder. She corrals her shiny brown hair and reties it. “Why didn’t my mom save any of his pictures?”

“Can’t say. Maybe Enya thought it would upset your father.” Denise bats her false eyelashes. “Your father knew all the details before they were married.”

“I could see how it might upset him. What about the letters? Why did my mom keep those?”

“That’s a question I can’t answer. Enya never discussed it with me.”

Lisa glances around. “Don’t get mad at me, but if you knew Leo was my father, why didn’t you tell me when I first spoke to you?”

The older woman’s blush turns an even deeper shade of red. “I didn’t think it was my place. I knew you’d find out soon enough.”

“Guess it makes sense. I was wondering. Let’s change the subject. Tell me what my dad was like?”

Denise takes a sip of coffee as she digs inside her memory bank. “Let’s see. Leo was handsome, smart, and a big-time practical joker. The senior class voted him "Most Outspoken," from what I remember. He was a year ahead of your mom and me. Maybe I can find a fellow graduate of his and ask to borrow their logbook."

"That would be such a help." Lisa continues to sift through the pictures.

"Oh, my. Will you look at this," Denise says, pointing to a photo. "I think we were doing the Funky Chicken." She picks up another picture. "Here's your mom and Leo. There's me with my date, Ricky. My sister's next to him. These are so bad. We all look uncoordinated,"

"I love the scene. I want to use it as my back cover."

"Back cover? Of what?"

"My book."

Denise's mouth falls open. "You're writing a book?"

"Come on. You know I'm a journalist. I want to write about my search to find my father and expose how terribly America treats its Vietnam vets. Aside from physical wounds, so many have PTSD. I've already interviewed one man who served with my dad. I have the information on a second, and I plan on finding others."

"You're serious?"

Lisa makes a fist. "Of course, I am."

"Look, I don't mean to spray water on your bonfire, but do you think people are interested in such a subject? Isn't the Vietnam War passé?"

"Stories about wars are timeless. I've put out feelers to a friend of mine who's a literary agent in New York. She's asked me to e-mail a proposal."

Denise plays with her coffee cup. "Hmm. Your concept is good, but I don't know if it'll work."

"It will. I'm excited about it. We might even secure a visit with Sterling Jernkowski, my mom's killer. He's locked away in the Central State Hospital in Milledgeville. Travis has a friend who works in the Atlanta mayor's office." She taps on her watch. "He's there right now, trying to arrange a meeting."

"You're crazy, Lisa. If I were you, I wouldn't want anything to do with him."

"Well, you're not me. I want to sit across the table, look the guy directly in the eyes, and ask why my mother's dead."

"For sure, you're Enya's daughter. You have the same stubborn streak I always admired in her. When she felt she had right on her side, you couldn't get her to budge an inch."

"I guess I'm more like my mom than I thought. Right now, finding my dad and telling the story is my sole purpose in life."

"Here, here, girl. You've convinced me." Denise raises her coffee in jubilation. "You have my vote, and I want a signed copy."

10

Wednesday Morning, September 24

Travis checks his rearview mirror as he passes the Hammond Drive exit, driving south on Georgia 400. They have a ten o'clock appointment at Central State Hospital in Milledgeville, a facility serving as a home for the criminally insane.

Lisa lowers her orange juice container. "Thanks again for this."

Travis's lips curl into a wry smile. "Anything for you."

"I'm going to owe you big time." She shoots him a timid smile. "I think this meeting will let me close the door. You know how tough it's been to get over my mom's death."

Blue flashing lights reflect inside the car. Lisa turns and peers out of her window. A tow truck and two other vehicles sit on the shoulder while two paramedics roll a gurney toward the rear of an ambulance. The acrid odor of seared motor oil is unmistakable.

Travis presses the brake pedal and switches lanes. "We're lucky Randy's connection inside the Department of Corrections paid off. It's six-thirty now. The drive should take two-and-a-half hours."

Lisa yawns. "Don't forget, it's the early bird who finds the worm."

"I think you've taken liberties with the expression. But what does it even mean?"

She waves a finger at him. "Don't arrive late, or you'll lose out on your date."

"Nice comeback. Listen. I hear there's a great Thai restaurant on Columbia Street. After the interview, we can check it out."

"Do you always have food on your mind?"

"I'm a big guy. You know I need a bunch of calories."

"Turn right at exit 4A, take I-285 East," instructs the navigation system's robotic female voice. Travis signals and guides his Sl-550 Mercedes into the right lane.

Lisa pats him on the hand. "I'm sorry, honey…my nerves. I didn't mean to take it out on you. My stomach's churning. I have no idea what to expect."

"I wouldn't count on him telling you too much. He's nuts and locked up for a reason."

She stretches across the console and kisses him on the cheek. "This is important to me. Meeting Jernkowski isn't an obsession, but it's close to it. I can't tell you how much I appreciate what you're doing."

"No problem. Whatever I can do to help. You know I love you. I'd move heaven and earth for you if I could. All I want in return is a personally autographed copy of your book."

"You're such a wise guy. Denise said the same thing." She lays a hand on his thigh. "I'll sign one for you, but only if you're willing to pay full price."

"And, you say I'm the one with the wacky sense of humor."

••• ••• •••

Their car pauses at the tiny gatehouse. One of the guards standing outside holds a muscular black German Shepard on a short leash. The second, inside the little building, reaches out his hand. "Access authorizations, please."

Travis presents their passes. The gate slides open, and he follows the signs leading to the Payton B. Cook building's parking area, the lone structure still active in the once impressive lunatic asylum.

They pass dozens of decaying structures whose exteriors display varying stages of neglect and disrepair. The once overcrowded sanatoriums, shuttered since 2010, are now jam-packed with broken windows and overgrown ivy.

"Places looks spooky, Lisa."

"You're right. I Googled this place. Any number of paranormal experiences have taken place here over the years. Did you know there are thirty thousand people buried on the grounds?"

"Thirty thousand? My God, that's beyond tragic."

"You can say that again." She points to a run-down two-story structure. "The majority of the buildings are gutted. During the sixties, this was the largest mental hospital in the world. Can you imagine what went on in here? I'm nervous. What if Jernkowski won't talk with us."

Travis's fingers brush her cheek. "How can anyone resist your charm?"

"I knew I liked you for a reason. But seriously, what if the prisoner's uncooperative?"

Travis guides the car into the parking spot. "Jernkowski wouldn't have agreed to see us if he didn't want to talk. Maybe, he's ready to get things off his chest."

"This guy is certified bonkers. Who knows what he has to say?" Lisa gathers her bag from between her feet. "I'm all set. Let's do this."

••• ••• •••

"Empty your pockets and remove your shoes," orders the pudgy female Correctional Officer stationed inside the entrance of the building. "And I'll need to see a photo ID and your pass."

Travis obliges on all counts, and as instructed, enters the walk-through metal detector.

Lisa hands her driver's license to the officer. He compares the picture on the laminated card to the live version. "Okay. Now, empty your bag on the belt and remove your shoes."

The first-time visitor doesn't make waves and dumps the contents in a grey bin resting on the conveyor belt. Her pumps take their place behind her purse, makeup, and usual paraphernalia.

The second guard, a tall black man, finishes Travis's pat-down and hands back his license. "You can put your belonging away. You're cleared to proceed."

"Thank you." Travis tucks his wallet into his back pocket. "I know you've got your job to do. Must be tough."

The male guard shows no emotion. "Thanks," he says before turning and walking back to his post.

The female officer hands Lisa her ID. "Okay, you both can follow me."

She leads them to a grey metal door marked with black stencil: Room 102. "Go right in. The prisoner's already inside."

"We appreciate your help, officer." Travis pushes open the heavy door.

Sterling Jernkowski waits within the windowless room. Aside from a table and three plastic chairs, the space is barren. Shackles, fed through the tabletop eyebolt, hang over the sides of the prisoner's seat. They make standing upright impossible. He doesn't seem perturbed by the restraints and wears a dumb-looking sneer on his face as Lisa and Travis take positions across from him.

The prisoner studies his guests. "Zookeep told me you were coming. He said it's okay to talk with you."

Lisa opens her pad. "Thanks for agreeing to meet with us."

Travis sinks into his chair and tries to get comfortable.

Sterling's head dips. "Who's this guy? Your bodyguard? He's a hefty dude, but he doesn't look all that tough to me."

Lisa improvises. "He's not. He's my assistant. You don't have to worry about him. He helps organize my thoughts."

Sterling tries on an Elvis snarl. "I bet he organizes a lot more than that. If you know what I mean." He cackles.

Lisa's face turns a hue of deep pink. "We're here to talk about you and this Zookeep fellow. Why do you call him that?"

"Simple. Zookeep is good at making sure all the animals stay in line." Sterling squints at the fluorescent light. "He's like a trainer with a stool and a whip. He teaches all of them what will happen if they cause us trouble." He narrows his eyes. "I'm not stupid. I know who you are."

Lisa, a bit flustered, stares at Travis. "You do?"

"Course I do. You're my new instructor. Here to school me on proper table manners." He twists his manacles and makes a show of rubbing his butt cheeks on the edge of the chair. "Crack's mighty itchy. Can't seem to get at it." The glint in his eyes confirms his irrationality. "Can you help me out?"

"No way. And I'm no teacher. I'm here to talk to you about my mom's death."

The guard unfolds his muscular arms, steps away from the slate-grey wall, and turns toward the prisoner. He aims an index finger at Sterling's head. "Cut the crap, or I'll take you straight back to lockup. Understood?"

The wild-eyed expression fades from Jernkowski's face. His thin shoulders sag. "No. I don't want them to leave. I warned Zookeep to calm himself. He got upset with me and left the room."

The beefy corrections officer backs off and crosses his arms again. "No problem, but you better watch what comes out of your mouth."

Lisa glances at the nameplate on the guard's blue shirt. "Thank you, Officer Randall. He didn't upset me."

"You see?" the prisoner quips. "They like me. Zookeep's the one who annoys them. I'm innocent. Don't you understand? He's the one who committed the crimes."

The guard grits his teeth. "Don't put any trust in anything he tells you. This guy's a complete fabricator." The rattle of the prisoner's chains provides background noise as Randall shuffles his feet. "The psycho's segregated from gen-pop and locked up in max security. He talks to himself all the time and get this; part of his conversation is with a piss-poor English accent."

"Not true," Jernkowski blurts out. "Me and my roommate have discussions. Zookeep's from London and knows stuff. He gives me good advice."

Lisa sees her opportunity. "What about my mom…Enya Partainian? Did he give you any advice about her?"

"Enya Partainian? Who's that?" He sets his jaw. "Never heard of her." The chains rattle again as he jiggles around on the chair. "Weird name, Partainian. That Jewish?"

"No, Armenian."

"Say, Amen," he shouts. "Sound's funny. What's it supposed to mean?"

"Armenia is a country. It's right next to Turkey. More than a hundred years ago, the Ottoman Empire swallowed a good part of it. Two of my great-grandparents were born there. They came to the U.S. as kids after

World War One. My family is Christian and persecuted by the Muslims in charge. The government tried to eliminate anyone who practiced a different religion."

"I don't need no damn history lesson, lady." Jernkowski taps a forefinger on his temple. "That kinda stuff puzzles me. I like to keep it simple." His eyes grow foggy. "Who are you again? Why are you here?"

Travis's patience has worn thin. The sharp edges of the chair have taken their toll on his backside. "This guy is bonkers, Lisa. I don't see how he can help you."

She points two fingers at him. "Take it easy. Give it a chance." She turns back to the prisoner. "Sterling, I'd like to ask you a question."

He leers at her. "The answer is no. I won't marry you."

She ignores his remark. "You were in a focus group with my mom, Enya Partainian. Do you remember her?"

"Remember her? No. Why should I?"

Lisa tenses up. "You knocked her car off the road. She's dead."

Jernkowski's self-confidence recedes. "It wasn't me. I swear." He bangs on the table. "Guard, I don't want to talk anymore. Take me back to my cell. I ain't feeling good."

The guard presses the button on his portable transceiver and growls into the microphone. "Command, this is Randall in conference room Bravo. I need manual transport for Jernkowski, prisoner number one-four-two-seven. Over."

"Roger, that," crackles a deep male voice through the tiny speaker. "Transport team to respond ASAP. Command. Out."

Lisa jumps to her feet. "You can't take him out of here yet. I have more questions."

Randall steps away from the wall. "This meeting is voluntary. As screwy as Jernkowski may be, he still has rights. Time for you to go."

"Not as far as I'm concerned. This awful man murdered my mom."

Travis stands and lays his hands on her shoulders. "Calm down. We're guests here. You're making a scene. Be cool."

"Listen to your boyfriend, young lady." Randall points to the side door. "It's easier if you're gone before the security detail gets here. Doctor

Mendez said he'd like to speak with you on the way out. You can't miss his office, to your right, second door. His name's on it."

Lisa scowls as she collects her belongings. "This guy stole my mother's life. I don't feel any better. He's not sorry in the least."

Travis leads the way from the room. "I told you not to expect too much. This dude is screwed up."

"You're both going to die," Jernkowski shouts. "Don't worry. I'll be leaving here soon. You two better watch out when I do."

He's still spewing threats as the door to the interview room closes.

••• ••• •••

Travis lets the auto idle while he and Lisa stare at the grim reminder of the tens of thousands of people whose bleached bones lay beneath the fields of Central State Hospital.

Gooses pimples prickle her arms as she reads off the printed numbers on the metal grave markers. "This place creeps me out."

He offers an upturned palm. "Uh, huh. What did you expect? It's a cemetery."

"Yes, but these poor people. There are no names on any of the graves, only numbers to show who they once were. No one knows the actual amount of patients who died here over the years. This place was lobotomy central. I bumped into a woman who worked here as a nurse. She told me each of the operating rooms has tiled floors that tilt downward toward the center. They're angled that way so the blood will run into the drain and make clean-up less of a problem."

Travis grimaces. "That's disgusting."

The two can't take their eyes off the hundreds of mini-grave markers. The entire grounds are rank with untended grass and massive clusters of thick weeds.

Lisa pulls a tissue from her bag. "So many forgotten souls. Emptiness and sadness are all that reside here now."

"Please, enough with the negative thoughts. You've got to alter your outlook and think positive, babe."

"Well, I'm positive of one thing, Trav. Doctor Mendez is as weird as his patients. Did you see how he kept twirling his pen around when he spoke? What's with that?"

"Beats me. I admit the shrink was strange, but at least we learned about Jernkowski's conditions. You can write about that."

Lisa digs into her bag. "Hold on. I jotted it all down."

She skims through her notebook. "Ah. Here we go, and I quote: 'In my professional opinion, Jernkowski's suffers from dissociative identity disorder. Additionally, his neurological impairment is exacerbated by acute schizoaffective disorder. The subject identifies with an alternate personality and demonstrates antisocial and violent behavior. Ergo, he lives in a world of fantasy and tangles with pronounced bouts of depression, contributing to his social anxiety disorder.'"

"That's a mouthful." Travis grins. "In other words, he's got several screws missing."

She stuffs her spiral pad into her bag. "It's difficult to have any sympathy. All I know is my mother's gone, and he's responsible. There's no forgiving him."

"Please, babe. Let's forget him for right now. It does no good to dwell on what we can't change. Hateful thoughts will not bring your mom back."

"Oh, he gets me so mad." She leans back against the seat. "I guess you're right. There's no point in channeling negative energy."

Lisa digs inside her bag and pulls out a tube of lipstick. She pops off the cover and stares at her reflection in the vanity mirror. After adding texture, she places an index finger into her mouth and closes her lips around it.

Travis wears his surprise like a kid trying chocolate ice cream for the first time. "What the heck. Why'd you do that?"

She draws out her finger and shows off her bright, shiny teeth. "Keeps my pearly whites nice and clean, doll. Who wants red teeth?"

"Aha. I didn't know. My ex-wife chased me out of the room whenever she put on her makeup."

"Didn't you think that's weird?"

Travis shrugs it off. "Never thought much about it."

A tiny half-smile lifts the right corner of Lisa's mouth. "Hey, listen," She taps him on his arm. "I'm hungry, after all. How about we try the Thai restaurant on Columbia?"

11

October 12, 10:30 A.M.
Carter Avenue, Marina Del Ray, California.

Lisa and Travis troop through the double row of potted cactus plants that lead to the marble steps at the front door.

"Wow. Who designed this place? It's from a Jack Kerouac novel," he says, gaping at the angular architecture of the mid-century retro modern home.

Lisa holds onto the railing as she climbs and strokes the stones in the door frame. "It sure has a futuristic motif. How old do you figure?"

Before he has a chance to answer, a voice hails them. "Hey, kids, I'm down here."

They clamber down the stairway and find the homeowner.

He's perched on a stool, his long grey hair braided and tied back into a ponytail with a twelve-string resting across his legs. He stops fingerpicking and looks up. "Okay. I give up. You found me."

"Mister Blake? Hi, I'm Lisa, and this is Travis. Remember, we spoke on the phone."

"Apple-solutely. Of course, I remember. I'm glad you came. Please, sit with me." He points to the circular arrangement of chairs surrounded by a cluster of palms. "Everyone calls me Hobie. I've been working on a new song. Wanna take a listen?"

She shrugs. "Uh, sure."

Travis breaks into a wide grin. "Of course. I'd love to hear it."

Hobie plays a blues riff but stops in mid-note. He drops his hand and gives Travis the once-over. "I know you, don't I? Yeah, I do. You're Travis Gentry, the sneaky-fast left-hander. I loved your herky-jerky pitching motion. You were good in the clutch most of the time."

He leans his guitar against a chair and points to the Dodger's tank top he has on. "I was at the Stadium in oh-nine, game two of the Division Series. We were down a run when you came in with the bases loaded and struck out two men in the ninth. You got the win when Martinez whacked a two-run homer in the bottom half of the inning. The team should've won the whole shebang that year. Too bad you guys choked and got creamed by the Phillies in the League Championship Series."

Travis boosts an eyebrow. "You're right. It would've been great to win. You do your best, but you can't always control the way the ball bounces."

"Yuk, yuk. Amusing guy, you got here." Hobie rises from his chair and stretches out his hand. "Good to meet you, Ace."

The former major leaguer grabs it. "Sorry, we didn't pull it out for you."

The homeowner throws up an OK hand gesture. "No biggie. We'll get them next year."

Travis grunts. "This is 2012. You're talking 2009. I'm retired. I quit pitching two years ago."

Hobie squeezes Travis's bicep. "Come on. Look at those guns. I bet you can still bring the heat. It's like a bike. You should jump right back on. Right?"

Lisa's face shows her discomfort, but she rolls with it. "Travis is a special person, but we're not here to talk about his baseball career."

"I'm sorry." Hobie grins. "I couldn't help myself. Maybe when we have time." He throws out his arms. "Come here, girl. I want a hug."

Lisa's a bit ruffled but steps forward.

He gives her a short embrace. "You're here because of Leo."

She holds on to his arms. "Yeah. I am."

"You told me on the phone you saw Bobby Caswell. Glad to hear he's okay. We wrote to each other a couple of times, but I haven't seen him since Nam."

Lisa notices the long scar along Hobie's right bicep. "Yes. We visited him in Knoxville. He's never fully recovered from the war, but he's hanging in there. Bobby's one tough clam. We had a good talk."

"He's a good old boy, like Rip and your dad. We used to give those rednecks a load of crap because of their accents. Please don't take what I say the wrong way. I love those guys. We're all brothers."

"Well, I do declare, honey-chile." Lisa overemphasizes her southern drawl. "Do you know Rip's last name, and where's he lives?"

"I sure do." The laugh lines on Hobie's face stand out. "His last name's Ripton. He's a Bayou baby, from Mississippi, outside Biloxi. Saw him at a reunion two years ago." He points to the side door. "Wanna come in. My lips are dry. I require quenching. Either of you thirsty?"

Lisa pulls out her pad. "What's Ripton's first name?"

Hobie's blue eyes sparkle as he twirls the ends of his gray handlebar mustache. "Let me think for a minute. We always called him Rip. He had a long-ass first name. Hmm, I think it's Bartholomew. Yeah, his name's Bartholomew."

She makes a note. "You said you have an address."

"Yeah. I do. I got it inside."

••• ••• •••

Travis gawks at the large color photograph and three Gold Records hanging on the wall in the den. "These are yours?"

Hobie wiggles his eyebrows. "Yep. All certified."

"Lisa, do you have any idea who this guy is?" Travis points to the two Grammy awards decorating the shelf beneath the glass-encased records.

"A friend of my father's?" She moves closer to the wall and inspects the statuettes.

Travis smirks. "That's rich."

"Okay, then. Who?"

"Didn't you ever hear of The Snakeskin Prophets? Hobie was Viper, their vocalist. The group had four or five big hits in the late seventies. When I was in the minors, a couple of the boys would play their music on the bus. The band had a good sound. Each of their members had reptile names, like Rattlesnake and Cobra."

"Don't leave out Copperhead." Hobie points to another wall filled with photographs. "There we are, in all our glory."

Lisa studies the pictures. "Nice vests. Were they real snakeskin?"

"Alligator, man. Only our pants and headbands."

Travis checks out the subwoofer at the bottom of the surround sound system. "Do you still play professionally?"

"Yeah, with a local blues band. I still get a rush when I'm on stage." Hobie pulls out a small rectangular wooden box. "Wanna smoke some weed?" He holds out a pre-rolled joint. "Thai Stick…smooth and steady. I'll put on some sounds. Set up a groove."

Startled by their host's forwardness, Travis catches Lisa's eye, but neither says anything as Hobie walks to the silver stack of electronic components and inserts a CD. The rumble of thunder and Ray Manzarek's sparkling keyboard work introduce the opening of "Riders on the Storm."

Hobie twists both ends of the joint and adds flame to one side. He takes a hit and coughs. The skunky smell of smoldering marijuana and grey smoke fills the room. Lisa reaches out for the cannabis.

"Jim Morrison was my biggest influence." Hobie's left eye quivers as he speaks. "I'm in full agreement with the people who claim the Lizard King was a genius. I won a Grammy for my tune 'Daggers of Light.' I mimicked the opening of this song, changed it a little."

"Really," Lisa says, blowing out a cloud of smoke.

"Yeah. Songwriters do it all the time." He shuts both eyes and hums along. "I gave Jim kudos on our second album, *A Spoonful of Venom for a Rainy Day*. The Doors had their fingers on the pulse of society for their first two albums. Morrison was a modern-day prophet. What a bummer he died so young. Are you aware he's an original member of the 27 Club?"

Travis shrugs. "Twenty-seven club? Never heard of it." He takes the joint from Lisa.

Hobie smacks his thigh. "You're kidding? Janis Joplin, Jimmie Hendrix, and Jim Morrison, the Big Three, all twenty-seven years old when they died. Drugs figured in each of their deaths."

Travis nods to the beat of the music. "No way. I thought Morrison died in a bathtub in France from some respiratory thing."

"Not true. That's what the establishment wants you to think." Hobie rubs his chin. "Jim died from a heroin overdose. No one ever did an autopsy on his body. The listed cause of death is bogus. It's a damn rock and roll conspiracy." He reaches for the joint and sucks on what's left of it. "You know, there are other musicians who died at twenty-seven, like Al Wilson, from Canned Heat, and Brian Jones, from the Stones. Spooky shit, man."

Lisa does a search on her phone. "Listen to this. Amy Winehouse. Curt Cobain. Pigpen, from the Grateful Dead. They're all members of this 27 club."

"See. Your girl knows." Hobie walks to the glass doors facing the marina and slides one open. "Why don't you come outside? Check out the view."

Lisa steps out on the deck and rolls her head back. "Wow. What a wonderful refreshing smell, and check out this view. It's phenomenal."

Travis comes down the steps and snuggles into the soft cushions of a lounge chair. "When I lived out here, I loved to watch the boats bobbing on the water inside the marina. I forgot how much I dug the salty scent. You know what? I think I'm going to take a stroll and look around while you guys talk."

Lisa parks herself at the edge of a lounger. "Sounds good." She leans back and follows Travis with her eyes as he walks along the concrete path snaking around to the water's edge.

Hobie collapses into a chair. A green-and-white umbrella juts out from the center of the table and provides shade for him and his guest. "Travis is right as rain about this place. But you didn't come all this way for the scenery. I guess you have some questions for me. I'm living alone. Both my kids are in Oregon, and I'm happy for your company. My wife, Mary, died five years ago." He sighs and lifts his head. "She was with me from my garage-band days. The sweetest person I ever knew. I miss her terribly. I hurt every day cause she's gone."

"I'm so sorry. Do you mind if I ask you how Mary died?"

"I don't mind. A pile-up on the freeway."

Chills run through Lisa's body. "My mom also died in a traffic mishap. In her case, it was murder. A crazy person had it all planned out. He broke my heart. Travis and I visited him in jail. I thought it would help me get over it. I didn't learn too much, but the trip inspired me. I have a chapter in my book about it. Today's meeting with you will be another."

"I'm so sorry about your mom. I know how you must feel. Something like that is impossible to get over."

"I know." Lisa removes the recorder from her bag and holds it out. "You don't mind if I use this for the interview, do you? It makes my job easier."

Hobie's eyes wander. "Why should I mind? Fine with me. What would you like to discuss?"

"Bobby told me about the battle at the schoolhouse in An Khe. He gave me a few details, but he said he blacked out once he was wounded. Can you break it down for me?"

"I recall the day like it was last week." He takes a sip of lemonade. "The weather was dry and hot. We got neck-deep in the shit that day. A dozen Viet Cong were waiting for us in the bush outside the village. Luckily, we had only one KIA. It could easily have been a slaughter." Hobie shudders. "Your dad saved our asses."

"Please, go on." She angles the recorder close to his mouth.

"Okay. Here goes." Hobie leans forward. "Uh, yeah, I remember. Your dad and two of the guys, Bobby, and Rip, I think, tried to outflank the enemy. The rest of us stayed back and gave support. Then, it got crazy. An RPG landed in front of our position. It kicked up a lot of smoke and debris, but we lucked out. The round was short."

Hobie gulps and brushes the back of his hand across his forehead. He takes a sip of his lemonade. The worry lines on his face betray his emotions. "It's hard to talk about it. You can never forget the overpowering smell of bitter smoke and the God-awful stink of rotten eggs."

"Rotten eggs?"

"Yeah. It's the sulfur, part of the chemicals in gunpowder. Smells like crap." Hobie frowns and looks out at the marina.

"We can stop if you like." Lisa strokes his hand.

"No. I'm fine. It's been a long time, but the memories cause pain."

"Don't stress. Take it slow."

"I'm okay...It's weird. That day, I remember shouting out we needed to move. I thought the VC could have us bracketed. I was right, but already too late. The gooks sprayed our position with automatic weapons fire. Bullets zipped all around us. You can never forget the sound; it stays with you for life. I thought it could be over; all of us were about to die. Doc Freeman took a burst and flew backward. I crawled over and rolled him over. His face was gone."

Hobie's eyes fill with tears. He uses his shirt lapel to wipe them away. "I didn't feel it at first, but I took one in the arm." He points to his right bicep and the elongated scar. "Carter grabbed a bandage from Doc's bag and wrapped it. Lucky for me, the bullet went straight through, no bone damage."

"How awful. What happened next."

"Your dad made it back with the guys. Bobby had taken one in the chest and another in the shoulder. Sarge had Davis radio headquarters; give them our sit-rep."

Charlie sure had our nuts twisted in a vice. God must have been watching out for us because we lucked out big time. Two Cobra Gunships were on patrol nearby and got to us in less than two minutes. Your dad popped smoke and gave instructions to the pilots. The choppers iced the bastards. Kudos to the Air Cav. Saved our asses, big time."

Hobie's face shows the strain of his admissions. "Sorry about the language. I got carried away."

Lisa's unfazed. "No biggie. What about the students inside the school?"

"What about them? The inside of the schoolhouse was an overcooked shit sandwich. The teacher was dead—her throat slit. Three of the students lay dead in a pile. Their bodies were ripped apart by automatic weapons' fire. Five other kids were safe. But finding those bodies walloped your dad hard, like a stiff kick to the nuts. The pain's too difficult to describe."

"Were the children killed by the enemy?"

"I'd like to think so, but I can't say for sure. The Viet Cong killed the teacher. The children…it could have been either side. Wrong place, wrong time, caught in the middle of a firefight. Hard to say for sure."

"I'm sorry. You guys went through so much."

"Yeah. A medivac took me out, along with Bobby and Doc Freeman's body." Hobie pulls out a handkerchief and wipes his eyes. "That day was fubar, like the whole freaking war."

"What's fubar? Never heard the term before."

"Fucked up beyond all reason. It's screwed up the way the lifers bragged about us winning a big strategic victory. As far as I'm concerned, it was just another day humping the boonies and nothing more. The skirmish didn't mean a thing, except for poor Doc Freeman and his family. For them, it only meant heartache."

12

October 15, 7:12 A.M.
4.3 miles N.W. of Milledgeville

A stream of raindrops continues to attack the windshield glass as John Renfro takes a quick bite of his donut and guides the Chevy passenger van along GA-212. The vehicle seats twelve, but today, the corrections transport carries a lone prisoner, a guard, and the driver.

Jernkowski has a court date in downtown Atlanta. He's fully restrained and immobile. A belly chain holds his cuffed wrists, and leg irons restrict the movement of his lower quadrant.

"Hey, Delaney. I need to take a leak," Sterling blurts out, looking to aggravate the heavyset corrections officer sitting a row back.

The uniformed CO glares at the back of the prisoner's head. "You had your chance, birdbrain. Hold it in, jerk, and no accidents. You understand me?"

"Stupid asshole," Sterling mutters. "You're way too easy."

Delany slaps him in the ear. "How's that feel, idiot? Too easy?"

Jernkowski drops his head. "What the hell's wrong with you? Got no sense of humor?"

The sun breaks through the clouds. The wiper's rubber blades scrape against the dry windshield glass, taking its toll on the driver's nerves. Annoyed, Renfro reaches for the lever on the side of the steering column. He averts his eyes from the road surface for only a second. It's one second too long.

The van swerves right as a twenty-pound wild turkey slams into the driver's side of the windshield. As the glass shatters at the point of impact, the Chevy careens over the grassy embankment. Renfro's chest smashes against the steering wheel as the thick trunk of an oak tree brings the van and the driver's life to an abrupt halt. Delaney receives equally harsh treatment. He's boosted from his seat and thrown forward—snapping his neck against the reinforced metal partition at the front of the passenger compartment.

Sterling is lucky. He lays in the aisle, momentarily dazed. The force of the collision separated his chains from the guardrail and bounced him against a seatback. He gathers himself and crawls forward. "Zookeep, you got to give me a hand. Help me find the keys."

His shackles jangle as he climbs over a destroyed seat. He turns over Delany's body and struggles to pull the silver keychain from the overweight guard's belt. Sterling grunts as he wriggles them free.

"Got It," he shouts and hunts through the ring. "There you are." A metallic click, and then another. The chains fall away. He's free. "Who says I'm not a genius? Those suckers are going to find out who we are. Oh, yes, they will."

The prisoner reaches into the dead man's back pocket and pulls out his wallet. As an afterthought, he jerks the baton from the guard's belt holder. Sterling tries three keys before the lock on the cage door clicks. He grits his teeth and pulls it open.

The creature responsible for the chain reaction thrashes around erratically on the floorboards of the front compartment. One wing hangs at an odd angle, the splintered bones visible through the skin.

"Hey, Thanksgiving dinner, cut it out." Sterling stomps on the dying bird's neck and digs in his heel. The turkey stops moving. "You're an ugly one, ain't ya."

He hits the release on the driver's seatbelt and tips Renfro backward. The shirt fabric is bloody around the collar. He opens the buttons and works the uniform shirt off the lifeless body.

Sterling slips on the top. He rubs his bruised right wrist. Reaching up with his left hand, he feels wetness at the peak of his head. He uses his discarded prison top and wipes the blood from around the wound. "Not too bad, Zookeep. Could have been like these two assholes, D-E-A-D, dead."

The lunatic inhales and savors the metallic scent of the fresh blood. He pokes the driver's stomach with his boot. "No more cheeseburgers for you, fatso." He lunges forward and kicks out the rest of the fractured windshield. "Got me my disguise, scumbags."

Closing the buttons on the oversized shirt, he climbs over the dashboard and drops to the ground. Sterling crawls up the embankment and crouches next to the black skid marks. Within a few minutes, he hears the roar of an engine.

A powder blue BMW convertible skids to a stop. The front door bursts open, and a blond-haired female jumps out. "Are you alright? What happened?"

The psycho in the bloody shirt laughs and bashes the good Samaritan in the face with the black baton. "I'm peachy-keen, moron." He clenches his jaw. "I'm better than alright. So, you want to know what happened? This is what happened."

As his victim staggers forward, Sterling swings his weapon again and contacts the back of her neck. The do-gooder is unconscious before her face smacks against the asphalt. A small pool of blood stains the ground around her head, a byproduct of ruptured gums, a cracked skull, and a busted nose.

Jernkowski climbs behind the wheel of the luxury auto. The man with the pseudo-identity, who lacks even the vaguest idea of right or wrong, wends his way toward the big city. Sterling caresses the smartphone he finds on the center console and digs inside the oversized red bag resting on the passenger seat. Two credit cards and one-hundred-and thirty-eight dollars in cash lay buried inside. "Thank you, missy. I appreciate your kindness." He turns up the radio. "Zookeep, we're free at last."

••• ••• •••

October 17, Nighttime

Sterling has spent the last two days incommunicado. Bored of watching television, he's existed on cold cereal, cans of SpaghettiOs, and baked beans. A well-stocked freezer does him little good with his lack of microwave expertise limiting his food preparation capabilities.

He reaches into the cupboard and grabs a tin of cat food. Sterling cracks it open. With two fingers, he squeezes his nostrils shut but can't bring himself to swallow the pasty goop. He spits the Savory Salmon Feast into the garbage and dumps the can. "Yecch! It tastes like two-day-old liver. I guess we need to consider ourselves lucky, Zookeep. Beggars can never be too fussy." The spoon lands in the sink as he squints at the clock and follows the sweep of the second hand. "Ten-forty-three."

Jernkowski's strokes the top of his head. His fingers come up dry. "Good. Time to tend to the rest of our scrapes." Strolling into the attached half-bathroom, he stares into the mirror and admires himself in the oversized Atlanta Falcons jersey and rolled-up pair of jeans appropriated from an upstairs bedroom.

Sterling grimaces and flexes the fingers on his right hand. "Ouch. My wrist's still sore." He rolls it over and frowns at the grotesque shade of deep purple. He rests his backside on the toilet seat, removes his right shoe, and pulls down his sock.

The adhesive tape securing the gauze pad needs a bit of coaxing. "Hey, not too bad. The cut's already scabbing over."

He reaches across the sink, opens the bottle of hydrogen peroxide, and dips a couple of cotton swabs into the mouth of the container. Sterling swishes them around and dabs at the reminder of his lucky escape. "The system can't hold us, Zookeep. No way. We're too smart for those suckers. You know I'm right?"

The self-proclaimed criminal mastermind spreads Neosporin over the cut and rewraps his ankle. Once that's done, a gob of Cortisone 10 finds its way to his wrist. He pats a washcloth doused with water across the top of his head and checks the terrycloth for any trace of blood. "Ah. We're good to go, Zookeep. It's almost time for the eleven o'clock news."

He rushes into the living room and pushes aside the purple drapes. "Hey, Zookeep, it's mighty nice here on Bethany Bend. The street's nice and quiet."

Two nights earlier, Sterling dumped the stolen Beamer in a park down the road and walked the three blocks to get here. An open window around the back made getting into the house easy pickings. So far, no setbacks or complications to mess up his reality. "We're honkey-donkey. Those bastards will get their comeuppance. We'll make sure of that."

The familiar theme song from the eleven o'clock news lures Sterling away from his daydreams of payback. He falls back on the couch and boosts his head with a pillow.

The frontal view of a female reporter appears on camera. She's standing next to a map of the Southeastern U.S.

> *"Good evening. It's eleven o'clock, and here's what's happening. The FBI is spearheading the search for Sterling Jernkowski. The investigation has expanded into thirty-four counties and over four states. A joint task force is hard at work and reports it's close to apprehending the escaped killer. Jernkowski is considered extremely dangerous and last seen driving a black BMW, car-jacked from his latest victim."*

Both the front and side view of Sterling's mugshots settles on the screen.

> *"As reported earlier, Jernkowski was on his way from Central State Hospital in Milledgeville to Fulton County court for final disposition of his case. A freak traffic accident caused the death of two Corrections Department employees and allowed the prisoner to escape. Dubbed the "Zookeep Killer," Jernkowski is charged in the deaths of six people. If you see him, do not approach. Please call the authorities immediately."*

The photograph disappears from the screen.

"Did you see me? I'm famous." Sterling runs a hand through his long red hair. "Looks like I could have used a trip to the barbershop. They mentioned your name, but they should have said more about you. You're the guy with a hot temper. Ain't that right?"

The lid of his left eye flutters as his facial muscles stiffen, and his demeanor takes a more serious tone. "Bloody hell, mate." His pitch is an octave lower and sports a peculiar cockney accent. "I'll slice off the *bullocks* of anyone who tries to stand in our way."

"Appreciate it," Jernkowski says, reverting to his usual speaking voice. "I like the way you look out for me."

"It's because we love each other, lad." The voice once again carries the Londoner's accent. "You know you can always count on me. No need to get your knickers all in a twist. I'll never tell you to piss off."

Sterling doubles over with laughter. "I love the way you talk. Half the time, I'm not sure what you're saying, but your East End accent gives me a charge."

He aims the remote control at the television. "I'm grumpy, and I'm sleepy." He exposes his upper teeth as he guffaws at his Disney-like simile. "Please, don't make any jokes about Snow White and any of her dwarfs. Okay?" He stretches out and sinks into the seat cushions. "Gonna grab a nap. You keep an eye out for trouble, Zookeep. Wake me if those idiots show up."

The man with multiple psychological disorders and vicious nature conks out.

••• ••• •••

The long-distance airline travelers have timed their return flight to perfection. Traffic is light, leaving Hartsfield-Jackson. The Mercedes moves along I-85 and turns right onto GA-400.

Lisa checks the time on her phone, 11:17 P.M. "We should make it home before midnight, hon."

"That's good. This trip wore me out."

She sees the blue notification LED flashing on her phone. It's a reminder there's a voicemail message. She presses the speakerphone button and hits play. A familiar voice fills the car. "Hello, Ms. Partainian, this is Detective Collins. I wanted to give you a heads-up. There's no reason to get stressed out, but I received a call from Milledgeville. Their van had an accident this morning, and Sterling Jernkowski escaped. Please call me back when you get this message."

Lisa fumbles with her phone. "Good heavens, Travis. The message is two days old."

"Yeah, but I wouldn't read too much into it. Jernkowski's long gone. He wouldn't stick around Georgia. He's at least two or three states away by now."

"You may be right. Let me give the detective a call."

"It's past eleven. Don't you think it's kinda late?"

"Guess we'll find out." She dials the number and listens as the message machine engages. "Hello, this is Detective Collins from the Alpharetta P.D. Sorry, I missed your call. Please leave a message, and I'll get back to you as soon as I can."

Lisa wears her disappointment like a rushed aromatherapy facial. "You're right. There's no answer." She stashes her phone in her bag. "I'll call him back tomorrow." She drums on her cheek with two fingers. "It's too late to pick up Molly from Denise's house. I'll get her tomorrow. I miss the furry hairball." Lisa sighs.

Travis signals right. "I'm a dog person, but I must admit your cat acts almost human." He exits GA-400 at Winward Parkway and makes a left.

"Oh, yeah. I have an idea."

"What's that?"

Lisa edges back against the seat. "The house is big. We should adopt another cat. Molly could use the company."

He shakes his head. "I don't know about that. What about a puppy? How about a Yorkie or a toy Poodle? You could carry one around in your pocketbook."

She pokes him in the arm. "As long as you walk it. I'm not fond of picking up dog poop. You're one sick puppy yourself. I think you need a bit of counseling."

Travis makes a right onto GA-9 and pulls up to a red light. "Not true, babe. You're all the help I need."

"No way. You need a lot more than I can give you, though I do have considerable talents you aren't aware of yet."

"Not true. I'm well aware of your qualities. That's why I'm in love with you."

Lisa narrows her eyes. "Oh, yeah? I'm like a leaky tube of Crazy Glue. I'm stuck on you. I love you more."

He blows her a kiss. "Let's not have an affection contest right now. There's no need to argue about love."

"Fine." Lisa rolls her eyes. "Then, we'll call it...almost even."

"Almost? Well...okay. Sounds good to me." Travis turns right and applies the brakes.

••• ••• •••

The napping fugitive is roused by the vroom, vroom of the high-powered motor, as Travis guides the car into the driveway. The engine cuts off. The sound of two car doors slamming shut brings the time for confrontation ever closer. Sterling cradles the baton in his left hand and hefts a ten-inch kitchen knife in his right. "I'm ready, mate; it's game time."

He dashes into the darkened kitchen. "They should be coming this-a-way, right through the side door and into the kitchen," he whispers—his voice trembles with anticipation.

The nocturnal riffs of the Cicadas and Katydids increase in volume as the front door opens. Lisa and Travis's jovial banter drowns out the insects and adds an unwelcome exclamation point to Sterling's excitement.

Guided by the glimmer of the crescent moon, the killer modifies his plan and skulks toward the living room, following the trail of voices. As he sidesteps a chair, his right elbow dislodges a wood-bordered wall calendar. It clatters to the floor.

••• ••• •••

Lisa flips on the hall light. She takes a step back, startled by a loud crash, and shrinks back.

"Hold up." Travis raises a hand. "There's someone in the house."

"I know. What should we do?"

Before he can answer, a figure charges at them from the darkened dining room. Travis reaches for the clay flowerpot sitting next to him on the end table. He cradles the five-inch eucalyptus plant, rocks back, and fires. The muscles in his arm twitch as the potted plant explodes from his hand and hurtles at the home invader.

The high-velocity heave slams into Sterling's forehead. As he falls, the kitchen knife and baton fly from his hands and land at the feet of the baffled couple.

Travis's cheeks turn bright pink. "Holy crap. Let's move." He collects the weapons from the floor and guides Lisa through the front door. "Call 911. Tell them we'll be outside."

He deposits the knife and baton in his car's trunk and exchanges them for a wooden Louisville Slugger.

"Yes. Thank you. Please, hurry." Lisa drops the phone into her bag and grabs her hero's arm. "Stay with me. I'm scared."

After what seems like light-years, the wail of distant emergency sirens slices through the nighttime silence.

Travis points in its direction. "They sound close. He pivots toward Lisa. "Why don't you stand behind me, just in case he wakes up?"

Her feet stay planted. "I'm not moving." Instead, she throws an arm around his waist. "You're my superman. You saved my life."

He smacks the bat against his open palm. "Don't worry. No one's going to hurt you."

••• ••• •••

Sterling's head throbs. *It feels like I got an army of frogs jumping around inside my skull.* He licks his lips and tastes the blood dripping from the split at the bridge of his nose. The fugitive jumps to his feet and runs into the kitchen. Grabbing a dishtowel from the oven rack, he runs water over it. "Ouch. That hurts," he says aloud, blotting his face. "Zookeep, we gotta go."

Jernkowski tilts his head as he listens to the shrill screech of the approaching sirens. Plucking a piece of blue-handled cutlery from the wooden block on the kitchen counter, he swipes at the air and sprints toward the door in the back hallway.

He twists open the lock and teeters across the backyard's manicured lawn. His eyes slowly adjust to the scant moonlight. He lifts the bottom of his shirt and swipes at his nose before hoisting himself over the four-foot-high wooden fence.

As his heels dig into the grass, he's startled by loud barking. The weapon drops from his hand. He bends and gropes in the dark to retrieve it. From the corner of his eye, he sees a grey blur storming toward him. "Oh, shit." His fingers wind around the handle. He sprints across the yard, but before Sterling can boost his body over the next fence, sharp teeth puncture his skin and dig into his left calf muscle.

"What the fuck?" He reaches back and plunges his knife into the jaw of the Pit Bull. The enraged animal yowls and releases its grip. Blood spurts from its wound. The muscular canine whimpers and rubs a paw over its muzzle. Quickly retreating, the dog races to find sanctuary beneath the porch.

The killer has no time to lick his wounds. Limping across the grass, he hops another fence. This time, his luck improves. No dogs are roaming the grounds. He scrambles through two more yards and cuts over a driveway. The wail of sirens grows more distant. Ignoring his pain, Sterling stays on the move.

He settles on the steps of a Baptist church. Slicing off the bottom of his pant leg, Jernkowski winds it around his wounded calf and ties a knot. He lifts his head and stares at the beige steeple. "They will pay for this. I'm not sure when, but soon enough."

13

Three police cruisers sit outside the split-level on Bethany Bend. Their sirens are now silent, but the flash of blue emergency lights bombard the neighborhood with fluctuating shades of illumination. A trio of officers charge from the vehicles and swarm up the steps. They enter the residence through the half-opened front door.

A fourth, with sergeant stripes on his sleeve, clambers from the car's passenger seat nearest the house and slowly saunters toward Lisa and Travis.

He raises a hand and taps a finger against the front of his cap. "Hello. I'm Sergeant Reynolds. The 911 operator reports you can identify your assailant." His tone is cordial, his pronunciation precise.

"Yes, we can," Travis replies. "It was Sterling Jernkowski, for sure. There's no doubt. He was the one who came at us."

"I see." The officer scribbles on his notepad. "Please, explain what happened?"

"Sure. Lisa and I arrived home at about midnight. We got out of the car and came into the house through the front door. We turned on the light and heard a loud noise. Then wham. He came out of the dark through the dining room. I saw his face for a split-second, but for sure, it was Jernkowski."

The sergeant makes another note. "And you, ma'am. You recognized him?"

"Yes. I've no doubt it was Jernkowski. I'll never forget the face. He's my mom's murderer."

"I know. I read the report on the onboard computer. So sorry. Please, would you continue, ma'am?"

"Sure. Anyway, Jernkowski came charging at us." She points to her boyfriend. "Travis saved our lives. He knocked the guy on his butt."

Reynolds raises an eyebrow. "What did you do? Punch him?"

Lisa barrels forward. "No. He hit him right between the eyes with a flowerpot. It was a perfect shot."

A male voice crackles through the speaker of Reynolds's intercom. "We checked upstairs and the basement, Sarge. The house is clear. We've got traces of blood on the floor in the dining room and the kitchen. Over."

The sergeant taps a button on his radio. "Roger. Forensics is on the way. Check the backyard and surrounding area. Out."

Travis points toward his car. "I have Jernkowski's weapons in my trunk. I'll get them for you."

The sergeant lays a hand on his shoulder. "No, don't. We'll have forensics sift through the evidence."

"It's so strange," Lisa says. "On our way home from the airport, I listened to a message from Detective Collins telling us Jernkowski escaped, but we never expected this."

"Good to know." Reynolds turns his head at the sound of an approaching engine. "I gave Collins a call and woke him up. He's on the way."

A black SUV angles toward the curb. Two men wearing crumpled blue suits push open the doors. They pose for a few seconds as they examine the surrounding area.

"They're FBI," the sergeant says, his voice a hoarse whisper. "Excuse me a minute." He stuffs his pad into his belt pouch. Reynolds leaves his interviewees and walks toward the "big guns."

"Hi, Agents. I'm Reynolds." He offers his hand. "We've got two witnesses. They've made positive IDs. It's Jernkowski. It looks like he's branching out. I have my officers searching the grounds."

The dark-skinned agent pulls out his ID as the three men saunter toward their witnesses. "Hello. I guess desperate people attempt desperate acts. I'm Special Agent Cobb." He points to his partner. "This is Special Agent Simmons. Would you explain what happened when you arrived home?"

"Again?" Travis asks.

Reynolds furrows his brow. "We've set up an eight-block perimeter. GBI's put out a BOLO. This perp isn't going to get away this time."

••• ••• •••

Unfortunately, for the general public, the police officer is dead wrong. The subject of their all-points bulletin is miles away, driving southwest on Pleasant Hill Road. In the Chevy Malibu trunk lies the body of its owner, a middle-aged male, who made the mistake of his life by opening the door to his car in a CVS parking lot.

Jernkowski's face carries a smug grin. "Zookeep, I admire how you take care of business. You're getting mighty good at this."

"I told you, mate, no problem's too difficult to handle as long as you sharpen your butcher's hook," he says, switching to his half-assed cockney accent. "Jack the Ripper ain't got nothing on us. Don't forget to keep your peepers open. We've got to avoid the bobbies."

"I know." He reverts to his natural drawl. "I love how you talk, Zookeep. Can you give me lessons sometime?"

"I can't teach you the King's English, mate. The way I speak spreads like natural butter. Don't be daft. You're the one with the sweet and fancy talk."

Sterling notices the McDonald's Restaurant with the "Open 24 Hours" sign hanging above the plate glass window. He makes a right and guides the Chevy through the parking lot and into the unoccupied drive-through lane. He opens his car window and reads the menu.

"Can I have your order?" the caustic-sounding female voice asks through the outdoor speaker.

"Yeah. Gimme a Big Mac, large fries, and a Coke."

"What size drink?"

"Supersize me." Sterling's eyes widen. "You know what? Make it a strawberry smoothie instead."

"Large?" the dispassionate voice asks.

"What'd I say? The biggest and, give me an apple pie. Make sure you warm it. I don't like it cold. Hot and gooey is the way I like it."

He puts the car into gear and rolls to the pay window.

The black-haired female millennial inside the booth taps on the register. "Nine-sixty-nine."

Sterling drops a ten-dollar bill into her palm and narrows his eyes. "I'm a big sport, chickie. Keep the change, but don't spend it all in one place."

He drives to the next window, unaware his latest victim's blood is dripping from the undercarriage, and left a puddle on the asphalt below the pay window. Another crimson pool is developing while the car sits idling at pick-up.

The window slides open. "Here ya go, big spender." The same female worker holds out his order. "Big Mac, large fries, large smoothie, and a *super-hot* apple pie."

He reads the nametag pinned to her blouse. "Thank you, Shirley. You know I like mine hot. Hey, you look mighty familiar," he deadpans.

"You don't say?" The worker is oblivious to the sarcasm. "I should look familiar. I took your money at the other window. We're short-handed, just two of us on tonight." She stares at his deep-set eyes. "Don't act like such a creep."

Sterling plucks the bag of food from her hand. "I'm a creep?" His eyes telegraph the pure malice pumping through his heart. "Is that a fact, sugar?" He peers over her shoulder and eyes her coworker, who's busy flipping a burger on the stove and skimming over a page in his book. "Just the two of you, huh? Interesting."

He reaches into the bag and rips off the wrapper from the plastic straw. "Lucky for you, we don't have time right now. Ain't that right, Zookeep?" He slides the straw into his drink and hits the gas.

The girl's hands tremble. "R-R-Reggie, get over here. Look at this, will you." She stares at the small puddle outside the pickup window. "This doesn't look like engine oil or brake fluid to me. I think it's blood." She shoves her head out of the window. "Look." She points. "There's more at the other window."

Reggie slams his book closed. "Stop being a pain in my butt. Can't you see I'm going over my lesson? I've got to study." Her coworker is a hundred pounds too heavy and moves in slow motion. He thunders out from the cooking area. "Okay. You got my attention. Show me."

Shirley's arm trembles as she points. "Right there. Take a look." She taps a forefinger on her chin and sighs. "You know what?"

"No. What?" Reggie squeezes next to her and leans over the ledge of the pickup window. "Hmm. Yeah, I see it. You might be right. It looks like blood."

"Reg, I'm sure he's the escaped killer the police are after. It's been all over the TV. What'd they call him? Animal keeper?"

"You mean the Zookeep Killer?"

The hairs on Shirley's arms stand at attention. "Yeah. He's the one."

"You're shitting me. That psycho could have killed both of us?" His sleep-deprived brown eyes are the size of golf balls. Reaching into his pants, he fumbles for his cell. "I'm gonna call 911."

••• ••• •••

The fluorescent light inside the tiny interview room blinks intermittently.

Collins flips open the cover of his notepad. "Sorry. I know it's annoying. I need maintenance to change it for me." He drops a pen next to his pad. "You two are fortunate. Jernkowski's as crazy as they come. I think his brains dropped off a coconut tree."

"You have a fascinating way with words, Detective." Lisa tugs on Travis's arm. "If it weren't for my big guy here, we'd be two more of his victims."

"It was quick action on your part, Mr. Gentry. Do you have any idea why he would come after you?" Collins asks.

Lisa smacks her palm on the table. "I do. It's my fault. Travis and I visited Jernkowski in Milledgeville. He got angry at me. Like an idiot, I had told him my mother's last name. There aren't many Partainians left in the world. When we were leaving, he threatened to get us. He must have remembered the name and found the address."

Collins drops his hands on the table. "Makes sense. I don't understand why he would want to hurt you. Thank God you're okay. We found his blood in the dining room, kitchen, and on the back door at the crime scene. Uh, I mean your house. He left his fingerprints all over."

Lisa shudders. "I won't feel safe until he's behind bars."

The detective uses a thumb to rub the edge of his chin. "We found a stolen car in Roswell Area Park. It had a body in the trunk. We've put out an APB. Jernkowski's on the run again, but we'll find him. In the meantime, I'll station a patrol car outside your home."

Travis waves him off. "Thanks, Detective, but we're staying at my condo in East Cobb. The jerk doesn't have a clue who I am, and a corporation owns the property."

"Sounds like a plan. I'll keep you apprised." Collins rises from his chair. "Stay safe."

••• ••• •••

November 5, 9:45 A.M.

Lisa and Travis have adapted well to the home on Sandy Hills Road in Marietta. Molly loves the new digs too. Most mornings, sunlight fills the four-bedroom, three-thousand square-foot home with warmth and stimulating energy.

Today is different.

Lisa stares at her laptop. "I've hit a wall, Trav. I feel so uninspired. I'm frustrated." Tears streak her face. "Maybe this project isn't meant to happen."

"Not true. I have faith in you. You'll work your way through this." He walks to the stereo and reaches for a Michael Bolton CD.

"You already know how much I appreciate the confidence you have in me. Without you, I think I might have given up, but the reality is, I'm no closer to finding my father today than I was two months ago."

Travis finds the track he wants on the CD and hits play. "You just need a kick start. We have an appointment with Ripton in Biloxi next week. I'm certain he'll have plenty to tell you about Leo. He'll get you back on track."

Lisa grabs a tissue. "I hope, but I can't be sure."

"Well, I am, and I also know I'm madly in love with you." As Michael Bolton's silky voice filters through the in-wall speakers with his rendition of "When a Man Loves a Woman," Travis reaches into his jeans pocket and drops to one knee. "I want to spend the rest of my life with you. He opens the tiny customized oak box. A sculpted band of 18-carat gold holds the sparkling four-carat diamond in place. "Will you marry me?"

Lisa gasps. "Yes, of course, I'll marry you." She falls to her knees. Black mascara drips down her cheeks. "You've made me so happy."

Travis places the ring on her finger. "I'm even happier. I've loved you since the day we met in high school, and even more now."

"I'm in love with you too. Lisa dabs at her face. "If only my mom could be here for this."

"She is, babe. She's smiling down on us right now."

Their eyes meet.

Lisa's cheeks are aglow as she pulls him closer. "You're right. I know she is."

Travis kisses her passionately.

"Mmmm, you taste so good." she relaxes and stares into his eyes. "Look at these goose-bumps." Lisa holds out her arm. "They're all over me. I can't believe this is real. And the best part is you're making me into an honest woman."

"Not me. You're the most truthful and honest person I know….and the most beautiful." He kisses her flush on the lips. This time, she returns the kiss with even more enthusiasm.

14

11:45 A.M.

"You want a sandwich, babe?" Lisa asks, dipping her butter knife into the jar of Miracle Whip.

"No. I need to go out for a while. I'll get something to eat on the way over to my lawyer's office."

"Your lawyer? What do you need with him? Something I should know?"

"It's no biggie. My business manager thought it would be wise if we had a prenup drawn up."

Lisa's jaw juts forward. She loses her grip on the knife, and it slips from between her fingers. The dull edge of the blade bounces off the table and tumbles to the floor. "What? Seriously? You've never mentioned a word about this before. I can't believe you're springing this on me."

"I think it's only fair."

She flings her sandwich into the sink. "Fair?" She rips off the engagement ring and tosses it at him. "Here. You keep this. Tell your lawyer to add it to your inventory."

Travis scoops the ring from the floor. "Why are you getting so upset? I don't think a prenup is that big a deal."

"It's a matter of trust. I'm not looking for your money. I don't need it."

"Come on. Don't make such a big deal out of it."

The veins in Lisa's neck protrude, and her muscles throb as she glares at him. "Of course, you don't see a problem. I can't believe this is happening. I can't stay with you."

"I need to be careful. My first wife raked me over the coals."

"Well, mister. You've carefulled your way out of this relationship. You blew it. I'm packing my things. I'm not marrying you." Lisa storms from the kitchen.

••• ••• •••

2:00 P.M.
Holiday Inn, Powder Springs Road

Lisa pulls the cord on the beige drapes and gooses the temperature control on the wall-mounted thermostat. She lays her cell on the end table and presses the button for the speakerphone. "Hello, Suzie. Are you still there?"

"Yeah. I was waiting for you to say something. I don't know what to say. I'm flabbergasted."

"I know. I can't believe this happened." The distressed female flops on the queen-sized bed and moans as she rolls over. "How could money be more important to him than our love?" Lisa tucks a pillow beneath her stomach. Digging her elbows into the mattress, she props up her head with her hands and sniffles.

"Did you forget men are from another planet, sweetie? They don't think like us. How many times have they let you down in your life?" The sarcasm in Suzie's voice slashes through the tiny electromagnetic speaker.

Lisa kicks off her shoes. "I know, but I'm in love with him. What am I supposed to do now? He blindsided me. I don't need his money, but I'm not about to sign anything like that. Can you blame me? Oh, Suzie, I love him so much. Do you think I'm acting foolishly?"

"No way, girl. I agree with you. I would be doing the same thing. It's the principle. He's playing you dirty."

Lisa dabs at her eyes with a tissue. "You're right, but all I think about is Travis. I see his face in front of me. I don't know what to do."

"Listen. Why don't you meet me at the French coffee shop on Highway 92, corner of Sandy Plains? The Café du Croissant, you know the place.

It's right next to the smoke shop. I'd rather talk with you face to face. Let's see. It's one o'clock now. How about we meet in an hour? I know what you need."

"What's that?"

"You need a Suzie Noyes made-to-order pep talk. You've got to snap out of your funk. You don't deserve to be unhappy."

Lisa frowns and glances at the clock. "Uh…Oh, okay. I know you're right."

Molly leaps onto the bed and presses her nose on her owner's cheek. Lisa sits up and lifts the cat onto her lap. "See you at three, Suzie."

••• ••• •••

Sandy Hills Road Condo

Travis collapses on the cobalt blue couch and runs a hand through his hair. *How could I have done something so moronic? Why did I listen to my business manager? Lisa is more important to me than any amount of money. I need to make this right.*

He picks up his phone and hits the speed dial again. It goes straight to voicemail.

Travis lays the phone on his lap and shakes his head. "Heavens to blazes. How stupid of me. Now, what do I do?"

His head collapses against the black cushion as he stares at the white stucco ceiling. The ringtone on his cell gets his body to jerk forward. He brings the phone up to his ear. "Hello. Who's this?"

"This is someone who's going to do you a big favor. It's Suzie."

"Suzie? What do you mean? What kind of favor?"

"That's right. Just play dumb, especially since you've made the biggest mistake of your life."

"I know. I blew it." Travis jumps up and paces across the room. He lifts the slat on the blind and stares out of the window. "Did Lisa ask you to call?"

"No. She has no idea. This is my idea. Tell me. What were you thinking? Do you know how much damage you've done to the woman who loves you? She doesn't need your money. I can't believe how much you've hurt her."

"I want to tell her how sorry I am." Travis's voice trembles with heartfelt emotion. "Do you know where she is? Lisa left the apartment and won't pick up the phone. I know I'm a fool. I have to see her. I need to apologize."

"I'm meeting her at the French coffee shop on 92 and Sandy Plains Road in forty-five minutes. You better not make a scene."

"I promise I won't. I want to tell Lisa how much I love her and beg for forgiveness. I'm willing to do almost anything to get her back."

"That's good, Travis. Listen. I don't want to surprise her, so make it three-fifteen when you get there. That'll give me a chance to speak with her first."

"Sound's great. Suzie, I appreciate what you're doing."

"Don't mention it. I'm doing this for both of you as well as for me. I'll see you there in an hour."

••• ••• •••

The Café du Croissant

The door chime echoes gently as Travis steps inside the upscale brasserie and considers the surroundings. He catches sight of the ladies immediately. They're sitting at a small circular table on the right side toward the rear of the shop. Aside from two employees standing behind the showcase, only one other table appears occupied. The three college-age girls look up, then go back to typing on their laptops.

The crewcut barista leans forward and rests his chest against the corner of the glass counter. "What can I get for you, monsieur? Would you care for our homemade chicken salad on Brioche?"

His customer shakes his head. "No, thank you. I'm not hungry."

"Well, then. How about a pumpkin spice latte? It's our special of the day."

"Yeah. Sounds fine," Travis answers, paying no attention to the worker's tan tee-shirt with brown lettering that advertises "Coffee Makes The World Go Round," Instead, he focuses on the back of Lisa's head and the blond streaks accenting her long brown hair. "You can bring it over to me, please."

"Got it. A squirt of caramel? Brightens the taste."

"Sure. Whatever you say." Travis motions toward Lisa and Suzie. "I'll be right over there." As he strides to the table, he reaches into his jacket and removes a folded piece of paper.

"Hey, Travis," Suzie says, pointing to an empty chair. "Sit."

Lisa turns her head and lifts her eyes. Before she has a chance to say a word, Travis hands her the note. "I'm so sorry. Please, read this. I want you to know how I feel about you." He locks eyes with her. "I adore you."

She uses a napkin to wipe her tears before staring at the handwritten lettering.

Dearest Lisa,

I want you to know how much I cherish you and how sorry I am for causing you pain. Please forgive me for my stupidity and shortsightedness. You've brought me more happiness than I've ever known. I thank God for every day we're together.
Your influence makes me a better person. Your attitude and love of life inspire me more than you'll ever know. I learn something new from you every day. Without you, I feel I'm unable to survive. I refuse to allow the riptide to carry away the sands of time. Please, I beg you to forgive me.

I love you so much,
Travis

Lisa pushes her chair back. She strokes her fingertips over the tabletop as she rises. Her eyes glisten as she throws her hands around Travis's neck. "My God, your words, they're so tender, so…so sincere. I feel the same about you. I love you so much."

Suzie doesn't say a word. A satisfied smile graces her face while her eyes follow her friend's movements. She throws her head back and sighs.

Travis places a hand on either side of Lisa's face and caresses her cheeks. "Please, forgive me. I'll never do anything to hurt you again. You're the best thing in my life, and I can't lose you. I promise to make it up to you."

He digs into his jacket and drops to one knee. "Lisa, you're the only woman in the world who makes me happy. I love you with all my heart and soul and want to share my life and all that I have with you. Please, accept my apology." He holds out the ring.

Lisa coaxes him up and looks into his eyes. "Oh, yes. I accept. I love you and feel the same way about you." She slips the ring on her finger and presses against him. "I forgive you."

Oblivious to their magic moment, the barista carries a cardboard cup to the table. "That will be six dollars and seventy-two cents, please. Anything else, sir?"

Lisa and Travis glance in his direction. They both chuckle and lock their eyes on each other. Suzie opens her purse and reaches for the check.

15

November 12, 10:15 A.M.
435 Hummingbird Lane, St. Martin, Mississippi.

Lisa leans forward against the white wooden rail of Rip's front porch and looks out over the Back Bay. She tunes out the dog's barking and shivering, zips up her lightweight jacket. "Brrr, it's nippy. Thought it would be warmer here in the Gulf."

The thin-as-a-rail Vietnam vet opens the door and joins his two guests outside. "Chill's in the air. Bout usual for this time a year."

The canine's constant yapping becomes more excited and increases in volume.

"Quiet on down there, Dexter. Leave those dang birds alone." Rip leans over the rail and waves at the floppy-eared hound hooked up to the tall metal pole. "They ain't a bother to no one." He claps his hands twice. "Cut it out."

The dog cowers and allows the long-billed interlopers a temporary respite from his racket.

"Good dog. We got us company today."

Dexter's tail wags. He barks and dashes after it.

Rip's left hand smacks the railing. "Crazy damn dog's a pain in my you-know-what, but ain't no better tracker. Whitetails are in season for the next week or so. Me and Dexter got plans to bag us the limit. If you do it right, the smoked deer meat lasts till spring."

Travis glances at his fiancé. "Never hunted much. We find most of our meat at Longhorn Steak House."

Lisa groans. "Oh, you're so bad."

Rip howls. "No. I get it. They got a couple of those restaurants around here. How about coffee?" He points at the door. "Only take me a minute."

Lisa eyes the vacant acreage next door. Rotting wood, scraps of metal, and extraneous garbage litter the concrete foundation of what was once a home. Uncut grass, overgrown bushes, and patches of weeds cover the rest of the property. "What happened. Why's it look so bad?"

Rip spits a glob of mucus off the edge of the porch. "Long story, but these birds sure took to the real estate." He points to the gaggle of sandpipers who've staked their claim. "Come inside. I'll tell you all about it over coffee. Got a box of chocolate donuts to boot."

Travis raises his right fist. "That's great. There's no food or drink at the motel, and we could use something. Lisa was too anxious to drive out and see you. We didn't stop for anything."

"I'm honored you think I'm so important." Rip's bushy grey eyebrows elevate. "Hope I don't disappoint y'all."

His guests settle into kitchen chairs while their host pours tap water into the coffee maker. "Katrina did the damage next door."

Lisa perks up. "I'm interested. Tell me how you made it through."

"That feisty lady was a nasty one. Katrina took a big bite out of this parish. The Christophers, the people who owned the house next door, both drowned. The poor souls ignored the orders to evacuate. County cleaned up a bunch of the mess, but the Fed's still haven't released the money." Rip checks the coffee machine. "With the owners dead, there's a bunch of legal mumbo-jumbo holding it up. I don't know who owns the land now. When I tried to find out, the Sheriff told me I'd better keep moving along and mind my business."

"Hmmm." Lisa scratches her head. "Do you have any idea why they warned you to back off?"

"Lawyers and politics. Those local public servant types always have their hands out, and the lawyers get paid by the hour. I can't say for sure, though. What I do know is Katrina was one crossfire hurricane. She chewed up the whole shebang and spat it out."

"Uh, huh." Lisa taps a finger on her chin. "How quickly did the Feds react?"

"Took them a while to send help. FEMA finally came through with the money. My new place is three years old now. The house is sturdy, made from brick. I don't have a wife or kids. Two bedrooms give me plenty of room. I bought a new boat. It's at the dock." He points toward the bay and lays three spoons on the kitchen table. "I've been all over these waterways, know every inlet, all the best fishing holes. Got them locked away right here." He raps his knuckles on his forehead. "I've loved it here when I was a kid. I love it here now. I plan to die here, but not yet, I hope. My life's in the Lord's hands. He's the one who decides who lives or dies."

Rip reaches above the sink and pulls out three mugs from the cupboard. He places them on the table, and lifting the coffee pot, fills each with dark liquid. "Sugars on the table."

"Sure," Lisa stirs in a spoonful of the white granules. "I'm curious. I hope you don't mind if I ask, but how did you survive Hurricane Katrina?"

Travis lifts his cup. "Yeah. I'd like to know too. You have any cream?"

"Sure," Rip says, opening the refrigerator. Don't mind telling you." He lays the carton of milk on the table, and raising an arm above his head, waves his hand. "It was like the alligators decided to have a barn-raising party. The winds blew the darn possums right out of the trees — one-hundred-and-twenty mile-per-hour. The fifteen-foot storm surge wrecked the entire coast. We lost all the docks and every single fishing boat in the fleet."

Lisa's brow wrinkles. Her lips turn downward. "How awful. You're lucky you survived."

"Yeah, good for me. Too many people thought the emergency warnings were bogus. I paid attention to the weatherman and drove inland to Southaven. I stayed with a cousin right near the Tennessee-Mississippi border. I came back a few days after the storm broke apart and couldn't believe my eyes. Hancock and Harrison counties lost a lot of people. The storm surge was over twenty-five feet. They say our community, St Martins, lost fourteen of its citizens."

Travis lays down his cup. "How awful."

"Yeah. I know? But, after surviving Nam, I consider the rest of my life gravy. These hurricanes are part of living here. You want more coffee, Lisa."

She bites off a hunk of a chocolate donut and wipes her lips. "No, thanks. I'm good. Can we speak about my dad? Bobby and Hobie told me about the firefight at the schoolhouse in An Khe. I don't know if you realize it, but today is forty-one years to the day. Can you believe that?"

"No way. It seems like yesterday. I'm glad to do whatever I can to help you. I owe my life to your dad. In the bush, Leo kept my shit straight." Rip covers his mouth with a handful of fingers. "Oops, pardon the language."

Lisa grins. "Not a problem. Relax. Do you mind if I record our interview?"

"Course not."

"Travis, I hope you don't mind, but I left my bag on the porch. Would you be a doll and grab it for me?"

"Sure. No problem." He's out the door and back inside the house within a few seconds.

"Thank you, babe." Lisa reaches inside the bag and takes out her digital recorder. She places it on the kitchen table.

Travis points toward the living room. "Mind if I watch TV?"

Rip bobs his head. "Of course not. Help yourself. The remote's on the coffee table."

"Thanks." Travis takes a donut from the Entenmann box on the way out. "You two have fun."

Lisa turns on the recorder. "As I told you over the phone, I've interviewed two of the men from your squad so far."

"Yeah, you said. Bobby and Hobie."

"That's right. Do you know where any of the other guys are?"

Rip stands and pulls open a drawer in the cabinet next to the sink. "I got a clipping to show you. Here. Take a look at this."

Lisa's eyes widen as she peruses an article from the New York Post. "Holy Toledo."

"Yeah, I know, it's awful. A buddy mailed it to me. Carter's in Riker's Island, been there for ten years. I saw him and his better half at a reunion in Las Vegas in 98. Carter kept popping off like a piece of field artillery. Guess his wife dying wasn't a big stretch after him being put away for domestic violence before. He had huge mental problems. The V.A. wouldn't help him."

"Seems like getting screwed over by the government isn't that uncommon. I've read articles in the medical journal and reviewed several studies."

"PTSD is one heartless bastard. The shrinks can't figure out how to fix it. I know a couple of vets who stopped trying and took their lives. In an article, I read that three times as many Vietnam vets have committed suicide than were killed by the enemy in Nam."

Lisa rubs her jaw. "Wow. I know more than fifty-eight thousand men died in combat. Triple the number boggles the mind."

"It's as true as God's green earth." He crosses his heart with his finger. "Our government doesn't seem to give a damn what happens to us. Too many of our guys are homeless, and the politicians won't lift a finger to help. They would rather let us die off. We remind them of a war we didn't win. For me, the bad memories won't fade. I have nightmares almost every night."

"How horrific and unfair." Lisa feels her blood pressure rising. "Well, I plan on reminding the public and the government the people who serve our country need our attention. My book will reference the shabby treatment you and your fellow veterans have received over the years."

"God bless you." Rip takes hold of Lisa's hand. "My life took a strange direction after I came home. People thank me for my service now, but the memory of how it was forty years ago won't ever fade."

"I understand. America should cherish their veterans." Lisa sniffles but corrals her emotions. "How about my dad? Did you ever talk to him after you came back home?"

"No, I never did, but I do have a surprise for you." He reaches into his shirt pocket. "Here's Randy Davis's phone number and address. He's another member of our squad, lives in Concord, Mass. I also have information for Captain Vargas."

"Who's he? The names not familiar."

"Not to you, but Captain Vargas was our commanding officer a good part of my tour. He put your dad in for his Silver Star. We bumped into each other at a reunion in Virginia two or three years ago and exchanged information. He's stayed connected with his men, most of 'em, anyway."

"Terrific." Lisa stores the piece of paper in her bag and takes out a notebook. "I have a list of questions I've jotted down."

Rip puts down his cup and leans back. "I'm ready for you. What would you like to know?"

"Tell me about the firefight at the schoolhouse in An Khe. What do you remember?"

He scratches the crest of his bald head. "Mind if I smoke?"

"This is your house. You can do whatever you like. But please don't blow smoke on me."

"No sweat. I'll take a few drags outside. I'll think about the day and fill you in when I come back in."

She shuts off the recorder and brings her cup to the coffeemaker. "Take your time. I'll watch TV with Travis in the meantime."

Rip lifts the Lucky Strikes from his shirt pocket and pulls one from the pack. "I won't take long." He flips open his Zippo and takes a drag before walking out the door.

The gusty breeze blows the harsh smoke Lisa's way. "Achoo." She reaches for her napkin.

"Bless you." Travis yips.

"Uhhh, I can't stand the smell of smoke." She wipes her nose and dumps the soiled napkin in the trash.

"What d'you say, sweetie?" Travis mutes the sound on the TV.

Lisa leaves the kitchen and nestles next to him on the couch. "What? Oh, I was talking to myself. Rip went outside to grab a smoke."

She admires her pear-shaped engagement ring and shows it off to her fiancé for the umpteenth time. "I still can't believe how beautiful this is. Can I ask how much you paid?"

He forces a laugh. "You can ask, but I'll never tell. Besides, you know your love is way more precious to me than any amount of money. I showed you that."

"I know, silly. I feel the same way about you." She snaps her fingers in mock frustration. "You can't blame a girl for trying. I'm naturally curious."

"It's more fun to keep you guessing." Travis kisses her on the cheek.

"Oh, you'll tell me. I have my methods." She raises an eyebrow to emphasize her point. "What's taking Rip so long? He should have finished his smoke by now. I'm going to check on him."

"I'll stay here and guard the TV." He gives her another peck on the cheek and turns on the sound.

"Isn't watching TV your specialty?" She huffs. "You're attached at the hip."

"Oh, come on, only during baseball season. Can't ever hide my love for the game."

"You're a big softie," she mutters as she struts from the room. "Still such a big baby."

••• ••• •••

Lisa grabs hold of the porch rail as she stumbles over her feet. "Travis, get out here right away. I need your help. Call 911. Rip's in trouble."

The source of her anxiety lies face down.

She falls to her knees and, channeling a burst of energy, rolls him over. Lisa's fingers probe the side of his neck. She finds his pulse— the rhythm's weak. "Hurry up. I need you out here now."

Travis rushes outside. "I got through. An ambulance is on the way. What's wrong?"

"He's unconscious. You can see how pale he is. What do we do?"

Travis bends and takes hold of Rip's calves. "We need to elevate his legs, get the blood flowing back to his brain."

"Where'd you learn first aid?"

"Rookie League, my first year in the minors. They forced us to take a course. Guess it stuck with me. Loosen his shirt collar and belt."

"Sure thing."

••• ••• •••

It takes several minutes for a hint of color to return to Rip's cheeks. His eyelids flicker several times before they remain open. He coughs and spits out a gob of mucus.

Travis helps him sit up and leans him against the rail.

"What happened? My head's sore." Rip reaches his hand around to the back of his head. Traces of blood stains his fingers.

Lisa bends next to him. "You must've hit your head when you fell. I'll get a roll of paper towels."

Rip wipes his hand on his pant leg. "Can't remember. Look in the bathroom. I got a first-aid kit in the medicine cabinet. There's a bag of candy inside the kitchen, right next to the sink. Would you bring it with you?"

Lisa hustles inside.

"I'm a damn fool for sure." The vet shakes his head. "Should've swallowed a scoopful of sugar. That son-of-a-gun Agent Orange gave me a dose of reality I'll never forget. I got type-two Diabetes. I let my blood sugar get too low. A doctor at the V.A. told me the disease comes with the territory. Nice payback for going to Nam and serving Uncle Sam."

As Rip attempts to stand, Travis grabs his shoulders and helps him into a rocking chair. "Please, stay down. Let's fix your head."

Lisa swings the door open and hurries outside. She's holding the first aid kit in one hand, a damp hand towel, and a bag of Skittles in the other. "Let me have a look at your head," she says, stooping over and handing the candy to Travis.

He rips open the bag and drops three pieces into the sugar-deprived vet's hand. Rip swallows them in one gulp and cranes his neck forward. "How's my head look? Stings a bit."

Lisa wears a phony grin. "Doesn't look too bad." She wets the cloth with peroxide. "Try not to move. I'm going to clean it."

She wipes around the wound as the sound of a distant emergency siren cuts through the Back Bay community.

Rip's lips press together. "I hope you didn't call an ambulance."

Travis jerks his head back. "Yeah, I did. We were worried about you."

"Quick, call them and cancel it. The hospital will charge me a fortune."

It's already too late. The wail of the siren breaks off as the emergency vehicle backs into the driveway. Two paramedics skip around the sides of the ambulance and open the back door. They remove their bags and lift out the gurney.

"Don't worry. I'll pay for it," Travis says. "Don't get up, war hero. Let the medics check you out."

"I ain't a war hero. I served with a bunch, though." Rip frowns. "Hey. I don't want you paying for me."

Travis pats the older man on the shoulder. "Don't worry about it, and stop being so modest. Lisa and I know who you are. You're a brave man and, in our book, a true American hero."

••• ••• •••

The slim female paramedic rubs an alcohol wipe over her patient's deltoid muscle and jabs a needle into it. Rip winces as she presses the plunger on the syringe. The spiky-haired redhead cleans the area again and stows the soiled antiseptic pad in her bag.

She holds out a clipboard and hands him a pen. "We need your signature right here, Mister Ripton," Her finger points to the bottom right corner of the page.

Rip scribbles with his left hand. "Yes, ma'am, whatever you say."

She opens a Band-Aid strip and covers the tiny red spot on his arm. "Okay. You're good to go. Do you have any questions for me?"

He shakes his head. "No. Thanks a lot for your help. My friends here will give me a hand."

"Let's go, Bonnie," her male partner shouts from outside the rear of the ambulance. "Quit doggin' it." He waves a hand. "Come on. We've got another call. Car pileup with a woman in labor."

Bonnie double-checks the minor abrasion on the back of Rip's head once again. "The injury isn't serious. Your blood glucose level is 112, fine for a person with diabetes. I've given you a tetanus shot." She closes her bag. "We're done. Gotta go."

The medic stops and turns toward them as she steps off the porch. "Look. You need to pay more attention to your sugar level. I don't want to come out here again. Make sure you see your doctor within a few days for a follow-up. I gotta go."

Rip fumbles with his cigarette pack. "Don't worry. I don't plan to see you anytime soon." He pulls out a smoke and lights it.

Travis hops down the steps toward the paramedic. "Wait a second. So, he's all set?"

"Yep. The patient's vitals are fine. Blood pressure's good, heart rate's strong and steady. Time to go." She winks and walks toward the ambulance.

"Take er easy," Rip shouts and throws out a strident military salute.

The ambulance door slams shut. The ear-splitting wail of the emergency siren picks up again. A dozen miniature sandpipers, startled by the shrill noise, shoot skyward.

Rip points toward the house. "Why don't we head inside? We still got an interview to finish."

16

December 11
Condo on Sandy Hills Road, Marietta, Georgia

Lisa twirls a lock of her hair and stares at her laptop. The casters screech as she rolls the chair along the floor a few feet. "This is tragic, honey. You've got to come in here and read this article."

Travis is standing in front of the stove. He slides the spatula under his omelet and shuts the flame on the burner. Wiping his hands on a dishtowel, he hustles into the spare bedroom, which now doubles as the home office. "You okay, babe?"

"Can you believe this, Trav?"

"Believe what?" he asks, his eyes focusing on the computer screen.

"This is horrible. Twenty veterans a day commit suicide. Do the math. It comes out to more than seven thousand each year. Even one is too many. You know how passionate I am about this. What can we do to help?"

"Yeah, it's awful, but it's not up to you to save the entire planet."

"I wish I could, but at the least, I'd like to help our veterans. They deserve whatever assistance we can provide for them."

"Mighty noble of you. How do you plan on making this happen?" Travis grins and lays a hand on each of her shoulders. "You know the remains of near-do-wells litter the road of good intentions."

Lisa curls her lips. "Where'd you come up with the cornball simile? What's it mean?"

A satisfied smile crosses his face. "Even though you're the writer, I can get creative now and then. And don't you ever forget, I'm in your corner and want you to succeed in whatever you do. Because of your passion for veterans, it's opened me up to a whole new way of thinking. I have a secret to share with you."

"Oh, yeah? Travis, I see the strange sparkle in your eyes. What have you been cooking up?"

He drops into a computer chair and rolls it next to her. "I had my business manager check out a veteran's organization in Acworth. They're doing good work and can use some help. So! We've invested one-hundred-thousand dollars in the future of the Georgia Veterans Homeless Shelter."

Lisa's eyes twinkle. "You're serious?"

"Yes. I told you I support whatever you do. I owe you, and this is my opportunity to pay you back."

"Oh, my God, Travis. You're incredible."

"There's more. A good friend owns a cleaning service. He's planning to hire and train a dozen veterans. The job will give them a purpose and revitalize their sense of self-worth. I've scheduled a meeting for tomorrow at the veteran's facility. You don't have any plans, do you?"

"Well, let me check my schedule." Lisa closes the lid on her laptop. "It's not easy to find a partner who appreciates you for who you are." She closes her eyes and kisses him on the lips. "I thank God for you every single minute of every day. I don't ever have to explain myself to you. You get me."

Her body quivers as Travis pulls her closer.

Lisa collapses on his lap. "I love you so much. If my mom were here, she'd be thrilled to know how happy I am."

He kisses her on the neck. "You're the light of my life. You've shown me the way to happiness."

Her voice quakes with emotion. "I feel the same way. You've changed my life in so many ways."

••• ••• •••

December 12
Old Mountain Trace, Acworth

Retired Colonel Riley Nesmith guides the couple through the shelter director's open office door. "Byron, I'd like you to meet Lisa Partainian and Travis Gentry."

A man twenty years younger than the stout colonel sits behind a desk crowded with papers. He looks up and takes off his glasses.

Nesmith pats Travis on the shoulder. "These are the people who will be financing our new outreach and back-to-work program."

The crewcut director jumps to his feet and scrambles around to the front of the desk. He offers Travis his hand. "I thank you for your support. You're doing so much to help our veterans." He nods to Lisa.

"Here, look at this." Byron pulls a rolled-up paper from a shelf and lays it on his desk. "I want to show you the plans for the new extension." He unfurls the blueprint. "Travis, what do you think?"

"It's not what I think." He points to his female counterpart. "Lisa's the director of the project. She's the one in charge. I'm along for the ride."

The Colonel raises a hand. "I'm sorry. I didn't explain the parameters to Byron. With Travis's Major League Baseball credentials, it's a natural assumption. Miss Partainian, please accept my apology. We didn't mean to offend you."

"You didn't. I'm used to people asking him for autographs and selfies. I'm proud of what Travis has accomplished."

"Whew. What a relief." Byron offers a three-finger salute. "I promise I won't make such a mistake again."

Lisa's all smiles. "No worries."

"Your salute. You were a Boy Scout, Byron?" Travis asks.

"Yeah, made it to Eagle."

The colonel pats Byron on the back. "He also spent twelve years in the Air National Guard, served two tours in Afghanistan."

"Thank you for your service," Travis says, inspecting the array of pictures hanging on the wall behind the desk. "Is that you?" He points to a photo where the director, clad in a dress uniform, is shaking hands with Joe Biden. Several political dignitaries surround them.

"Yep. That's me. I'm all decked out. The Delaware state capital building, the day I retired in 2005. The governor gave me a medal. Two congressmen and the U. S. Senator were there."

"He's modest," the colonel says. "The governor pinned a Conspicuous Service Cross on his uniform. He may not look it, but Major Clifford was a crack pilot. He flew thirty-two missions and saved a lot of American lives. His last foray was over Baghlan Province. His F-16 stalled, and the major parachuted into the Hindu Kush mountain range. He broke his leg in three places and dislocated his shoulder when he hit the rocks. Rescuers took two days to find him."

Lisa lets out a long breath. "That's incredible. I want to discuss your experience when you have time. I'm a journalist, I mean writer." She giggles at her miscue. "I forgot myself for a minute. I worked for the *Birmingham Gazette* for more than five years, but no more."

Travis tilts his head. "Ask her about her book. She's a burgeoning author and the person responsible for our involvement with veterans."

Byron pulls in his lower lip. "A writer? What are you working on?"

"It's a book about my father." The sudden bright pink in Lisa's cheeks betrays her embarrassment. "Would you believe after my mother died, I found old love letters stashed at the bottom of a wooden memory chest? My mom's safe deposit box contained my original birth certificate and the details of her first marriage. It was all news to me. It turns out the father who raised me isn't my biological dad. He adopted me."

"You have my deepest sympathies for your mom," Byron says.

Colonel Nesmith sighs. "How awful. My sympathies."

Lisa sighs. "I appreciate the sentiment. My mom's death is complicated. A nut with mental issues murdered her."

"I'm so sorry." The director bristles. "Oh, my gosh. I had no idea."

"The Zookeep killer did it. You've seen the story on the news. He's a part of my story."

"My girl's a super-talented writer." Travis takes her hand. "I know her book will be a best seller."

"Thank you, honey. I appreciate your confidence in me. I couldn't do this without you."

She turns toward Byron. "I'm on a quest to find my dad. He had psychological issues after he came home from Vietnam. I've found some of the men who served with him. Travis and I have interviewed three of them so far, but I've exhausted my leads. One potential interviewee died three months ago, and another is serving a long sentence in prison. Their former commanding officer is somewhere in Europe, and I haven't been able to reach him."

"Your book sounds like it has potential." Byron raises a finger and plants it on his cheek. "Maybe we can help."

The Colonel hands Lisa his card. "I'm the statewide coordinator for the Coalition for Homeless Veterans. Our organization has access to the V.A.'s nationwide database. Send me whatever information you have, and I'll see if I can find any information for you."

Lisa bubbles with newfound hope. "How wonderful. Thank you so much."

Byron dips his head. "I dabble at writing. I have a collection of fictional short stories based on the devastating effect PTSD has on combatants. Do you mind if I send you one? I would value your opinion."

"Of course. I'm happy to read it." Lisa reaches into her bag and hands him a business card. "My e-mail address is on there. Send it, and I'll give you my honest opinion."

"It's all I can ask." Byron rolls up the blueprint and points toward the doorway. "Please, follow me. Let me give you the grand tour and show you how we plan to spend your money."

17

December 15

Lisa spins her laptop around so Travis can see the screen. "Byron e-mailed me his story. I think you should read it. He's a terrific writer. His work needs a round of technical editing, but he has a strong voice. His work's important."

"Okay." Travis plops into the chair and sets his coffee cup on the desk. "I've got oatmeal in the microwave. Would you keep an eye on it for me?"

Lisa points to her face. "What about my nose? I can smell all the cinnamon you loaded in it."

Her fiancé plays along. "What about the flaxseed and wheat germ? I add them for fiber."

"You're such a health freak." She pinches him on the cheek. "I'll bring in the bowl. Meanwhile, check out Byron's story. Tell me what you think."

"Sure. Whatever you say." Travis grabs her laptop and scrolls to the top of the Word file.

OVER THE EDGE

A Fictional Work by Retired Major Byron Clifford

"These damn stools ain't made for me," Patricia Bustamante mumbled, unable to get comfortable. Shifting her body weight gave zero comfort and served only to fuel her irritation. She stubbed out her Newport and scowled. "Yecch! This cigarette tastes like shit." The detective was incredibly antsy this morning. She's suffering, but the wounds were the emotional variety.

Patsie took a swallow of the coffee and grimaced. As she laid the half-filled cup on the counter, it tipped, and most of the murky liquid spilled. *Perfect. This brew tastes like quicksand anyway. Oh well, today looks like it's going to be one hell of a day.*

With a wave of her hand, she broadcasted her coffee bean S.O.S. "Hey, Doris, how about brewing us a fresh pot of java? This batch is only good for mopping the bathroom floor."

The waitress exhibited a fake smile. "Sure, sweetie, coming right up. Give me a minute."

The off-duty APD detective nodded. "Fine. I'll wait. Right now, all I have is time."

Patsie's unhappy with the pathway her life has taken. She'd walked through the gates of the Atlanta Police Academy in February of 2006 and traversed her twenty-week course by navigating through a maze of male egos. She excelled and graduated at the top of her class. It had taken her five years to earn her detective shield and awarded a plum assignment with the Criminal Intelligence Unit.

She partnered up with Detective Sergeant Quinn Bridgeway, a "by-the-book" hard case. Quinn had served eight years as an Army Ranger, with multiple combat tours in Iraq and Afghanistan and a closure rate that set him apart from the others in the detective squad.

The animal magnetism took hold immediately. It wasn't long before Patsie and Bridgeway shared plenty more than their work schedules, meals, and overtime. She knew it was a troublesome move to get involved with her partner, but the relationship kicked into high gear after a drug bust inside the Cyclone, a seedy dance club in Little Five Points.

As Patsie toyed with her pack of Newports, thoughts of the fateful night flitted through her head.

"Look out," Bridgeway had screamed as he shoved her out of the line of fire.

She covered her face as two rounds whizzed past and burrowed into the wall. Her partner fired twice. The suspect hurtled backward and collapsed on the dirty grey carpet.

Quinn raced over and kicked the gun aside. "No more dope for you, motherfucker." He cocked his pistol and poked it into the perp's face. "Don't you even think about it!" He rolled his prisoner onto his stomach and clamped on the bracelets. The suspect groaned as the detective trundled him back over.

The detective clicked on the safety and shoved the dealer's weapon into his belt. "You're going away for a long time, you piece of crap. You have the right to remain silent..."

The cuffed suspect tried to sit up, oblivious to the reading of his Miranda warning.

Quinn's left hand pushed him back down. "Lay there, twerp. Don't move."

"Shit. Cut me a break, Bro. How was I supposed to know you two were cops? I thought you were another brother trying to rip off my stash."

The irritated detective pulled the dealer's shirt aside and inspected the shoulder wound. "Just because I'm black, I ain't your brother. You can explain your sad story to the judge. You know, you're one lucky son-of-a-bitch my aim was a little off. The bullet cut right through, no bone damage."

He squeezed the suspect's left cheek. "Don't twitch a muscle."

The detective dug inside his protective vest and hauled out his Motorola scanner. "Zone Five command. This is Bravo One. Pickup. Over."

"Roger, Bravo One. This is Zone Five Central. Over."

"Roger, Central. We have a ten-seventy-one. The suspect is down. We need a bus at 124 Borland Road, inside the Cyclone Disco."

"Roger that, Bravo One. I copy. Bus to 124 Borland Road. On the way. Out."

Quinn helped his partner to her feet. "You okay?"

"Yes, thanks to you."

That was when the real trouble began.

*****

"Here's your coffee, Detective."

Patsie's eyes slowly refocused. The chubby waitress poured a fresh cup from the carafe.

"Thanks, Doris. You're the best." She raised her cup and gave the waitress the thumbs-up. "Yeah. Much better. I guess there's still hope in the world."

"I never doubted it. Hey. Where's that good-looking partner of yours?"

"I'm gonna see him later. He had a meeting with the brass."

"Doris, pick up," the cook barked. "Adam and Eve on a raft with frog sticks on the side."

Patsie loved to listen to the workers dishing out their diner-talk. It made her feel like a character lost inside a Fifties novel."

"I love your lingo, Doris. It makes me think I'm floating on the river, taking a slow boat to China."

The baffled waitress shook her head. "Whatever."

*****

Patsie wondered how the relationship lasted this long. Quinn, quick to anger and hesitant to forgive, carried an overprotective male attitude that caused undue tension both in their private lives and on the job. Desperate for a solution, couple's counseling became the last resort.

Yesterday's session was a prime example of her frustration. After twenty minutes of argumentative patter, the exasperated doctor dropped his notepad and offered what he considered critical advice.

"Mister Bridgeway," he said. "Before we can delve any deeper into solidifying your romantic relationship, I suggest you check out the V.A.'s Clairmont facility in Decatur. They've instituted a top-notch program for combat vets and have made great inroads with alternative treatments for PTSD. I strongly urge you to call them and schedule an appointment. I'll give you their number."

Quinn's face turned a bright scarlet. "Save it. Been there, done that. The place doesn't do it for me. I don't need any help. I'm fine."

He vaulted from the chair and rushed to the bank of windows facing the street. "Ask Patsie." He angled his fingers between two of the shades and stared at the street traffic.

"How about it, Patsie?" the counselor asked. "What do *you* think?"

She hesitated, formulating an answer. "I think it might be a good idea if you listened to Doctor Scanducci. What about your panic attacks? You wake up at night with the cold sweats."

She pulled out a tissue and wiped her eyes. "If you won't do it for yourself, please, Quinn, do it for me."

"Don't I get a say?" He pounded his knuckles on the desk. "This therapy crap is a bunch of bullshit. I don't need this. I'm gone."

He stormed out before either the doctor or Patsie could say another word.

*****

That was yesterday. Today, Jocko Vangelise stood behind the bar in Riley's Roadhouse cleaning shot glasses. He finished counting out the register just as Saint Theresa's Church bell clanged to signal the arrival of the noon hour. The heavy wooden door to the pub swung open, and Detective Quinn barged in. The bartender nodded to his first customer of the day.

The muscular black man settled on a stool and pointed to the dozens of bottles lining the mirror behind the bar. "Gimme a Johnny Walker Blue Label... You know what? I feel like crap today. Better make it a double."

Quinn plucked a cigarette from his pack of Marlboros and tossed the box on the bar. He lit it and took a deep drag. Grimacing, the detective let the fresh smoke fall to the floor and ground his heel into it. "Ain't got no taste."

Jocko ignored the belligerent display. He opened the Scotch and poured the drink. "You're here mighty early, Detective. Where's your partner?" He returned the bottle to the empty spot in front of the mirror.

The detective lit another smoke. "Don't make me answer no questions. Okay? Mind your business."

Jocko's angular face registered surprise, but he played off the remark. "Yeah, sure. It's your dime. Only making conversation."

"Well, don't."

"Fine, but you know you can't smoke in here." The bartender pointed to the sign on the wall behind him. "I don't mean to bust your chops, Detective, but would you put the cigarette out?"

Bridgeway scowled at the bartender. "Hell, no. Why don't you do us both a favor and don't ask me again? I ain't in any mood." He gulped his double shot of eighty proof whiskey and grimaced as the desensitizer fought its way to his stomach.

The detective glanced around the pub. He and the bartender were alone. Quinn took a long draw on his Marlboro and blew out a large cloud of white smoke. The tinted mirror behind the bar turned the billowing haze a light shade of blue. The detective paid no attention and dropped his head on the counter.

The bartender stopped cleaning the shot glasses and threw the rag into the sink. "Shit, Detective. What's wrong?"

Bridgeway ignored him. After a few seconds, he raised his head and fumbled around in his pocket. He strolled to the corner of the tavern and dropped two quarters into the Wurlitzer retro jukebox. He punched the yellow buttons. The old mechanical monster clicked several times and whirred into action. The melodious strains of "Georgia on My Mind" filled the room.

Quinn spun around. "I love the way Ray sings this song. What about you? You like this or Willie Nelson's version better?"

Jocko didn't quite know how to answer. "I like 'em both. Want a refill?"

Singing along, a touch off-key, the detective worked his way back to the stool. His eyebrows raised in his attempt to reach the high notes, but to no avail. "You know what? Give me the bottle."

The bartender placed the Johnnie Walker in front of the detective. "You got it. Hey, what do you think about those Falcons? It looks like they got a real shot to win the division this season."

Quinn shrugged. "Who gives a shit? You know they'll choke again." He sighed. "Patsie always rubbed it in. She grew up in New England and thought the Patriots were kings of the hill. Well, she can't anymore."

Quinn's statement didn't sit quite right with Jocko. "Why can't she?"

The detective rolled the whiskey around on his tongue and swallowed. "There was a shootout last night. Patsie took two in the face. That answer your question?" He measured out three fingers of Johnny Walker and glared at Jocko. "What's it to you? She's freakin' dead. All right? Now you know."

"Shit. You two were in here last night. How'd it happen?"

Quinn reached under his jacket and pulled his Smith and Wesson M&P .40. He laid it on the bar. "Leave me the hell alone. I don't want to talk about it."

The bartender took a step back. "Are you serious? Your partner's dead?"

"Yeah. I'm serious. I wouldn't joke about Patsie's death." He pointed toward the emergency exit. "I don't want to hurt you. Go. Get the fuck out of here."

Jocko trembled. He wanted to run, but he couldn't move.

Quinn seized his handgun and pointed it at his unlucky victim of circumstance. "Go on, move. I told you to leave. I mean now, not tomorrow. Out. Move."

Jocko reached for his keys and shoved them into his jeans. He slid out from behind his workstation and ran. His metal taps echoed as he ran across the floor to the emergency exit. He smacked both palms against the panic bar and forced open the metal door. The screech of the security alarm pierced the relative quiet of the North Highland Avenue neighborhood.

Quinn blocked out the blare of the high decibel horn. Pouring another drink, he chugged it. Tears streamed down his face as he toyed with the pistol grip. "Why? Why'd you want to leave me, Patsie? I loved you. I'm so sorry. I didn't want to hurt you. I couldn't help myself."

He stared at his reflection. "What are your plans now, stupid? You've got no way out."

*****

"Ain't gonna be no happy ending to this one, Lieutenant," Quinn screamed into the phone. "Don't you send anyone in here, or I'll blow them away. Your guys are lucky I didn't take a pot shot when your team was setting up their perimeter outside the door."

More than half the bottle of scotch was gone. Both Quinn's arms tingled. His brain worked in super slow motion, encased in an alcoholic smog. "I know the score," he mumbled. "Nobody gives a crap what happens to me. Patsie's the last person who'll ever hurt me. I don't care about anything anymore."

His bloodshot eyes inspected the telephone keypad before he pressed the receiver against his face. "Oh, yeah, and I suppose you'll give me a lollipop if I come out? Well, there's no way. Keep your people out of here. I've warned you to leave me alone. I don't want to hurt anyone else."

Lieutenant Savage's voice echoed through the handset. "Don't worry. My people aren't coming in. They disconnected the panic alarm earlier. I'm telling you the truth. I want to work this out with you." He paused for a few seconds. "Let me come inside and talk with you. Remember, I'm your advocate, but we still need to maintain proper tactical crisis protocol."

Quinn cracked up. "Oh, that's rich. I know I'm only another perp to you. What do you think? I'm an idiot?" He tossed the phone on the countertop and stared at his reflection. "Look at yourself, fool. They think you're a skell. Pathetic. You didn't want to shoot her. She made you do it. Or maybe…it was the devil." He laughed maniacally and caressed his pistol with both hands. Twin streams of tears dribbled down his face.

The boom of the bullhorn startled him. "Detective Bridgeway, pick up the phone."

Quinn almost tumbled from the stool as he roared into the receiver. "I got nothing more to say to you." He grabbed hold of the bar's silver railing and steadied himself.

Swallowing another double, he mumbled into the phone. "Yeah, okay. I know I got to set the record straight. What the hell do you expect me to say to you?" He wobbled on the stool and grabbed the rail again. "Okay, I admit it. I killed my partner. There's no excuse. I'm guilty. I did it."

"We can get you help." The lieutenant tried to sound confident, but it was a charade. He'd run out of ideas. Stick to procedure, find a way to diffuse the situation. Don't lose this one. "Believe me, Quinn, I understand your pain. What caused the rift between you and your partner?"

"I don't know?" Quinn blubbered, massaging his right cheek with the barrel of his gun. "The Army, it messed me up. I'm a terrible person. What I've done over there still rips me apart."

He took another snip of Johnny Walker. "My God. How would you feel if you watched your buddies blown away in front of you? You feel helpless and can't do a damn thing to save them. You can't ever forget those times. My pals come to visit me at night. They won't leave me alone."

Quinn drank more alcohol, this time straight from the bottle. "I loved her. I loved Patsie so much. You've got to understand. She wanted to put an end to our relationship. The thought of her with another man pushed me over the edge. I didn't want to do it. I couldn't stop myself. It was as if something possessed me."

"I understand, Detective. We have people who are experts and can help you."

"AARGH." Quinn's hi-pitched scream vibrated through the phone.

Outside, the screech of sirens drowned out the sounds of his suffering.

The detective heaved the bottle of alcohol against the mirror. The broken glass cascaded over the counter. "I don't deserve to live anymore," he croaked. "Please, God, forgive me."

He opened his mouth and slipped the business end of his Smith and Wesson between his teeth.

The walls reverberated with the report of his weapon. The round burrowed through bone, brain matter, and cartilage, drilling a massive hole in the rear of Quinn's skull. His body cartwheeled from the stool and crashed to the floor. A pool of crimson swelled beneath his head. Tributaries of blood filled the cracks of the ceramic floor tiles as his life ebbed away.

"Bridgeway, are you there? Bridgeway, Bridgeway, answer me." He knew he'd lost and closed his phone. "Jesus H. Christ! Detective, what the hell did you do?" The Lieutenant's shoulders sagged as he stared blankly at the flashing red traffic light swaying above the intersection.

Lieutenant Savage, his mind tuned into another wavelength, didn't notice his phone slip through his fingers. It bounced off the concrete and rolled onto the roadway.

"I failed," he gasped and turned to the sergeant sitting with him at the command post. "The poor bastard's gone. Bridgeway ate his gun."

18

Lisa munches on a piece of celery. "So, what's your opinion of Byron's story? I think he's hit an exposed nerve. The plight of our veterans has been so understated. He writes of the need to help them fit back into society rather than allowing them to become lost within the system."

Travis's ears perk up, but he can only understand part of her comment due to her noisy chomping. "Don't you think his story is a bit too violent? I'm not sure how the general public would receive this genre." He frowns and averts his gaze. "Would you please take human bites? Don't you know it's rude to talk with your mouth full?"

"Sorry. I wasn't thinking. I guess I'm too comfortable with you." She skips behind his chair and throws her arms around his neck. The celery stalk dislodges from her hand and drops into his lap.

"Get this out of here." Travis retrieves it and takes a bite. "Uhm, taste's good. I think I like it better with peanut butter."

"No fair. Stop being spiteful. Please, give it back."

"Oh, no. I think I'll hold on to it. You stole my oatmeal."

"Borrowed, you mean. You want it back?" She falls into his lap and fakes jamming a finger down her throat. "If you keep it up, I can arrange to chuck some up for you."

"Oh, you're sick. I bet you would too."

The screen on Lisa's phone lights up. She reaches across the desk and brings the device to her face. "Hello. Who's this?"

"Is this Lisa?" a female voice asks.

"Yes. It is."

"Hold for Colonel Nesmith, please." The curt voice cuts off.

A deep baritone rumbles over her phone. "Hello, Lisa. How are you?"

"Why, hello, Colonel. I'm fine. How about yourself?" "I'm good, thanks. I want to continue an earlier conversation."

"Uh, what conversation is that?"

"The discussion you and I had about your father. I told you I had access to the V.A. database. Well, I've managed to find him. He's alive."

Lisa's heart pounds. "Oh, my goodness, how incredible."

"Yes, isn't it. Your dad's living in Prescott, Arizona. He'd been a patient at the V.A. hospital there. That's how I found his address. Get a piece of paper. I'll give it to you."

"Oh, my word. Please, hold on a sec." Her mind is spinning out of control. *Could this be real? I've exhausted all avenues, and now, the Colonel is ready to show me the way.* Lisa sets her phone on the desk and bobs on Travis's legs as she reaches for a pen and pad. "Honey, he has my father's address."

"Great, babe. Where's he live?"

"Shh. Hold on. I'll tell you in a second. I need to write this down."

She lifts the phone. "I'm ready. Go ahead."

"Okay. It's 2415 Pleasantville Circle, Prescott, Arizona, 86305."

She jots down the address and repeats it aloud.

"That's correct. Unfortunately, the V.A. didn't have a phone number listed."

Lisa's ecstatic. "You can't imagine how much this means to me."

"I do, and I'm pleased we could help. Listen, I don't have access to the complete health records, but three months ago, your dad spent four days in the hospital."

"My father's sick?"

"Would point to it, but I can't say. No diagnosis appears on the forms, only general information. I wish you luck on your mission. I imagine you're going to go out there."

Lisa nods. "Definitely. Thank you again. This info is invaluable. You can imagine what this does for me."

"Glad to help. Talk to you soon, young lady." The line goes dead.

She waves the piece of paper. "Got it, Travis."

He hugs his fiancé. "That's great. I know how important this is to you."

"I can't believe I've found him. I didn't get a phone number, but I have an address."

"I heard. Now's the time when I tell you I'll rent a plane and fly us out to Arizona."

"What? For real?"

"Of course. I told you I have a pilot's license. What a perfect time to use it."

Lisa bounces a finger on her upper lip. "I don't know...Why don't we head to the gym? We can burn off some calories while we discuss it."

••• ••• •••

December 17

With endless possibilities developing for Lisa and Travis, a double-sided coin of unbridled lunacy has sprung up in the Georgia woodlands.

Nestled in the underbrush north of Island Ford, the fugitive unzips his sleeping bag, climbs out, and slips on his jacket. "You know I'm right, Zookeep. There's no way we'll ever stop looking for that broad and her musclebound goon. She should never have disrespected us the way she did." He takes a bite of a nutrition bar and washes it down with a swallow from an orange juice container. Sterling lifts several branches from the stack next to him and strengthens the wall of his lean-to. Camouflaged by leaves, but with the handlebars uncovered, an Italian racing bicycle lies a few feet away.

"I like your style, mate." The cockney accented voice kicks in. "Glad you picked up goodies from Walmart. I like the Clever Mike you borrowed from the parking lot."

"Yeah. It's a ten-speed racer." A thoughtful expression cut across his face. "Do you think I'd let you go hungry? Ain't my style. I'm always looking out for you."

"Appreciate it. You know I can always use a plate of fish and chips. The granola bar tastes rank, not my cup of tea."

"I know, Zookeep. Don't you worry. We'll hit the big time soon. You know me. I told you before. I got plans. Christmas time is almost here."

The crunch of leaves catches the madman off-guard.

"What the hell is that sound? Do you think it could be a deer?" He pokes his head around his make-shift wall. "Oh, shit." His eyes catch sight of the approaching park ranger. Sterling knows his patchwork of twigs and stems presents an insignificant barrier against detection.

He grabs the tire iron lying next to his knapsack. "We gotta keep quiet, Zookeep." He coils his body.

The National Park Service employee sidesteps the semi-circle of stones serving as the intruder's lavatory setup. He wrinkles his nose, revolted by the rank odor.

The ranger unclips the Motorola walkie-talkie from his belt. "Central, we have a trespasser squatting on government property. The location is five hundred meters east-north-east of Robert's Road. I'm about to investigate. Will advise. Over."

"Roger that, Charlie. Big Momma at Central. Out."

Before the red-bearded ranger has a chance to refasten the wireless transceiver to his belt, Sterling steps out from behind his sanctuary and smashes the public servant across the top of his skull. The body crashes to earth, bounces off the small pile of stacked firewood, and comes to rest on a clump of dead leaves.

"Yeah. Now you see what happens when I'm disturbed," screams the hominid beast of the Chattahoochee National Forest. "No one tells us what to do. Right, Zookeep? We're the masters of our universe." He drops his weapon and gathers his possessions. "We've been here too long, partner. Time to move." He kicks the unconscious park ranger in the side of his face with the point of his sneaker. "Thanks a lot, troublemaker."

19

December 23
Twelve miles east of Prescott, Regional Airport.

Travis checks the skies around his cockpit. "We're prepping to land. Sit back, relax, and enjoy."

Lisa plays with her headset. "I'm good." Her voice wavers slightly, but not because she has any question about her fiancé's prowess as a pilot. Oh, no. It's the uncertainty of finally meeting her biological father. "I'll keep quiet and let you concentrate."

"We'll be on the ground in twenty." Travis goes through his checklist. He flips on the landing lights, checks his gauges, and cuts back the engine's RPMs. He flicks a button on the console. "Flaps engaged. About to enter the 45-degree entry angle."

Lisa raises an eyebrow and listens to her fiancé's aeronautical repartee.

Travis adjusts the headset microphone with his left hand. "Prescott Tower, this is November Lima Echo One-Zero-Three-Alpha. I'm twelve miles out from Prescott Regional, altitude fifteen hundred feet. Requesting permission to land. Over."

The tower's reply is immediate. "Roger, November Lima Echo One-Zero-Three-Alpha. Welcome to Ernest A. Love Field. You have permission to land on runway twelve. Pattern altitude is twelve hundred feet. Confirm right-side feed. I repeat, Romeo. Over."

"Roger that. Romeo, Prescott Tower. Will enter landing traffic pattern in thirty seconds. Over." Travis lowers the flaps another notch and glances at the airspeed gauge. It reads eighty-three knots. "We're looking good, Prescott tower. One-Zero-Three-Alpha, out."

Lisa rolls her head back and rests her neck on the edge of the foam-filled seat rest.

Travis completes his turn and brings the Cessna 172 SP Skyhawk in for its final approach. He decreases airspeed to seventy knots and verifies the plane's alignment with the centerline of the runway. Within a few seconds, he raises the nose of the aircraft and touches down.

••• ••• •••

3:30 P.M.
Stone Lake Retreat

Lisa's eyes light up as she examines the three-room suite. "How did you find this place? It's delightful and so roomy. Look at these log-cabin walls and the rustic decor. I feel like I've walked into a house in the old west."

Travis drops his suitcase on the bed. "When I was in the Arizona League, me and three of my buddies chipped in and stayed here for a week one off-season. I knew you'd like it."

"Like it? I love it." She opens the porch door and steps outside. Travis follows right behind. The December breeze whips over the vinyl coverings that provide a modicum of protection for the wicker furniture.

Lisa shivers and grabs the collar of her jacket. "Chilly…but what a dynamic view of the surroundings, and, oh, look at the lake below us. It's magnificent." She draws in the clean fragrance of the mountain air. "Travis, take a whiff. It smells like…umm, happiness."

"I figured this place would impress you. Stone Lake Manor, exactly the way I remembered. Boy, it's been fifteen years. This place hasn't changed one bit. Okay. I got one for you. I bet you'll never guess the town's motto?"

Her eyes fill with confidence. "Too easy. It's "Everybody's Hometown." Right?"

Travis looks puzzled. "How'd you know?"

"Simple. I took a brochure from the office when we checked in." She flashes the paper.

"Ah-hah. Another reason I like you. Aside from your good looks, you got brains."

Lisa kisses him on the cheek. "Thanks. Let's go find my father."

"Good idea. Don't you forget, Leo's going to be my father-in-law. I can't wait to meet him either."

••• ••• •••

Travis taps his finger on the dashboard clock. "It's almost five. We've been sitting here for an hour. We're not sure when he's coming home. Why don't we find a restaurant and come back later?"

"Okay." Lisa digs into her bag. "Let me leave him a note."

"A note? What will you say? Something like, your daughter, who you've never met before, was here to see you?"

"Yeah, sure. Leo will figure out my identity quickly enough when he sees my last name. I'll leave my cell number."

"I give you credit. You have this all figured out."

"I wish I did, but thank you, my prince. What if he doesn't want to see me?"

Travis sets his jaw. "I disagree. Why would he have created a trust fund for you if he didn't care?"

"I know you're right, but I can't help having doubts." She double-checks the address on the notepaper. "Give me a minute."

"Um-hmm." He watches his fiancé climb from the car and stride toward the door of the modest ranch-style house.

She tries the bell one more time. There's no answer. Lisa knocks on the door before she pokes her head over the POW/MIA decal and presses her face against the window. The flash of lights on the tabletop Christmas tree and a small bird fluttering inside a cage are the only signs of life.

She stuffs her telephone invitation into the mailbox as Travis starts up the Ford Explorer.

••• ••• •••

DeJulio and Sons Pizzeria on Cortez Street

"Yes. I'm so excited. See you soon." Lisa shoves the phone into her bag. "Holy cow. He wants to see me. I feel faint. I don't know if I can do this."

Travis chuckles and rests his beer glass on the table. "Calm yourself, sweetie. There's no need to freak out."

Her body quivers. "I keep telling myself I shouldn't, but I'm worried. What if I disappoint my father?"

"Oh, please. You're super intelligent and the kindest person I've ever known. You care more about other people than you do about yourself. Leo's fortunate to have you as his daughter." Travis cuts off a piece of Stromboli. "How much time do we have?"

"My father expects us at eight." She glances at her watch. "It's seven-thirty now."

He takes a long swig from his draft. "We're good. He's a ten-minute drive from here. Let's finish up."

"I want to order a sandwich for him first. There's no way I'll go there empty-handed." She hops up from her chair and shuffles to the cashier. "Excuse me, miss. Can you help me?"

The girl in the Santa hat and matching red and green nails, hands change to a customer and closes the register. "Yes. What can I do for you?"

"Let's see." Lisa taps her foot on the floor as she decides. "I'd like a meatball hoagie with mozzarella cheese and half-a-dozen garlic knots to go."

Santa's helper spins around. "Hey, Mario. Give me a meatball parmigiana and an order of knots for take-out."

The chubby chef lifts a fresh Italian bread from the top of the rack. "You got it. Coming right up."

The cashier presses her fingers on the computer screen. "Twelve-ninety-five, please." The register drawer slides open.

Lisa pulls a twenty from her wallet and passes it to the young woman. "Thank you."

"Here's your change, and Merry Christmas," says the cashier.

"Thank you. Please, let me know when it's ready." She points to Travis. He's wiping his mouth with a napkin and swallowing the last bite of his food. "I'll be at the table."

"Sure, sweetie. Won't take long. I'll bring it to you."

Lisa walks to the table. She sits and toys with her salad.

"You should eat." Travis gulps his beer. "You'll be sorry later."

"I can't. I don't have much of an appetite. My stomach's been upset. I guess I'm too nervous about this whole thing."

He lifts a napkin and pats his lips. "I understand, but you should eat."

She pouts and plunges the prongs of her fork into the center of a plump cherry tomato. "You happy now?" She wrinkles her nose as the bright red berry disappears between her lips.

The cashier drops a small brown bag on the table. "Our garlic knots are made in-house. We look forward to seeing you again."

"Thank you." Lisa picks up the bag. "I don't think so. We're not from around here."

••• ••• •••

Travis switches on the headlights, shifts into drive, and inches away from the curb.

Lisa wears her emotional distress like a flag caught in a gust of wind. Her stomach churns. She's excited yet blanketed by a massive array of self-doubt.

Her fiancé stops the car and swivels around toward her. Lisa's eyelids blink in double-quick time as she kneads her hands. Her usual self-confidence has evaporated; a frown of uncertainty accents the worry lines at the outer corners of her mouth. She's mindful of Travis's icy stare, but she's still unable to curb her outward signs of stress.

"Come on. Get over it, babe. You're going to fulfill your destiny and meet your dad. Go with the flow, and don't worry about the minor details. You've been yearning for this."

She rocks back and forth. "I'm not like you. I don't have ice water in my veins. You can deal with pressure. You had thousands of people hanging on your every move each time you stepped on the pitcher's mound. I can't help but feel the way I do. I'm scared. All right?"

He lays a hand on her shoulder and kisses her on the cheek. "That's not the woman I know and love. I'm right here for you. Don't worry."

"Travis. I love you. You're so good to me. How did I ever survive without you in my life? You make me whole." Lisa sighs and leans toward him. "You always know how to make me feel so much better. I'm ready. Let's go."

She yanks down the visor and digs out the miniature tube of deep-red tint from her bag. Travis jerks the car forward as she angles the vanity mirror. The uneven road surface forces her to wait for the right moment to fix her face.

As the vehicle slows to a stop at a red light, she, ever-so-daintily, adds a bit more character to her lips and a dab of powder to each cheek. She completes her quick makeup job just as the light cycles to green.

Her pocketbook erupts with the sound of Jimmy Page's ear-piercing guitar riffs. Lisa grabs her phone and presses the "talk" button, paying extra care not to smear her lipstick. "Hello, this is Lisa."

"Hi, Miss Partainian, this is Detective Collins. I hope I'm not calling too late."

"Hello, Detective. No, it's not too late. I'm in Arizona right now. I told you about my search for my biological dad. Well, I've found him. We're in Prescott and on our way to meet him. I'm surprised to hear from you. Why are you calling?"

"Sterling Jernkowski has resurfaced. We found his fingerprints at a crime scene at Island Ford in Sandy Springs. There's no telling what he might have planned."

"That's not what I want to hear. When are you going to catch this guy and put him away for good?"

"We have a task force in pursuit." Collins pauses. "You know first-hand how dangerous he is. I wanted to keep you in the loop."

"Is it the detective?" Travis murmurs.

"Yeah. Shhh." Lisa waves a hand.

"I appreciate you letting us know, Detective. We'll be back home in a few days. I'll call you then."

"Okay. Talk to you when you get back. Merry Christmas to you and your boyfriend."

"Merry Christmas to you. By the way, Travis and I are engaged."

"That's terrific," Collins says. "Congratulations."

"Thank you." Lisa hangs up and lays her phone on the center console. "I wish they would catch Jernkowski already."

Her fiancé presses the brake pedal and brings the SUV to the curb. "We'll worry about that later. We're here." He motions with his head. "Look. The outside light's on."

"Let me grab his food." Lisa reaches over the seat. "Umm. I can smell the garlic and tomato sauce."

Travis takes the bag from her. "You ready?"

"Guess so." She opens her door and steps on the sidewalk. "Is it normal to have the chills and an upset stomach?"

"For you? Sure. No one ever said you were normal in the first place?"

Lisa chuckles. "Chalk up another reason why I love you. You always know how to knock me out of my funk. You're my hero."

As they approach the house, the door flies open. A man with a trimmed grey beard stands inside the doorway. He lifts his black cane. "You must be my reinforcements."

She springs up the steps. "In a manner of speaking. It's me, Lisa. I'm... your daughter." She wraps her arm around his neck. "I can't believe this moment has come."

Leo rears his head back. "Your pictures don't do you justice. You've grown into a woman more beautiful than I could've imagined."

"You have pictures of me?"

He nods. "I know this must sound strange. Your mom sent them to me, though the last one I had was from your eighth-grade graduation. She stopped after that. I guess she figured it would be best. He squints at her companion. "Who's this big fella?"

"This is my fiancé" Her voice trembles as she hip-hops over a minefield of confounding emotions. A tiny grin lifts the corners of her mouth. Tears trickle down her cheeks.

"HI, I'm Travis." He reaches out a hand. "It's great to meet you. You're all Lisa talks about."

Her dad's eyebrows pinch together. "I'm honored. Why don't you two come inside? I have trouble standing for too long. My leg's a bit unstable."

Lisa nods. "Sounds like a good idea. My whole body's shaking."

Travis's eyes dance. "Sure. Sounds good to me too."

Leo kisses his daughter on the cheek. "Talk about surprises. I'm more surprised about this than you. I always hoped this day would come, but I stopped thinking about it years ago. You were never a part of my reality, yet here you are."

She gazes at her father. "It's crazy."

"Your daughter brought a meatball hero for you." Travis jiggles his bag. "You hungry?"

"Not right now. Stick it in the fridge. I'll have it for breakfast." He motions toward the interior of the house. The couple's eyes meet, but both let his comment on his morning food choice pass. The three of them walk through the foyer and into the living room.

Travis holds up the paper bag and walks toward the kitchen. "I'll put this away."

Lisa stares at the birdcage in the center of the room. "A canary? What's his name?"

"Hoppy, and he's a female."

She moves closer and tries to catch a glimpse of the bird's underbelly. "Interesting. How can you tell if it's male or female?"

"I can't. The clerk told me when I bought her. She's my therapy bird."

A slight grin runs across Lisa's face. "What's a therapy bird? Is it something new for PTSD?"

Leo chuckles and falls back into his rocking chair. "No. It's my creation. I used to have a dog, but I got tired of cleaning up after him. When he died two years ago, I decided to try a new approach. I bought the tiny chirper from the pet store at the mall. She cheers me right up, great emotional support. Ain't that right, Hoppy?"

As if on cue, the bird cheeps, jumps off its perch, and pecks at the stainless-steel seed dish. Lisa inches closer and pokes a finger into the cage. "Hello, Hoppy. I'm pleased to meet you. You're a pretty bird. Yes, so pretty."

The canary flaps its wings and wraps her tiny claws around Lisa's finger.

"Oh, my goodness. Will you look at this?"

"She likes you, girl. Must smell my Miller DNA in you."

Travis falls back onto the sofa. He doesn't say a word.

"Hey! How'd you find me?" Leo asks.

Lisa tilts her head. "It's weird. We became involved with an organization that helps veterans with housing and job training. I found your address through them."

Her dad rocks back and forth in the chair. "I'm glad you did. How's your mom?"

She looks dumbstruck. "You don't know?"

His eyes narrow. "Know what?"

"With all the excitement, I didn't have a chance to tell you on the phone…Mom's dead. She died a few months ago."

"When? How'd it happen?"

"August the sixteenth. A crazy person knocked her off the highway. The police caught him, but he escaped."

"Oh, my Lord. How terrible." Leo groans. "I feel so overwhelmed." He pulls out a handkerchief and dabs at his eyes. "Enya was the love of my life. I've never gotten over our breakup. It was all my fault. I'm the one who messed it up. I mistreated the only person who ever loved me." He slumps in his chair.

The canary hops onto the center perch. Lisa pulls her hand from the cage and crouches next to her dad. She lays a hand on his shoulder. "You're wrong. She's not the only one who loves you."

He leans forward. "What do you mean?"

Her eyes find her father's. "I care about you. I've waited to tell you this from the moment I first learned you were my father. We're flesh and blood. *I* love you. It took me thirty-nine years to find you, and I'm not about to let you go." Tears cloud her eyes. "You and I are stuck with each other."

20

December 29, 3:15 P.M.

After spending the night in Amarillo and a scheduled refuel in Pine Bluff, the Cessna's on approach to their destination, the Peachtree-Dekalb Airport in Chamblee, Georgia. The Jetstream's cooperated nicely and saved Travis and his passengers an hour of flight time.

Lisa rotates her body and looks into the back seat. "How are you and Hoppy doing back there?"

Leo fidgets with his shoulder harness. "We're golden." He checks the water level in the canary's plastic bowl. "Still wish we had a seat belt for my little pal." He laughs and taps the pilot on his shoulder. "What time do you think we'll land?"

Travis tinkers with his right earphone and checks the altimeter. "Thirty minutes until we're on the ground," he answers, reducing the plane's airspeed, and increasing its pitch.

The backseat passenger leans forward. "That's good. You know, I thought about learning to fly when I was younger. Too much was going on back then for me to follow through. After I became involved in the construction industry and opened my own contracting business, I stuck the idea on the back burner and left it there."

Travis does a quick check of his instruments. "Oh, yeah? If you want, I'll take you up and give you lessons. It's all by the numbers. Excuse me, but right now, I need to tune in to the Automatic Terminal Information Service."

"Whoa. Sounds impressive. What's it do?" Leo asks.

"It's a prerecorded transmission, cuts out the crosstalk and radio chatter. The broadcast gives current weather, range of visibility, active runway protocol and conditions, and other important data." He reaches over to the radio stack. He hits the Com2 button and switches to the ATIS frequency."

••• ••• •••

Sandy Hills Road, Marietta

Lisa sets the toiletry bag on the bed. "What do you think? Do you want to keep Hoppy in your room?"

Leo lays his boxers in the top dresser drawer and brushes them with a hand. "The living room is a more social location. That would be a better choice once my regular cage gets here. We can mount it from the ceiling and keep it high, away from your cat. Good idea?"

"Yes. I agree. I'm certain we can train Molly. She'll learn to coexist."

Her dad continues to fill the drawers. "For now, I'll keep Hoppy in my bedroom and leave the door closed. The rest of my stuff should arrive in a couple of days."

Travis admires the new shoe rack he's finished attaching to the closet door. "I think that's a good plan. We wouldn't want a confrontation. Matters wouldn't end well for our feathered friend."

Leo's posture stiffens. "Yeah, we gotta be careful." He closes a dresser drawer and parks himself on the edge of the bed. "I still can't believe I'm here. How the heck did I let you two talk me into this?"

Lisa snuggles next to him. "Oh, no. Don't blame us. You suggested the idea. Don't you remember? You said retirement didn't agree with your constitution. That's exactly the way you put it. You wanted mental stimulation. Besides, you're going to help me finish my book. I need to pick your brain. You promised."

"I know, I did." Leo screws up his face in mock frustration. "Guess I'm going to have to dig deep and pull a rabbit or two out of my hat.

How about we start tomorrow. I'm tired from the flight and could use a nap." He slides his suitcase under the bed and stretches out on the mattress.

Lisa stands and straightens the assorted items on the top of the dresser. "I'll wake you in an hour. Travis is ordering Chinese food. Any particular dish we should order for you?"

"Nah. Whatever you get is okay with me. Err, come to think of it, nothing with duck, too chewy to suit me."

"Not a problem," Lisa comes around the bed and examines the worry lines on his face. "I have a slight issue you might help me with."

"What's that?"

"What should I call you?"

"For right now, Leo's fine." He yawns as he fights to stay awake.

"Well, okay. Glad we straightened this out. I see you're sleepy. We'll get out of here and let you take a nap."

Her dad rolls over and gets comfortable. Lisa bobs her head and waves a finger at the doorway. She and Travis tiptoe from the room.

••• ••• •••

December 30, 8:30 A.M.

Lisa stares at her new Steve Madden sneakers as she waits in line at the CVS drugstore. She's missed her period and has been sick to her stomach each morning for the past week. Her intuition tells her she's pregnant, but scientific confirmation is sorely required.

"Next, please." The skinny brunette cashier waves her over. "May I help you, miss?"

Lisa glances at the rows of cigarettes lining the shelves as she lays the package on the counter. "Yes, charge, please."

The cashier scans the Clearblue Pregnancy Digital Test package and smiles. Oh. I wish you luck." She rings the register. "I hear this is very accurate."

"I hope so..." Lisa digs into her wallet and passes over her credit card. "...Especially since they guarantee it is on the package."

Her gynecologist appointment is next week, but waiting until then would be torture. Is she, or isn't she? Lisa needs to know now.

The young woman smiles and hands Lisa back her credit card. She drops the kit into a white bag.

Lisa brushes back her hair. "Thank you. I appreciate your help." She slides her card into her wallet and tucks the purchase underneath her arm.

"You go, girl," says the cashier. "I wish you luck."

Without much thought, Lisa hops behind the wheel of her Prius and drives onto Windward Parkway. She hasn't said a word to Travis about her missed period or suspicions. *How will he feel about becoming a father? I'm sure he'll want a son; take him hiking and teach him how to play sports. The baseball doesn't roll far from the pitcher's mound.*

She laughs aloud at her play on words. *Will our son grow as big as his dad, become a professional athlete? Hey. But what if the baby's a girl? Think of all the fun we'll have together. I'll tie her hair into pigtails. The two of us will play dress-up, and when she's big enough, we'll go shopping together at the mall. How about dance lessons like my mom gave me?* The thought of her mother brings on the waterworks. *Geez, I miss her so much. I wish she were here to share all this with me.*

••• ••• •••

BEEP! BEEP! BEEP!

The loud blast of an automobile horn yanks Lisa back to the reality of the morning rush. She applies the brakes as traffic comes to a dead stop. A police officer points and waves her over to the left lane. A cruiser, with the emergency light flashing, idles behind him. A second police car sits on the adjacent sidewalk bordering a Japanese Sushi restaurant. The driver's side door is ajar.

As Lisa's car inches forward, she notices people milling about on the asphalt. Two SUVs and a black BMW are parked haphazardly at the edge of the side street. The rear fender on a Toyota RAV4 has a huge dent above the wheel well. A broken left headlight dangles from the Bimmer.

As she presses on the gas pedal, the rotating red light of a fire engine appears in the rearview mirror. The blasts of horns and screech of sirens echo in her ears as the traffic mess grows more distant. She boosts the sound on the CD player and takes a last look in the mirror. Both hands tap on the steering wheel as she assists Cindy Lauper warble about the philosophy behind girls wanting to have fun. Bubbling over with energy, Lisa makes herself a pinky promise to do her utmost to fulfill her pregnant possibilities.

••• ••• •••

"One, two, three, four, five." Lisa replaces the cap on the Clearblue Digital device and lays it on the laminated countertop next to the sink. Hummingbirds flutter about in the pit of her stomach.

The window on the digital wand indicates the "Smart Countdown" has begun. Scuffling with apprehensions, Lisa taps a foot and waits. The mirror above the vanity betrays her distress as she tries to assure herself of the outcome. "Let's make this a double positive, pregnant, and healthy."

An excess of information explaining pregnancy risks is available online. Lisa's read way too much and knows the percentages for a miscarriage elevate once you reach forty. That birthday is right around the corner. The thought sends chills through the middle of her back. "Please, God. I want to have a baby, and it needs to happen now."

The screen on the tester goes blank.

Lisa lifts the small white dispenser filled with procreative truthfulness and gawks at it. Moistness fills her brown eyes. She squints at the tiny display, takes a deep breath, and holds it. *Here comes the decisive moment.* The word *Pregnant* jumps out at her from the center of the screen.

"Oh, my God! Thank you, Lord," she shouts in jubilation. "What terrific news."

The excited mother-to-be floats across the tile floor and closes the white wooden door behind her.

••• ••• •••

Lisa presses the phone against her ear. "Hi, Travis. Are you at the veterans' shelter?"

"Yes. I told you I had a meeting with my buddy. Right now, I'm with Byron in his office."

"Perfect," she answers.

"Yeah. I know. There's a reporter from the Journal on the way. We might as well get whatever publicity we can. Hmmm. Why don't you meet me here?"

She thinks for a moment. "Okay, I guess I could. I'll have a chance to talk with Byron about his short stories. See you soon."

"Hold up a sec. Why don't you ask your father to come with you?"

"Seriously?" Lisa can't help herself and decides to have a bit of fun. "What about his bird? Should we bring her along too?"

"Since when did you start doing standup? You know what? I think you should attach a love letter to Hoppy's leg and show her a map of Acworth?"

Lisa snickers. "Now, who thinks they're the comedian? I have news I need to deliver to you personally. I wouldn't want a canary to carry my message. It's a big surprise."

"Tell me. What is it?"

"Oh, no, Travis. If I told you, it wouldn't be much of a surprise."

"I suppose not. I hate it when you do that. You're going to owe me big time."

"We'll see. Wait until you hear what I have to say. See you soon."

She turns off her phone and rushes into the kitchen. Leo's at the table, the contents of his bowl of oatmeal almost gone. When Molly sees her mistress, she mews and jumps up. Lisa lifts her. "There you are, girl. I need to go out for a bit. I don't want you to miss me too much. I'll be back soon."

She reaches beneath her kitty's chin and rubs.

Molly's eyelids flutter. She purrs and flicks her tail.

"Leo, why don't you come with me? I'm going to meet Travis at the veteran's shelter. We could use your input."

"My input? What do I know?"

"You know how veterans feel and the problems they face when they come back home."

He drops his spoon into the bowl. "It's the concept of war that's the problem. Ask anyone who's fought in one. The horrors live inside you for the rest of your life."

"I understand…Dad." Lisa catches herself. Leo wasn't too keen on the word when she'd asked him about it before.

He swallows the last spoonful of oatmeal. "You know what? If you'd like to call me Dad, that'll be fine." He walks to the sink with the empty bowl. "I'll go with you. Let me get my stuff."

21

Georgia Homeless Veteran's Shelter, Acworth.

Travis's eyes fog. "This is something. I'm a father at forty." He throws his arms around his fiancé and embraces her. "You've made me so happy. I love you."

Lisa hadn't planned on using Byron's cramped office as her official announcement headquarters, yet here they are. "I know. Isn't it wonderful? I have an appointment with Doctor Levin next week, but the pregnancy test is nine-nine percent accurate. We won't know if it's a boy or a girl for a few months."

"As long as we have a healthy baby." He kisses her on the hand and once on each cheek.

"For sure. Having a healthy baby is what's important."

He stares into her eyes. "I love you so much."

"Oh, no. I love you more."

"Here, we go again." He smiles and guides her to the grey couch across from Byron's desk. "Please, sit. You need to take it easy."

"Now, don't you start acting overprotective. I'm fine."

Loud noises and the uneven tones of a not-too-distant disagreement override their conversation.

Travis hops up. "I'm going to see what's going on. You stay here. I'll find out and let you know."

"Okay." Lisa frowns. "But you better hurry back. I don't want to stay by myself."

"He lays a hand on her cheek. Don't worry."

Another crash adds to the uncertainty of the situation.

"Oh, crap. Sounds like dishes breaking." Travis sprints out of the office and dashes through the communal area and into the kitchen.

He finds Byron in front of the stove, taking part in a face-off. The brawny shelter director grapples with a man trying to press forward. Tempers appear to cool when they see Travis.

A table lies overturned with shards of broken stoneware and remnants of an egg breakfast gone wrong scattered about the floor in the center of the room. Leo is helping a white-bearded man in a fatigue jacket rise to his feet. A beat-up Vietnam Veterans hat lies on the floor next to them.

Travis stoops and retrieves the hat. "What the heck happened here?"

"A disagreement," Byron answers. "Charlie, here, took exception to something Joe said."

The accused troublemaker explodes. "It ain't my fault. It's his. Said I cook like shit, wouldn't eat my food. He had the nerve to tell me I'd even mess up my own wet dream. Do you believe this old dirtbag's bull? He's the one who broke the dishes and knocked over the table."

The older vet throws out his hands. "Damn straight. And I'll tell you why. You make your eggs way too loose. Your recipe suck. You always add too much paprika and cayenne pepper." He throws up a middle finger. "I told you before; your food's too spicy. You don't listen. Pisses me off."

Charlie's body stiffens. "Oh, here we go again." He seizes Byron by the shoulders and tries to push him out of the way. With thirty pounds more muscle on his frame, the director doesn't budge.

Charlie releases his grip. "This old jerk thinks he's the baddest mofo in the valley. He may be older, but Joe's no different than me. He's just another fool the government threw into a ring of fire and discarded like a piece of garbage when they finished with him."

"Come on, guys. You two are brothers. Stop this." Travis doesn't raise his voice. "You're supposed to help each other. Life's hard enough. Don't make it any rougher."

"For damn sure." Joe scowls and points at Charlie. "This kid doesn't have any respect for us Vietnam vets. He thinks he and the guys who served in Afghanistan had it much worse than the soldiers of my generation. What a crock of shit."

Travis pats his father-in-law-to-be on the back. "He's a Vietnam vet too. The Major," he wiggles a finger in his direction, "served in Afghanistan and Iraq. You don't see the two of them disrespecting each other."

"Not yet, anyway." Leo keeps a straight face.

Byron loosens his grip on Charlie.

"Look. All of you put your lives on the line for this country." Travis emphasizes each word. "We're proud of you, no matter when or where you fought. You're all patriots."

Leo thrusts out his hand. "Welcome home, brother."

Joe grabs it. "Welcome home yourself, brother." A grin slowly forms on his face. "Listen, Charlie, I'm sorry. Your cooking's not half-bad. I messed up and got a big mouth. I know we shouldn't argue." He points at Travis. "He's right. If we don't look out for each other, who will?"

Charlie nods. "You got that right. Let's forget this happened. Blow it off as a big misunderstanding." He bounces a finger on his lips. "Hey, listen. How about you take a walk with me over to Waffle House? I'm buying."

Joe releases his grip. "What about my buddy here?"

Charlie waves a hand. "Sure. No problem."

Leo winks at Travis. "If it's okay, I'll keep them in line."

"That'll work. We're waiting for my buddy and the news reporter to arrive. You go ahead. Before you leave, you should talk to your daughter. She's got exciting news."

"Good. Tell me."

"Oh, no. Talk to Lisa." Travis points toward the communal area. "She's through there. I'm not going to spoil the surprise."

••• ••• •••

"What inspired you to become involved with helping veterans?" asks Marlon Wilson, the coco-skinned reporter from the Journal.

Travis taps his fiancé on the hand. "Lisa is the one who put the wheels in motion. Let her explain."

She takes a sip of water and places the plastic cup on Byron's desk. "Thanks for giving me credit, but honey, you made this possible."

I see." The reporter shifts in his chair. "Lisa, would you explain, please."

"Gladly. The story might sound convoluted, but it all began when my mother died."

Marlon lays his hands on his lap. "I'm so sorry for your loss."

"Thank you. So, I came home from Birmingham, and when I was going through my mom's things, I found a stack of old love letters written by a soldier serving in Vietnam. When I checked her safe deposit box, I found paperwork revealing this man, Leo Miller, was my dad. Evidently, he and my mom were much closer than pen pals when he came home."

The reporter rubs his chin. "I like the way you put that. How so?"

Lisa takes another swallow of water. "I discovered my mom's first and second marriage licenses, annulment papers for her and Leo, my original birth certificate with my biological dad's name on it, and the adoption record."

Marlon sucks in a quick breath. "Wow. That's amazing."

"Mind-blowing. You can imagine my reaction. I felt as if my whole life up to that point was a lie."

The reporter checks his recorder. "I can understand your reaction. What did you do?"

"I decided to find my father, and while I'm at it, write a book about the experience. Travis and I ran into each other at the gym. We were high school sweethearts but hadn't seen each other in years. He's the major reason we're here with you today. This man helped transform my dreams into reality."

Her fiancé's chin dips. "Let's not get carried away here. I helped, but you're the galvanizing force."

"This might be true, but you've picked me up whenever I suffered a defeat."

The reporter wags a finger. "Enough with the explanation of inspirations. Please, Lisa, continue with your story."

"Oh, sorry. In one of the letters, I found the information on one of the men who served with my dad. I looked up his phone number and called him. He also had a letter from another of my dad's old buddies. The more

I spoke with the Vietnam veterans, the more I realized what a raw deal they've gotten, but I was still no closer to achieving my goal of finding my father."

She takes a sip of water. "Travis came with me on all my trips. He understood how I felt about our patriots and surprised me by creating the veteran's fund. It was a natural progression from that point onward. Colonel Nesmith, who's connected with this shelter, heard my story. He's the one who helped find my father."

"Please. Why don't you elaborate?"

She clears her throat. "This is getting mighty personal, but here it is. For the past forty years, my dad's been living in Prescott, Arizona. He has Diabetes, a by-product of exposure to Agent Orange. He's doing well now, but he spent time in a V.A. hospital, fighting off some complications. He's in Atlanta now and involved in our struggle to gain recognition for the plight of our veterans."

"Fascinating. What are your long-term goals?" Marlon asks.

"The rate of suicide for combat veterans is one-and-a-half times greater than for people who've never served. More than twenty vets commit suicide each day. There are several variables, but I believe we can help them and provide quality living quarters and sustainable employment."

The reporter drops his chin on his chest. "I had no idea the rate was so high. I'll try to convince the newspaper to solicit donations for your organization."

Lisa's face brightens. "Travis, do you hear that?"

"Yes. What a great idea. We could also ask for aid from the medical community, enlist psychologists or psychiatrists, and supervise group therapy sessions. Many of the vets have PTSD and other serious mental conditions. Imagine all we can do for them if we put our resources to good use. Could you mention this in your article?"

Marlon pulls out his cell phone. "Sure, but I have a better idea. A good friend of mine works for a TV station. Let me call and see if we can get some screen time. An on-air interview would go a long way in spreading your message. The public needs to hear this story."

He presses his auto-dialer. "Hello, Baron? Hey, my brother. Yeah, it's me. What's up? I'm calling to check if you're coming to Foster's tomorrow night. Terrific. See you at eight."

The reporter slides the phone into his jacket pocket. "We were roommates at Morehouse. Ever since graduation, a bunch of us meet at a place on Lawton Street to welcome in the New Year."

Travis hops up and pulls open the door. "Sound's great. Let's go inside. I'd like you to meet the shelter director and Bob Randolph, the owner of Randolph's Cleaning Service. His business is ready to employ our vets. We still have the details to iron out, but I'd like to get you in on it."

22

New Year's Day, 12:45 A.M.
Moreland Avenue, Little Five Points

Sterling wipes the blood on his victim's pants leg and closes the serrated blade on his hunting knife. "Can't ever say no to the Zookeep." The words glide from his lips, along with a small stream of saliva that disperses in the frosty air. He stuffs the dagger into his backpack and glances at the silver garbage cans blocking the rear entrance to the shuttered tattoo parlor.

"Right, mate." The tart reply resonates with a tasty helping of the pretentious British accent. "Shouldn't ever need to ask anyone more than once for their bread and honey."

He rifles through his victim's pockets, avoiding the blood oozing from the chest and stomach wounds. He digs deep and finds a set of car keys along with a brown leather wallet.

"Two-hundred-and-sixty-six bucks and two credit cards. Yes. What a nice haul, Zookeep." He tosses the empty piece of cowhide aside. "We better use this Visa and Amex quick."

Sterling grips both the corpse's ankles and drags the body further into the alley. A dim bulb at the entrance of a basement art supply store provides the only light. He stashes his victim behind a green dumpster and positions a trio of garbage cans as a barrier against discovery. "We can't get sloppy now. Can we?" He toys with the Hyundai keyless remote as he strolls from the alley.

The door to Milligan's Tavern opens. "Happy New Year," roars a reveler dressed in a red, white, and blue outfit and a decorative top hat to match. As the drunk stumbles onto the sidewalk, the brisk night air strikes him in the face. The party animal teeters and fights to regain his equilibrium.

A woman with long blonde hair, and one lock covering an eye, follows him outside. She carries her high heels in one hand and spins a noisemaker in the other. "Spider," she chirrups, "slow down. Wait for me,"

Another pair of partiers follow along in the New Year's Eve procession.

"Hey, George Washington," Sterling shouts at Spider, "you look like a trick-or-treater who doesn't know Halloween's been over for two months."

Spider's beyond tipsy and pays no attention. All four celebrants stagger across the street.

"Screw off," Sterling shrieks. "That's right. All of you, get the hell out of here."

He presses on the key fob and looks north. *No response.* He turns in the opposite direction and tries again. This time, he hears a beep. Seven or eight cars ahead of him, the headlights on a grey Sonata flash twice. *Yeah. There's my ride.*

The killer sidesteps an older woman with a long leash draped around her arm. A blimp of a dog waddles behind her. "Look, Zookeep. Damn beast looks like a balloon about ready to explode."

Sterling throws his bag in the back of the car and drops into the bucket seat. "Nice set of wheels we got. Huh?" It takes thirty seconds of trial and error, but the engine turns over, and the blower kicks on. A gust of frigid air hits him in the eyes. The car's temperature gauge registers forty-four degrees. He shivers, and fumbling with the vent control, redirects the airflow away from his face.

"Don't worry, Zookeep. Give her a minute. She'll warm up."

"Taint worried one bit, chum. We're all set now; scored us a nice stash of bees and honey." The maladjusted social misfit jerks on the rearview mirror and admires his yellowed teeth.

"Oopsy-doopsy. There you go with your funky talk again, Zookeep. You're right. We got plenty of money, collected over two hundred in cash nectar from the hive." He checks the fuel gauge and fastens his seatbelt.

"Half-a-tank. Plenty of gas to get us to Newnan. We need to pay a visit to two old friends."

He doesn't bother to signal and cuts off a grey Honda Accord. The pissed-off motorist slams on his brakes and leans on his horn. Sterling sticks out his middle finger and laughs.

It's bumper-to-bumper traffic for three blocks. Sterling shifts into neutral at the red light at McClendon Avenue and yanks open the glove box. "Let's see what we got here?" He brushes aside the papers and silver flashlight and stares at the grand prize. "Well, thank you."

Atop the manual, a box of .38 cartridges leans against a packed leather holster.

Alas, his happiness is short-lived. The repeated blast of a car horn intrudes on his world. "Okay. Hold your horses, asshole." He slams the glovebox closed and shifts into drive.

"Hey, Zookeep. You see what we got, right? Found us a legit widow-maker."

••• ••• •••

Sterling turns off I-85 and jumps onto GA-34. He hates Newnan. The bad memories of the sexual abuse, the beatdowns, and the nightmares, still haunt him. The time to avenge his past suffering has come.

He exits the highway and finds himself on familiar grounds. Sterling parks in front of 134 ½ Kellogg Place and shuts the engine. The wail of a distant siren is the only sound encroaching on the virtual silence of the witching hour.

Except for the soft amber glow of a nightlight, darkness fills the interior of the private residence. The three steps leading to the front door are visible through the porch light's hazy glow and two strings of leftover Christmas lights wrapped around the doorframe.

The dashboard clock shows 2:15 A.M. "We got us a good plan, Zookeep." He jerks open the glove box and cradles his latest piece of pirate booty. Pressing the release latch, Sterling flips open the cylinder.

All six chambers lay bare. He drops a hand into the glove box. "It's no problem. Easy peasy." He dumps the pack of cartridges on the passenger seat and loads his new toy. His skinny fingers snap the weapon shut.

"Let's rip these assholes a new one." He shoves the revolver into the backpack and flicks the switch on the car's electronic door lock. "I don't give a crap if they apologize and wave the white flag. We're going to get us payback tonight." He opens the door and looks around.

Sterling bypasses the front of the house and heads around the side. It's been eight years, but he remembers Tina Raymond's old habit of leaving the back door unlocked. In the moonlight, he can see the waist-high row of bushes beneath the screened-in porch. Patchy and unkempt, the Evergreen hedges need trimming. The overgrown grass and invasion of unwelcome wildflowers verify the dire need for a landscaper.

Doesn't anyone take care of this place anymore?

It's been a while, but the memory of the untold hours spent manning the mower and weed whacker reminds Sterling of the pain. The beatings old-man Raymond doled out were a small part of the misery. He can never forget the sexual liberties forced on him. Tonight, the scales of justice will dip in his direction. He plans to exact retribution for the fourteen-year-old who couldn't muster the strength to fend off his abuser.

The tip of his right sneaker sinks through the rotted wood of the top step. He pulls his foot away. As he opens the raggedy mesh door, it begins to break free from its moorings. Fortunately, the bottom hinge forestalls disaster. *I need to watch out, got to stay invisible.* He eases the splintered door back into place. The porch floorboards creak. He tiptoes to the back door and tries to turn the knob. *Shit. It's locked. Don't seem right. Okay. New Plan.*

Sterling burrows into his backpack. He unfolds his hunting knife and jimmies the door latch assembly. With an almost imperceptible click, the bolt slides free. He leans into the door and uses his body weight to push it open. "We're in business," he whispers, his eyes slowly adapting to the faint glow of the lone five-watt neon bulb. He visualizes the home's layout in his head.

"Wish we had a torch, mate. We could see our way up the blooming apples and pears," his alter ego says.

"Up the stairs? Don't worry, Zookeep. Follow me. I know the way."

He takes the ten carpeted steps two at a time. When he reaches the landing, he holds out the knife. The blade glints in the moonlight. Sterling creeps three quick steps and skulks inside the first door on his left. Empty. The next room is on the right side of the hall. Boxes and books line the walls. He walks to the end of the hallway and peers inside the doorway. A bulky comforter covers the bed. Sterling distinguishes the outline of a person beneath it.

He drops his backpack and races across the room. The dispenser of half-baked justice rips off the covering and stabs at the body. He connects to the upper torso, then to the diaphragm. The spurting blood soaks the victim's flannel pajamas. With each stroke of the blade, the life-sustaining fluid splashes on Sterling's face and clothes. He's unfazed and continues his blitzkrieg.

Sterling's victim moans and lifts both hands in a feeble attempt to fend off the onslaught. It's already too late.

The killer revels in his act of savagery. "Yeah, yeah, yeah," he screams, continually flailing his arm. The tip of his weapon pierces the ribcage and slices through to the other side, again and again. The self-proclaimed rectifier basks in his spiteful euphoria. With each stroke, he removes a bit more of the horror of his childhood exploitation. This act will eradicate the memory of adolescent torture and parental betrayal for all time, or so he imagines.

Exhausted, Sterling's breaths come in truncated bursts. The knife slips from his fingers. He switches on the table lamp and glares at his victim. "What? Who the hell are you?" he bellows. "I don't freakin know you."

The stark reality of Sterling's depraved act of misguided retaliation registers within his twisted brain cells. "You're not Mr. Raymond." The high-frequency scream demolishes his sensual orgasm of malevolence. He recognizes the voice. It's his own.

He grabs the lapels of his quarry's blood-drenched sleepwear. "I was looking for Mr. Raymond," Sterling sobs, but not due to regret.

"This sucks. Why'd you get in my way?" He pulls at the pajama top and bounces the target of his mistaken identity on the mattress. "I'm justified. So, what if you're the wrong person. It's your own damn fault for living here."

Falling to his knees, Sterling retrieves the knife and wipes the blade on the comforter. He hums the melody from Old Lang Syne.

23

January 16, 2013, 10:15 A.M.
Gunther Liebolt Studios on Martin Luther King Jr. Drive, Atlanta.

Benjamin walks toward the set and motions toward the trio of comfy-looking chairs. "Lisa, you can sit right here. Travis, right there. I'll sit between you."

The guests work their way around the wooden coffee table.

"Ah, purple, my favorite color," Travis says.

"Yeah, mine too," seconds the orange-haired young woman who's stepped out from the backstage area. Garbed in a Rainbow Coalition t-shirt, a large gold ring embellishes the skin of her left nostril. The earthy aroma of patchouli oil follows after her.

Ben takes a step forward. "This is Joanne, my production assistant. She'll get you organized. Relax. This experience will be fun."

The unorthodox appearing assistant smiles. "Good to meet you."

Benjamin chugs a Red Bull and belches. "Oh, yeah. Much better. Gotta feel it." He strolls toward the studio tech, who's busy adjusting the height of the pedestal-mounted camera.

The cameraman chews on the butt of an unlit stogy. "How long, you figure?"

His boss's eyes glisten with newfound vitality. "Should be about a fifteen-minute shoot." He tosses the blue and silver can into a pail.

Joanne digs into her bag and points to Lisa's chin. "Lift your head, please." She attaches a wireless lapel microphone to her blouse. Travis's shirt comes next. The production assistant clips one to his collar. "As Ben said, there's no pressure."

Scooting over to the two foreground lights, she trains them on the trio of chairs surrounding the coffee table, lifts the handheld light meter, and checks the numbers. "We're good, Bob. We're reading 750 Lux."

The cameraman raises a fist. "Right on."

Benjamin drops into the chair between them. Lisa and Travis watch as he rehearses his intro, occasionally throwing out a hand to emphasize a point. The reporter folds his paper and stuffs it into his shirt pocket. He looks across at his interviewees. "A word of advice. Watch me. If you make a mistake, don't worry. We can edit it out and reshoot in a heartbeat."

"Got it," Travis says, making himself comfortable and adjusting the placement of his size fifteen sneakers.

Lisa fluffs her skirt. "Me too."

"You framed up, Bob?" Ben asks.

"We're good to go." The cameraman gives a thumbs-up.

The host throws up a closed fist. "Follow my lead."

"No problem," Travis answers.

Lisa tries to appear cool and calm. "Whatever you say. You're the boss."

"Good, then we're set." Ben circles a finger in the air. "Ready, Action."

Joanne clicks on the audio recorder. "We've got sound."

"Rolling," Bob adds.

The TV reporter primps his collar. "Ladies and gentlemen, in the studio with us today, we're pleased to have Lisa Partainian and Travis Gentry. These are special people who've invested in the welfare of our homeless and stricken veterans. Their story is of great interest. I'm sure you'll feel the same way after you hear what they have to say." The host turns toward his guests. "Thank you both for coming."

Travis lobs a one-finger salute. "Thank you for having us."

Lisa clears her throat. "Yes, thank you."

Ben stares into the camera. "You people might remember Travis. He grew up right here in Marietta and pitched for the 1990 Lassiter High School State baseball champs. He enjoyed a successful major league baseball career with the Dodgers, and three years ago, he retired and moved back to Georgia. Now, he and his fiancé have found a way to give back to America's veterans."

Travis smiles at the camera. "Thank you. I don't mean to correct you, Ben, but you forgot the College World Series with Arizona State. We were runners-up in 94."

"Oops, sorry." Ben smiles and shifts his attention to Lisa. "Tell me, how does it feel to have a professional athlete as a life partner?"

"Why? Because he's tall and dreamy? Or because he has such a big mouth?" she deadpans.

The host wears a huge grin. "Okay. You got me. Why don't you tell the audience about your book project?"

"Yes. Thank you. This past August, I received the shock of my life when someone murdered my mother. Let me tell you, that's an experience I hope no other family will ever have to endure."

"You must have been devastated."

"No doubt. I was heartbroken, but my mom's death led me to an incredible discovery. I learned I wasn't the flesh and blood daughter of the man who raised me. My true biological father's identity came to light, a fact hidden from me my entire life."

Ben's eyes widen. "Must've blown your mind?"

"It certainly did. The revelation sent me on a quest to find him and create a written record of my odyssey. My book is at the editor right now."

"Terrific." The host applauds. "I congratulate you."

"Thank you. Even more amazing, I've found my father. Wilder still, Travis and I reconnected after more than fifteen years. We're getting married next month at the site of our re-date."

The look of surprise registers on the interviewer's face. "Lisa, please, tell me. What's a re-date?"

"A term I coined. You see, we were sweethearts during high school. As he mentioned, Travis attended college out of state. Long-distance love affairs usually don't work too well. We broke up, and the two of us traveled our separate ways. When we bumped into each other at the gym a few months ago, SHAZAM." She raises both hands. "The 11th Bomber Squadron is where it all began, again. What better place to have our wedding?"

Ben nods and turns toward Travis. "Makes sense. Please tell our audience about the Georgia Veterans Homeless Shelter."

"Sure. I'm happy to." He glances at his fiancé. "Lisa and I have created a fund in conjunction with the Georgia Veterans Homeless Shelter in Acworth. When the work is complete, the building will house fifteen veterans. We've also instituted a work-study program to help get them back on their feet. We're starting small, but we have big plans."

Lisa points at the camera. "America, we all need to wake up. Where is our compassion? Our humanity? These sons and daughters of liberty need our help. They fought for our freedom and have made great sacrifices. We need to secure their futures."

Ben's eyes gleam as his face breaks into a massive smile. "I agree, big time. Thank you both for sharing." He slides a forefinger across his Adam's apple. "Okay, Bob. Cut."

He stands and smiles at his guests. "You guys were great. We'll post the mailing address and phone number on-screen during my sign-off. You're going to have plenty of coverage. My boss said we're going to broadcast the interview through our statewide affiliates."

Lisa throws up a hand. "All right!"

Travis gives her a fist bump. "Sure is."

Ben claps his hands. "Okay. Enough chatter. Let's shoot a few close-ups, and you two can cut out."

24

The left turn signal indicator blinks as Travis waits for the light to change. "I'm so proud of you, hon. You sure let loose on camera."

Lisa plays coy. "You think so? I didn't do anything special."

"Oh, yes, you did. Your enthusiasm will capture people's interest. I bet we'll collect a bunch of contributions because of you." The traffic light turns green. Travis drives up the entrance ramp and onto I-285. "You demonstrated so much positive emotion. We couldn't have a better spokesperson."

Lisa shrugs. "I followed your lead. My life is so much better with you as a part of it."

"It works both ways, doll. You energize me on so many levels."

"You should look out, big boy. I have plenty of mysterious ways to charge your battery."

"Oh, you're so bad." He taps the left-turn signal and glances in the rear-view mirror. "I guess it's another reason I want to spend the rest of my life with you." He angles into the center lane.

Lisa rolls her eyes. "Oh, please. And I thought my gourmet cooking turned you on." She winks and wiggles in her seat. "I'm happier now than I've ever been. With you at my side, I know I can solve any problem. I have complete faith knowing I have you as my backup plan."

"It goes without saying. I'm confident you'll find the solutions for whatever dilemma you face. You have a special knack, always did."

"I love you so much. I believe in you, too." Lisa glances at the dashboard clock. "What time did you tell Byron we'd meet him?"

"Told him three. We can stop at our place first."

"Oh, good. With all the excitement, I forgot to take my prenatal vitamins."

"Sure thing. We'll be home in half an hour."

"You know, Travis, I'm thrilled my dad's gotten involved with us. He fits in so well at the shelter. It's surprising how he's brought a bit of calm to the place."

"I agree. Leo has a special rapport with the other vets. With his experience in the construction industry, we're fortunate to have someone who knows which end is up."

Lisa raises an eyebrow. "You better watch out with your dirty talk. I think you're looking for trouble."

"I guess you can see right through my plan. You're the best kind of trouble to get into."

Her cheeks turn a deep pink. "I have a new red nightie to try on for you."

••• ••• •••

Georgia Veterans Homeless Shelter, Acworth.

Travis and Lisa sidestep the partially filled dumpster occupying space next to the side entrance. As they walk into the building, a workman angles past them and grabs a piece of sheetrock from a chest-high pile inside the doorway. He hoists the forty-pound board onto his shoulders.

"I'm gonna check out the progress." Travis pivots away from her.

"Okay, honey. I'll be in Byron's office."

Lisa marches through the director's open office door and drops a thick manila envelope on his messy desk. Here's my first draft. *No Veteran Left Behind*, that's the working title. I'd much appreciate your feedback."

Byron folds his newspaper and checks the heft of the manuscript. "Sure, I'll be glad to."

She flops on the couch. "I know how busy you are, so no pressure. Did you hear from Marsha yet?"

"Yes. I sent a proposal and synopsis of each of my stories. When Marsha called me back, I pitched her an idea for a new stand-alone novel centering on government corruption and CIA involvement in Iraq. The tentative title is *View from Inside Armageddon.*"

"Wow, Byron. That sounds incredible. You're so prolific."

"I wouldn't go that far."

"Well, I would. Look at you. You're a regular word processor."

"Ha, ha." The director wears a thoughtful expression. "I haven't signed a contract with the agency yet, but I'm certain it'll happen. Marsha thinks she has the perfect editor. He's former military."

"I'm so happy for you."

"I can't thank you enough for your help."

"No, Byron. Your creativity speaks for itself."

"Come with me. I want to show you how much progress we've made. Your dad has been great and saved us a boatload of money."

"I'm so pleased." Lisa springs from the couch. "This couldn't have worked out better."

The director leads her through the common area. Two male residents lounge on a sofa watching television. Byron nods to them and pushes aside a strip of the clear plastic tarp hanging at the entrance to the new wing.

Leo's razor-knife flashes as he scores the paper backing of a piece of Gypsum-filled plasterboard. He lays his yardstick aside, pressing a knee on the four-foot by eight-foot piece of sheetrock, and breaks off the section. The master carpenter leans the custom piece against the half-finished wooden wall frame and rises.

Sliding the knife into his tool belt, he turns toward the new arrivals. "Hey, what's up? I have a good head of steam going. We're making quick progress here."

"Sorry to slow your roll," Byron answers. "I wanted to spread the good news."

"Good news? Hey. I have news of my own." Leo flexes his leg. "All this exercise let me get rid of my cane. I don't need it anymore. I'm moving around fine."

Lisa stares at his resurrected leg. "How marvelous! Miracles do happen."

Byron bounces on his toes. "For sure. I've got one even better for you. We have more sets of hands on the way, two former Twelve Whiskies,

Army Carpentry, and Masonry Specialists. They've agreed to move in and help with the construction. They're arriving tomorrow."

"Could be a good thing, but we don't need any lard asses causing us slow-downs." Leo sneers. "Their skills better be up to snuff, or they'll be outta here so fast, they won't have time to hammer nameplates on the ends of their bunks."

Byron chuckles. "It's good we have you around to keep our guys straight."

"Somebody's got to do it." He adjusts his carpenter belt. "We're almost finished with the drywall. I'll mud the seams later today. I figure we'll start sanding tomorrow. We can put your 12W boys to work, see how good they are with the paintbrush."

"Super. I told your daughter how lucky we are to have you. I'm speaking not only as the shelter director but as a former soldier who cares about his fellow veterans. I can't thank you enough."

Leo shrugs. "No biggie. I'm doing what comes naturally."

Lisa's eyes dart around. "Have you seen Travis?"

Her dad points toward the rear exit. "He's outside taking a call; said we were too noisy."

"Oh, okay. When he comes back in, please tell him I'm in Byron's office."

"No problem." He kisses his daughter on the cheek. "Let me get back to work." He reaches into his belt and lifts out a hammer. Spinning it in his hand, Leo retraces his steps to the newly cut piece of sheetrock.

••• ••• •••

Director's Office

The expression on Travis's face telegraphs his discomfort.

"What's wrong?" Lisa bolts from the couch and rushes to his side. "Who was on the phone?"

Travis doesn't answer.

Lisa frowns and tugs on his arm. "Please! Let me know."

"It was Collins, the detective."

She crosses her arm. "Collins?"

"Yeah. He called to let us know Jernkowski surfaced again."

"Jeez. When will the police catch this guy?"

"Soon, I hope. The psycho went on a New Year's rampage. The specifics are pretty graphic."

"Spare me. I don't want to know the details."

"Fine with me."

Her eyes widen. "Thanks. Listen, I need to powder my nose. I'll be right back."

"Okay, babe. I'll be right here."

Byron waits until Lisa leaves the office. "Travis. Tell me. I'd like to know."

"It's crazy. The sick asshole murdered a guy in Little Five Points. They found his body in an alley, stuffed under a dumpster. The story gets worse. He took his victim's car and drove to Newnan. The jerk didn't know his former foster parents sold their house two years ago. The new owner was asleep. Jernkowski stabbed him more than three dozen times."

"Whoa! Sounds whacked."

"For sure. And get this, the killer took a shower and made himself eggs? His fingerprints are all over the place. He left the car he'd stolen and switched it for the one belonging to the dead homeowner. They found it in the Anna Ruby Falls parking lot yesterday."

"What the heck. Why do you think that lowlife went there?" Byron's face brightens. "I bet I know."

Travis swallows the bait. "You do? Why?"

"What better place to go than Helen for a belly full of Bratwurst and a stein of lager to wash it down."

The two men crack up.

"I should be recording this," the director quips. "We sound like the crazy ones."

Lisa's footsteps echo in the hall.

"What are you guys talking about?" she asks as she reenters the room.

"Zookeep's reign of terror." Byron makes the sign of the cross. "The character is no joke. I know you two had a close encounter of the most dangerous kind."

"Tell me about it." Lisa squeezes her fiancé's arm. "He saved my life."

Travis's hand finds her shoulder. "Yeah, scary business. Thank goodness he didn't get the opportunity to do his worst. We were lucky."

Lisa's lips part. "Much more than lucky. You protected my butt."

Her real-time superman slaps three fingers over his heart. "And a firm one indeed."

Byron's face flushes. "Okay, enough of this backside talk. What do you think of the new wing? Never imagined we'd finish so soon."

Travis gives a thumbs-up. "When will the furniture be delivered?"

The director fumbles through the papers on his desk. "I've asked the company to push it up a week." He finds the purchase order. "Here it is. Originally, we had delivery scheduled for February first. Who knew Leo would make such a difference in our timeline?"

Lisa smirks. "Good old dad. He's a man of many talents. You've brought out the best in him."

Byron swivels his chair around. "I've done next to nothing. Your dad helps with much more than construction. He's terrific with the younger guys."

25

The Zookeep has accounted for the deaths of ten human beings, and at any moment, his body count has the possibility of ballooning. He's proven quite unpredictable and minus more than a handful of lug nuts. Inexplicably, he's remained one step ahead of the authorities. The self-righteous malcontent is on the move and searching for more fertile ground where he can sow his seedlings of irrationality.

Having grown weary of Helen's Alpine-style village, Sterling hitches a ride with a teenager who's tooling around in his daddy's blue Chevy Suburban. The driver is fortunate. His passenger merely says thanks and climbs from the vehicle.

Sterling approaches a one-story wooden cabin along the narrow dirt road and lays his palm on the hood of the Jeep Cherokee parked outside. "Aha, still warm, Zookeep. They must be inside." He brings a finger to his lips and rolls his eyes. "Gotta be as quiet as mice. No, let's stay even quieter."

The killer slithers up the trio of steps and peers through the front window and into the kitchen. There's a counter in the center of the room. Beyond it, in the main chamber, a television screen throws off rays of incandescent light. There's no other movement. Sterling digs into his knapsack, removes his knife, and flicks it open. The doorknob turns all the way. He pushes open the door and tiptoes inside.

Alerted by the murmur of voices and sound of splashing water, Sterling pauses in midstep. The scent of mint fills his nostrils. Creeping past the flat-screen, he stops and peeks around the partially open porch door. The heads of a male and female are visible above the rim of the hot tub. Gathered atop the crown of the woman's head, a ponytail holder keeps her gold-colored hair in place. The back of a hairless head is visible next to her. The man without a conscience cocks his head and listens.

"Oh, honey, stop with the politics," says Blondie. "You know it raises your blood pressure."

"Emily, stop telling me what to do," Baldy answers. "It's Obama with his dang gun control crap. That pisses me right the hell off. We need a Republican in there. Now we gotta wait another four years."

Sterling narrows his eyes and tightens his grip on the hunting knife. *These idiots aren't going to see four more minutes.*

He lays his bag on the floor and tiptoes through the doorway and onto the porch. Moving past the loveseat, he positions himself at the edge of the hot tub and clears his throat. As Baldy turns and looks up, Sterling plunges the knife into the soft tissue of his neck. The victim screams and tries to rise. The Zookeep's arm recoils and thrusts the blade forward, piercing the ribcage and puncturing his heart. The body goes limp and slides beneath the water.

Blondie's shrill wails provide her no quarter nor any opportunity to secure sanctuary. The long blond hair gives the killer a perfect handhold. Grabbing her ponytail, he jerks her head back and snarls as he slices through the layers of skin protecting her esophagus. The gurgling sound of his latest conquest choking on her blood is music to the killer's ears. Streaks of crimson discolor the bluish-green cast of the water as she falls forward and joins her husband's body floating a few inches beneath the surface.

Sterling jerks a towel from a wall hook and wipes his face. After cleaning the blade, he stuffs the Buck knife into his bag and carries it into the living room. He drops it next to the couch and tosses the towel on a chair.

"We gotta get out of these clothes, Zookeep. I hope this guy ain't partial to barbeque and French fries." Sterling heads into the wood-paneled bedroom and slides out the middle dresser drawer. He picks out a pair of pink panties, takes a whiff, and then examines his reflection in the full-length mirror. His nostrils flare. "Smell's fresh."

The underwear drops to the floor as he paces across the room and opens the top drawer of the twin mahogany dresser. Sterling flips it over, dumping the contents on the bed. "Yeah. Now, we're talking." Discarded clothes are thrown haphazardly around the room as he selects an outfit. "Okay, shower time."

The assassin strolls into the bathroom and adjusts the water temperature. He undresses, grabs the green bar of soap, and steps beneath the spray of warm water.

Sterling tilts the showerhead toward his head and lathers his face. "Ooh, yeah, feels good, buddy. What d'ya think, Zookeep?"

"Methinks, a *chicker,* and a *Chas and Dave* might set things right."

"Haircut and a shave? Hmmm. I guess we could. Sure. Why not? Did I ever tell you how much I love your cockney slang?"

The cascading water washes over him. He cuts off the flow and steps from the stall. Lifting a towel from the rack, he searches the open toilet bag on the countertop and finds what he needs.

••• ••• •••

Sterling thrusts his face six inches from the bathroom mirror and admires his beardless reflection. He lays a hand on his bald dome. "Shit. I look like the actor from that movie. You know the one, uh, *The King and I.* He's got that funny name. What is it, Yule Brinna, or something like it? Ah, screw it. Don't matter."

He slaps on a dash of aftershave. Bounding into the bedroom, the new-look predator pulls on a pair of socks and slips into an oversized pair of boxer shorts. The khaki bottoms are also too big, but the leather belt takes care of the problem. The Budweiser tee-shirt swims on him, so he tucks it into the waist of his new Dockers. Sterling stares into the mirror again. "I look tough, don't I, Zookeep?"

"Sure do, mate. No bloke better start no *argy-bargy*; they need to *ey up*."

"For damn sure. Any darn fool throws a punch at us, the fool better watch out."

The racket from the television shifts the double-edged maniac's focus. As if mesmerized, the clean-shaven miscreant glides into the living room. He settles on the couch and follows the action on the TV screen. The image centers on a group of people inside a stadium. They're on their feet, shouting, "Go Falcons, go Falcons." The audio comes across loud and distorted.

"Can you believe this? The noise is all about football, Zookeep? Who cares?"

A succession of commercials ensue. If you need new windows, a lawyer to sue a driver who hit you with their car, or relief for a bloated stomach, your dreams might have come true.

Sterling picks up a pillow and tosses it across the room. "Jesus, what bullshit."

The picture fades to black. After several seconds, Lisa and Travis's faces burst on the screen. The prerecorded interview, shot at Gunther Liebolt Studios, rolls.

Sterling leaps up. "Look at this. It's those assholes." He stands and gapes at the screen. "I was wondering what happened to you two."

He presses his fingers over the scab on the bridge of his nose. He seethes at the memory of the long-armed bastard who chucked the flowerpot and knocked him for a loop. "I owe you assholes, big time." He falls back on the couch. "Zookeep, we found 'em."

The interview cuts off. A sincere-sounding accident attorney takes the place of the subjects of Sterling's ire.

"Can you believe this crap?" He raises a leg and kicks at a lamp. "They're getting hitched at a place called the 11th Bomber Squadron Restaurant, and what the hell is the Georgia Veterans Homeless Shelter? We better check this shit out."

••• ••• •••

A moonless night. Torrents of rain cascade down all over God's green earth and the metal of the maroon-colored Jeep Cherokee as it turns off Georgia 515 and follows the ramp leading to Interstate 575. Sterling's in a foul mood. Dark and rainy aren't his favorite combination of driving conditions, but he's coping.

He reengages the cruise control and keeps the speedometer steady at sixty-five miles per hour. The clock reads 2:15. "Screwed up, Zookeep. We got us another hour of driving through this crap."

"Pleasure and pain give Mother Nature her early bloom, China plate."

"Yeah. I know rain makes the flowers grow. Zookeep, but it's winter. All this water ain't about to help that none."

The interior of the car explodes with sound. Johnny Cash's deep baritone voice decodes "Ring of Fire."

"Some nice ring tone," Sterling announces, grabbing the iPhone from the center console. A gleeful smile parks itself on his face. "Chicken Galore. Can I take your order?"

"Huh? Who is this?" answers the male caller. "What the hell is Chicken Galore? I want to talk to my dad. Put him on."

"You got the wrong number, stooge," Sterling snorts, not bothering to disconnect. He drops the phone on the passenger seat and yells at it. "You're an idiot!"

Thirty seconds after passing the sign for Cherokee County Airport, the rotating blue light pops on in his rearview mirror. "What the...gotta stay calm. I know, keep cool, but I'm better off being prepared."

Sterling reaches under his seat and yanks out the pistol. Stuffing the weapon beneath his thigh, He stares at the Bobblehead Jesus on the dashboard and flicks it with a finger. "Ain't no way we can outrun the heat in this weather."

The Georgia State Patrol cruiser flashes its high beams twice. The trooper's baritone voice trumpets through the public-address speaker. "Pull over to the side of the road."

The traffic stop recipient applies the brakes and swerves onto the shoulder. Turning on the hazard lights, he shifts into park. Flipping open the glove compartment, Sterling picks up his latest male quarry's wallet.

The tap on the window disrupts the rhythm of the raindrops drumming on the roof. A blinding beam of light hits Sterling squarely in the eyes.

"Open your window, please, sir," requests the unseen trooper.

Sterling lowers the tinted glass halfway. "Nice weather, huh?" The silhouette of the rotund officer comes into view.

"Shut your engine, please."

The killer's body tenses as he complies.

"Didn't you see the sign? You passed through a work zone. The posted speed limit is forty-five miles per hour. Do you know how fast you were going?"

"No, but I bet you're about to tell me."

"Don't act like a jerk-off." Frustration colors the trooper's voice. "The weather's bad enough. Let me see your license, registration, and proof of insurance."

Sterling hands the officer a North Carolina driver's license and attempts a friendly grin.

The trooper ignores him. "Do you know you have a tail-light out?"

"No, I haven't checked it lately. Do you think the ducks are having a grand old time in this weather?" His attempt at humor finds no audience.

The officer shines his light on the license and shifts it back to his detainee's face. "Roland Talbot? No way. This license doesn't belong to you. You're twenty years younger than the guy in the picture."

Sterling's expression morphs into a grimace. "I look younger because of my baldy haircut. You like me any better this way?"

The officer shifts the flashlight to his left hand and reaches beneath the all-weather parker with his right. "Let's go. Step out of the car."

The social misfit grabs hold of his pistol. "Wait. I have a much better picture for you."

The flash of light and roar of gunshots punctuate the early morning calmness. The officer's wide-brimmed hat spills to the ground as he pitches forward. His nose bursts apart as his face smashes into the edge of the roof. The two high-velocity puncture wounds in the center of his forehead spurt blood as the heavy-duty flashlight drops from his hand and bounces down the hill. The trooper's body tumbles to the ground. Spectral pulses of light dance across the tree line until the department-issued piece of battery-operated electronics crashes against a large rock and shines no longer.

"We showed him what he gets for screwing with us, Zookeep." Sterling twists the key in the ignition. The radio erupts with Johnny Cash's voice and the sound of chunky guitar chords. Sterling leans over the console and grabs the cellphone from the floormat. He chucks it out of the half-open window and shifts into drive.

"No more fooling around. We mustn't forget, got us a wedding invite."

26

January 18, Mid-morning
Georgia Veterans Homeless Shelter, Acworth

The new north wing is close to completion. Robbie Baxter, one of the former Army carpenters, finishes tying off the dozen leftover pieces of two-by-fours and climbs down from the pickup bed. As Leo signs the return authorization form, the truck lurches forward. The rope comes loose as the pile shifts, and the wood scatters.

"Look out!" Robbie shouts.

Leo spins away from the free-falling missiles. He manages to avoid them, but for an obstinate piece of yellow pine joist that rebounds off the sidewalk. The sharp, kiln-dried corner jabs the inside of his left ankle, gashing skin, and cracking bone.

"Yow!" He screams, stumbling backward and collapsing on the concrete. "Shit! I heard a pop." He reaches down and feels around the fragment of bone protruding through his skin. "Quick! Get a towel. Call 911!"

Byron hears the commotion from inside his office and sprints out the side door. He totes a roll of paper towels and rips off sheets as he races toward Leo. Dropping to his knees, the director presses the balled-up material against the wound.

Tyrone, the second military carpenter, dials the emergency number. "We have an injured man. Yes. 123 Cushing Avenue. Please hurry!"

Leo rocks back and forth. "This son-of-a-bitch hurts!"

Byron points to the doorway. "Ken was a medic in Afghanistan. Go inside and get him."

Robbie hustles inside.

"An ambulance is on the way," Tyrone barks.

Robbie, out of breath, returns with back-up. "Let him help. He knows first aid."

Ken squats next to Byron. "I got it." He takes the crumpled up toweling and checks the wound. "The bone sliced through the skin, but I've seen much worse. It doesn't look like any major arteries are involved."

"Aww, shit! I can't believe this happened," Leo moans

The former field medic stays calm. "It's under control, Major. I need a first aid kit and a basin of water. I want to clean around the wound."

Robbie shoots up a hand. "I'll get them. Be right back." He rushes inside.

Ken continues to apply pressure. After a minute, he rechecks the injury. "Looks like the blood flow's slowing down." He places the towel back on and peers over his shoulder. "Where's that water?"

"I'll go see." Byron takes a step toward the building but stops. "Shhh. Listen. Do you hear the siren?"

Robbie rushes from the shelter. "Here's the water and a washcloth. I couldn't find the first aid kit."

Byron waves a finger toward the back door. "In my office, behind my desk, middle shelf. Quick! Move!"

"Got it." Robbie takes off again.

The wail of the siren grows louder.

Tyrone points toward the street. "I'll go out front, make sure they see us."

Before he has the chance to take a step, the Metro Atlanta ambulance pulls into the driveway and screeches to a stop. The passenger door swings open. A young black female hops out. She's tall and thin, her black hair braided and accented by golden streaks.

The paramedic hurries to the rear of the vehicle. She removes her bag and rushes to her patient.

"It's his ankle," Ken says, keeping pressure on the wound but moving aside to give the emergency worker room to maneuver.

She removes the blood-soaked towel and examines the laceration. "You did an excellent job. The bleeding's stopped." The aid worker squirts saline solution over the area and pats it dry. "I'm going to wrap it. They'll sterilize and treat it at the ER," she says, reaching into her bag and pulling out a roll of gauze.

Her partner's partially open jacket reveals a sizeable beer belly resting on the gurney as he rolls it toward the patient. "How is he, Keisha?"

"Compound fracture of the left tibia, above the ankle. The patient is conscious, his condition stable. Bleeding under control. Just about ready for transport." She cuts two pieces of adhesive tape and secures the bandage.

"Roger, that." The driver lifts the backboard from the gurney and places it on the concrete. "You ready, Keisha? Watch his foot."

"No problem, Chuck." She zips her bag and takes a position on the side of the patient.

"Slip the backboard under me," Leo says. "I can lift my butt for you."

"No. That's alright," answers the driver, stepping to the right side of the patient. "Stay calm. We've got it. Ready, Keisha?"

His partner nods. "I'm all set. Waiting on you."

"Great." He places his hands under Leo's upper thighs. "Okay. Here we go. One, two, three, lift!" Chuck grunts as they hoist their patient onto the stretcher.

"Just relax, sir." He secures the safety straps. "Ready, Keisha?"

Byron rushes over. "I'll give you a hand."

The female medic raises a hand and gently shoos him away. "No. We got it. Insurance issues, but thanks."

The director wraps his fingers around the victim's hand. "I'll call your daughter, let her know what happened."

Leo grimaces. "Yeah, okay. Thanks."

Byron stares at the driver. "Where are you taking him?"

"Emory Trauma Center on Main Street."

••• ••• •••

1:15 P.M.

Lisa paces beside her father's bed. "How could this happen? You're always so careful."

"Accident. I was stupid. Should've tied off the wood myself."

She walks to the half-opened door and glances into the hallway. "Travis is trying to find out how long before they take you up to surgery." She checks the wall clock. "You've been here for almost two hours."

"I know. It reminds me of the Army, hurry up and wait. Hospitals are the same way."

Lisa frowns. "Doesn't sound too reassuring."

"Don't worry. I'm okay. They took X-rays, and the nurse gave me a Tetanus shot." Leo analyses the Cardiac Monitor. "Look. My BP is one-twenty over sixty-eight, and my pulse is sixty-three, normal readings. My right leg feels like crap. I also must have twisted the left knee when I fell. It's tender. I guess it could always be worse."

A cute blonde nurse with curves in all the right places nudges open the door and heads straight to the IV stand. "Shouldn't take much longer. We're prepping an OR."

"I'm his daughter. What about a pain killer? He's uncomfortable."

Leo sits up. "It's okay, Lisa. I told them I don't want one. I had problems with Quaaludes years ago. I'd rather deal with the pain."

The young nurse checks the splint on his lower leg. "We've treated your father's wound with Lidocaine. He's receiving Tylenol and an antibiotic through his IV."

Travis motors into the room. He's out of breath. "I spoke to the supervisor. Leo's going up for surgery in a few minutes."

One of the nurse's pencil-thin eyebrows raises. Her cheeks flush as she gets an eyeful of a piece of prime American male real estate. Slightly flustered, she casts her gaze downward and rushes from the room.

The young woman's reaction doesn't escape Lisa. "I think she was checking you out, hon."

Travis scratches his head. "I didn't notice. Besides, you know you're the only one for me."

"You got that right," Lisa growls.

The hum of muffled voices and the metallic clatter of castors rolling through the doorway cut off their conversation.

"Mr. Miller?" announces the blue-clad worker holding the side of the transport stretcher, "Hi. I'm Enos, ER tech." A human heart tattoo is visible on his upper right arm as the worker lifts the patient's chart from the bed rail.

"Finally." Leo lays his head against the pillow. "Been waiting to get the show on the road."

Dashing into the room, the cute nurse is a whirlwind of motion. Her fingers make quick work of the monitor wires.

Another male tech joins them.

The nurse lowers the bed rail. "Okay. Let's move the patient. Be careful."

The three lift Leo onto the gurney. Enos takes the IV bag from its stand and lays it above the patient's right shoulder.

Lisa plants a kiss on her dad's cheek. "We'll be in the waiting room. Don't worry. Everything will turn out fine. I love you."

He throws up a victory sign. "I love you too, sweetie."

She pinches her lips together and takes a sideward glance at her imaginary competition. The nurse pays no attention to the icy stare and helps roll the gurney into the hall.

••• ••• •••

5:15 P.M.
Second Floor Waiting Area.

The elevator door opens.

"Are you Miss Partainian?" asks the scrub-frocked gentleman with close-cropped blonde hair and wire-framed John Lennon glasses. "I'm Doctor Roseman, your father's surgeon."

Lisa seizes the arms of the chair and jumps up. "Yes, Doctor Roseman. I'm Leo's daughter. How is he?"

"Mr. Miller's fine. The operation was a complete success. We inserted a metal rod into his right tibia to promote healing. He'll be out of action for three months or so. His left knee has a slight patellar tendon tear. It doesn't require surgery, but he'll need to stay off it."

Travis jumps up. "Stay off his feet? For how long?"

The doctor's eyes narrow. "Who are you, exactly?"

"I'm Travis, Lisa's fiancé."

"Ah, hah. How do you do?" The doctor says, nodding.

"Fine. Good to meet you. Are you saying Leo will need a wheelchair?"

"Yes. For a time. That's the prescribed course of treatment. Leo's knee injury isn't serious but needs to heal. I estimate four to six weeks before Mr. Miller can discontinue using the chair and switch to crutches. Down the road, he'll need physical therapy."

Lisa taps a foot on the tile floor. "Hmm. When can we see him?"

"He's being transferred from recovery now. He'll be in room 212. I'd wait fifteen minutes; give him time to get his bearings."

She takes Travis's hand. "Thank you, Doctor. We appreciate your thoughtfulness."

"I'm glad to help. I've checked your dad's records. I know he's a veteran and has Tricare. We're sending over the paperwork to the V.A. They'll provide a wheelchair and will fill his prescriptions."

Lisa exhales. "That's tremendous."

Travis leans against the checkerboard wallpaper. "Yeah. Sure is."

"Here's my information." The doctor offers her a business card. "My dad flew helicopters in Vietnam. Anyone who served our country has my utmost respect. It's the least I can do." He glances at his watch. "I have a date with my wife for dinner. It was nice to meet both of you. My number's on there. If you have a question or if there's a problem, call me."

Lisa scans the front of the card. "I will. Thank you again, Dr. Roseman."

"If you haven't done so already, I'd suggest you become Health Advocate for your father. A social worker can help you fill out the paperwork. It will come in handy in the future."

Lisa nods. "Thank you. I'll mention it to my dad."

The doctor turns and presses for the elevator.

27

February 1

"Here it is." Lisa hands Travis a sheet of paper. "My guest list's complete." Blue lettering fills the first dozen-and-a-half lines of the page. "I have my maid of honor and her husband. My brother, Jared, and his new girlfriend, and I've also invited Maggie from the Birmingham Gazette, her date, and several of our friends from school.

"My dad invited three of the vets from the shelter. Hobie's going to fly in from California. He said he's stoked and wrote a new song for the occasion. Wants to play at the reception."

"Good. Should be exciting." Travis presses the remote and mutes the TV while he studies his list. "I have twenty-eight guests. With you, me, and Leo, and in case we have anyone last minute, I'll tell the restaurant to prepare the buffet for fifty-two."

"Sounds about right. I've called the people on my list and made sure they can make it. Can you believe this? Our wedding is twenty-three days from today. We haven't allowed our guests very much time for arrangements."

Travis pulls her toward him. "I don't think I can wait that long. I need you near me all the time." He pecks her on the cheek. "I want you to become Mrs. Gentry as soon as possible. We should've done this fifteen years ago."

"We're together all the time anyway." Lisa pats him on the shoulder. "No sense crying over it. Things happen for a reason. Hmm. What an old expression. I wonder who first said it?"

Travis smiles. "I think Forrest Gump. Do you remember the scene in the movie when he's jogging with all those people trailing behind him?"

She looks bewildered. "Uh-huh. So, what's your point?"

"I'm getting to it. You remember the part where Forrest takes a faceful of mud, and a guy strolls over with a yellow shirt and hands it to him?

Lisa smiles and shuffles her feet. "Maybe"

"Well, he uses it to wipe himself off. Then he hands the shirt back. The guy holds it up and is awed by the smiley face mud pattern on the fabric. That's when the Johnny-on-the-spot has his epiphany. He goes home and stencils: '*Shit Happens*' beneath the picture and makes himself a fortune."

"I saw the movie three times, sweetie. Sorry to tell you this, but you've got it wrong."

Travis's head jerks back. "What do you mean?"

"Your memory's in the toilet, honey. Tom Hanks hands the dirty shirt back and says: '*Have a Nice Day.*' That's the slogan below the smiley face."

"Are you sure?"

"Yes, Travis. It's after that when Forrest steps in a pile of dog poop, and a guy gets inspired to create a bumper sticker with your overused phrase."

"Wow. You're a regular Brainiac, Miss Partainian. One of the major reasons I love you so much." His eyes twinkle. "I bet you didn't know this, but I'm a sapiosexual."

Lisa purses her lips. "Sapio, what? Please don't tell me you're a sicko who likes to get it on with Maple trees."

Travis holds back his laughter. "You're a regular riot. I think you know me better than that. Sapiosexuals are people excited by brainpower. I'm in love with your mind as well as your body. Your intellect captivates me. It has nothing to do with saplings or pancake syrup."

Lisa wears a mischievous grin. "And here I thought you were looking to branch out."

"My goodness. Girl, you require some serious therapy. Even with your sick sense of humor, I'm thrilled you're marrying me. I can't believe how lucky I am." He pauses. "You complete me."

"Okay, Jerry McGuire. If you expect me to say: 'You had me at hello, you'll be waiting a long time." She points to the bedroom. "I have a much better idea." She grabs his hand.

Travis's eyes light up. "Oh, you're so sneaky. I love your style. You know, I'd follow you anywhere." He cradles her in his arms and carries her inside.

••• ••• •••

Veterans Homeless Shelter, Acworth

Leo glares at the younger man sitting across from him on the couch. "Hey, Air Force. Will you close the damn window? Ain't you cold."

The younger man in a baseball cap embroidered with an Iraq/USAF logo looks up. "No, I'm not. I've got thick skin." He grunts and pulls down the double-hung window halfway. "We'll compromise. Okay, old-timer?"

Leo rolls his wheelchair out of the direct path of the breeze. "Yeah, I guess. You better watch out with the old-timer crap. If I weren't in this chair, I might seriously kick your ass."

Air Force fights off the urge to laugh and removes his cover. He navigates a hand through his greasy black hair. "Look, I'm sorry. I didn't know you were so touchy. Byron told me, in your day, you had a reputation as one of the best point men in the business."

The older man scowls. "In my day? You're at it again. Watch that mouth."

"Okay, okay. Sorry." Air Force readjusts his hat. "Geeze, will you stop acting so touchy." He taps his knuckles on his chest. "Respect. I've read how people treated you guys when you got home. Wasn't right."

Leo plays with the leather pouch on his hip. "Ancient history, brother. Sorry, I didn't mean to come off like a jerk." He points to the cast. "Guess I'm on edge from this damn piece of plaster. My leg itches like hell."

"It's gotta be rough." Air Force extends a hand. "I'm Bunzie…Bunzie Martinez. I've been in Atlanta for a few weeks but got to the shelter yesterday. I'm still learning my way around."

"Ah, a newbie. Well, then I guess a welcome is in order." Leo angles his head. "Your name's unusual. Is it a nickname?"

"Nope, my given name."

Leo tries to keep a straight face. "Listen, don't mind my reaction. I never met anyone with the name before. It's different."

"Like my mom, who gave it to me. She's gone now, but she invented it. My dad told me she dumped out letters from a Scrabble game and came up with it."

"You're kidding?"

Bunzie makes the sign of the cross. "Hand on the Bible. I shit you not." He points to the coat rack in the hallway. "Listen, why don't I grab our jackets. We can hang out on the front porch and talk. I'd like to hear about your time in-country. It must have been tough."

"I don't want to talk about the war. It's too painful, but I'll go outside with you."

"Right on. You don't have to say a word about Vietnam. We can hang out, shoot the shit, talk about the weather, or whatever. Hold on a sec. I'll get our stuff." He scrambles into the hallway and makes it back before Leo has a chance to unlock the wheels on his chair.

Bunzie hands him his jacket. "Here, you go. Sun's nice and strong. It's chilly but not too bad." He winks. "Don't you worry. I got a strong pick-me-up. It'll keep us energized."

Leo plays with the controls of his wheelchair and scoots over to the front door. He gets some help from Air Force, who sidesteps the motorized buggy and lifts the front wheels over the doorway. Leo maneuvers his slick buggy outside and plants himself next to the beige wicker swing. Bunzie sits and unscrews the cap from his bottle of Southern Comfort. He hands it to his new buddy.

Leo takes a swig. "Where you from?"

"Originally, New Orleans, but I lived a lot of places."

"Yeah, okay. I should've figured by your accent."

Bunzie takes the bottle. "No way! A lot of people think I'm from New York cause of the way I pronounce my words. What about you? Where you from?"

"Me? Atlanta, born and bred. My head was so far up my butt when I got out of the Army that I couldn't see a ray of sunlight. I hurt all the people close to me, especially my wife. Our marriage was a disaster. I headed to the Keys for a while, then moved to Arizona. I've been living there for more than forty years."

"Wow. You said a mouthful. What brought you back here?"

"My daughter. She's a smart cookie. Found out where I lived and got me to come home. Glad I did. She's getting married in three weeks. Her fiancé's a great guy. I'm happy for them." He taps the side of his wheelchair. "I'll be rolling down the aisle in this contraption when I give her away."

Bunzie hands over the Southern Comfort, digs into his jeans jacket, and lights a cigarette. "You know, I was married once." He rotates his head and lifts his eyes to stare at the clear blue sky. He rolls his Bic lighter around in his hand.

Leo reaches into his jacket. "Divorced?" He pulls out a joint from his inside pocket. "How about a little fire over here?"

Bunzie takes a last draw on his cigarette and flips it over the wooden rail. It bounces off the sidewalk and rolls into the street. "Now, you're talking." He flicks the spark wheel on his lighter.

Leo blows out a cloud of smoke and passes the joint. "Nice shot, litterbug. You learn how to do that in New York?"

"I'm not from New York, never even been there. I told you, I'm from The Big Easy. I ain't no Yankee." He takes a toke, holds in the smoke, and exhales. "Ah, forget it."

"You're way too easy, Air Force. I'm playing with you. Whoever thinks you talk like a Yankee's got to have major ear problems. A Mississippi accent, maybe."

Bunzie draws in more smoke, then exhales. "I told you I was married, right? Well, I'm not divorced. My wife fell off the face of the earth."

Leo reaches for the joint. "Huh? What does that mean?"

"Marla's been missing more than two years and presumed dead. Messed up or what?"

"No, shit? How'd it happen?"

"She and a girlfriend took a trip to the Bahamas and never came back. The authorities say they hired out a boat, went sightseeing, and disappeared."

"Wow. You know you're talking about the Bermuda triangle. Plenty of boats and planes have gone missing in those parts over the years. You have my sympathies, man."

"Thanks a lot. I flew down there, but no one knew anything. The cops weren't any help at all. They told me to take a hike. Weird, huh?"

Leo hands him the joint. "Yeah, man, screwed up. Come on, take another hit. Mellow out."

Bunzie sucks in the smoke, then blows it out. "Sorry, man. I didn't mean to send you on a bummer." His face brightens. "I have a new girlfriend. I'll introduce you to her. He takes another hit. "Hey, I got a good joke for you?"

"Sure, man. Fire away. After what you told me about your wife, I'm about ready for anything."

Bunzie's face betrays his excitement. "Okay, here goes. Mary and Mickey Dunn are potato farmers. They live in Ireland and have three sons. When their oldest, Nealie, reaches twenty-one, he decides he no longer wants to plow fields and shovel cow manure all day. He tells his parents he wants to spread his wings and travel to New York, make a fresh start. Mary and Mickey are sad, but they believe America is the land of opportunity, and they agree to let him go. They drive him to Dublin airport and say goodbye."

Bunzie takes another hit on the joint.

Leo leans forward in the wheelchair. "I'll bite. What happened to him?"

"Hold up. I'm getting to it."

His audience of one smiles. "Okay. Well, get to it already, will you? I think I need to go inside and take a leak."

"Fine. So, two years pass, and they don't hear a peep from Nealie. Buddy, the second oldest, volunteers to try and find him. His mom and dad think it's an excellent idea and give Buddy a lift to the airport. When he gets off the plane at Kennedy, he jumps into a taxi and tells the driver to take him to Times Square in Manhattan. When he's dropped off at Forty-Second Street, he's thirsty and goes into a Blarney Stone. After eating a corned beef sandwich and polishing off a bottle of beer, nature calls. Buddy walks to the bathroom, but when he tries the door, it's locked. He raps on it. A muffled voice comes from inside: 'Hold your horses, buddy, I'm nearly done." Buddy's shocked. 'Nealie,' he shouts, 'I can't believe I found you. Where have you been all this time? How come you never wrote to mom?'"

Leo's head rolls back. "Oh, man, you blew the punchline. The guy in the stall is supposed to say, 'hold on, buddy, I'm nearly done, but I ran out of paper.' Then, Buddy says, 'that's still no excuse for not writing your mother.'"

Bunzie rolls around in his seat. "Your way's much better. I'll use it the next time. I'm working on a standup routine. I think I'd make a good comedian."

"You can't be serious. The joke is older than me, and like you said before. I'm old. You better find yourself a bunch of new material if you don't want people booing you off the stage. I heard there's one leaving in ten minutes."

The two men are too busy laughing to pay attention to the cream-colored Ford Escape that's pulled up in front of the house.

"Is this the Veteran's Homeless Shelter?" the driver asks, slowly climbing the steps.

Bunzie ducks his arm behind his back and conceals what's left of the joint. He points to the sign above their heads. "You read English?"

"Yeah, I can read. You know, my roommate is English. I left him home today. He was feeling tired and wanted to rest."

Leo scowls. "What do you want? Are you a veteran?"

"No, I'm not. I'm trying to find a woman."

"Isn't that what men do most of their life?" Bunzie chuckles.

"No. Not like that," the stranger answers. "This one's named Lisa. She has a boyfriend. I don't know his name, but he's a big guy with short black hair." He raises his hand above his head several inches. "He's tall and looks like he works out."

Leo sits up. "Why are you looking for them?"

The stranger's eyes dart from side to side. "Uh, I owe them money."

"Sounds like a bunch of crap to me." He motions toward the Chevy. "Go...take a hike. Ain't anyone around here like you describe."

Sterling sneers. "Mighty touchy, ain't you? No reason to get all bent out of shape."

"Who the hell is this guy?" Bunzie's lips tremble as he bellows. "Get lost."

The unwelcome visitor scowls. "If you ain't careful, I'll show you who I am. I'll bring my friend back. You two will be sorry if I do."

"Talk's cheap, asshole." Leo flips his pouch around and slides open the zipper. "If you decide to come back, I've got a special surprise for you and your buddy."

"You don't scare me, you old fart in a wheelchair." The interloper slowly backs down the staircase. "You two are lucky I'm in a good mood."

Bunzie swings his arm out from behind his back. "Right, jerk, skedaddle. You almost made me waste good weed."

Sterling doesn't say a word. Instead, he turns and unhurriedly walks back to his car. He waves his middle finger as he opens the door and climbs inside—the tires screech as he speeds away.

Leo closes his pouch. "Strange freaking asshole."

Bunzie passes what's left of the blunt. "Do you have a weapon in there?"

"Of course. I always carry one. You never know who you'll bump into, might as well keep a little protection."

"You're right. The guy's scary." Bunzie's eyes grow large. "How do you think he would have reacted if I hit him with my toilet paper joke?"

"Lucky for him, you didn't." Leo taps his pouch. "You know he would have been toast if he made a move. I like you, Air Force. You're okay in my book, even if your jokes are kinda lame."

28

February 2, 8:00 P.M.
11th Bomber Squadron Restaurant

Sterling cruises through "Outpost Oscar" and passes beneath the upraised checkerboard boom barrier. An old Jeep with a raggedy canvas top and a beat-up transport truck compete for his attention. "Look, Zookeep. Those things are as old as my mama's knickers."

"Stop being cheeky—your mum's dead," his counterpart answers.

Sterling frowns. "It's an expression. I know she's gone a long time. I don't even remember what she looks like."

He backs the black Ford Explorer into a parking spot, kills the engine, and climbs out. He freezes and admires the beat-up French tank guarding the outer perimeter of the main building. "Wow. Look around, Zookeep? This place is trippy, like a scene out of a World War II movie. Why do you think those two jerks picked a place like this to get hitched?"

"Right-o, mate. Don't get your *bollocks* all in a twist. We'll finish off their Otis Redding with a bing-bang," he replies, employing a little of his cockney rhyming slang.

His voice shifts back into his regular vernacular. "Yep. Going to be an exciting wedding reception."

The faded green Jeep with its white "Military Police" lettering stenciled beneath the windshield garners Sterling's momentary consideration. "Check it out!" He points to the miniaturized bomber mounted on the turf across the way. "Hey. Will ya look at the size of that propeller."

Nose art decorates the fuselage beneath the cockpit. "Why d'ya think they called the plane 'Sexy Sadie?'" He leers at the pin-up wearing the two-piece beneath the black lettering.

"I gotta give them credit. Someone sure knows how to pick 'em. The babe's a real beauty." He reads the inscription on the placard pounded into the dirt next to the plane and repeats it aloud. "B-25 Mitchell Bomber, Miniature Fiberglass Replica."

His ear-piercing whistle frightens the middle-aged couple who've just left the restaurant and walks his way. The woman grabs her date's arm as she looks to give a wide berth and avoid the potential troublemaker.

Sterling eyes the artillery piece perched behind a stack of sandbags and stutters past a small stand of trees. Laughing, he strolls beneath the external red-brick portico and yanks open the bulky maroon door. "What say we go inside and check this place out, Zookeep?"

Working his way through the foyer, he hangs a right and finds himself lost in a sea of people.

A young woman's head peeks out from behind an oversized hostess station. "Do you have a reservation, sir?"

He's caught off guard but counters. "Uh, no. I wanna sit at the bar."

She points past the restroom sign hanging over the wall of sandbags. "On your right. Follow the music. Have a good evening, sir."

"Okay. I plan to. I always do."

As Sterling works his way through the maze of people, he finds a corridor filled with black and white photographs featuring brave warriors who've put their lives on the line battling the minions of evil during WWII. Even if he were paying attention, the registry of American heroes would have no validity. His mission of revenge is all that fills his mind.

The vibrant pulse of the electric bass guitar keys his senses. The hollow thunk of the vibrating strings mesmerizes the first-time visitor. The rat-a-tat-tat of the drums and wail of amplified guitars add harmonious definition and draws Sterling closer to the wellspring of rock and roll. The clack of the cowbell adds the finishing touch. "Don't Fear the Reaper" reverberates through the ceiling speakers.

He pushes through the crowd of revelers and finds an empty spot behind the wooden rail. On his right is a rectangular bar jammed with people. Dozens of cocktail glasses hang by their stems above the counter. Beyond it, a dozen occupied hi-top tables fill the cramped area. Framed photos and campy memorabilia from an earlier time hang on the walls surrounding it.

The music nips at Sterling. The song's lyrics provoke mental imagery of repressed emotions and unleash a stream of malignant energy. Dark thoughts consume him.

You people should fear Zookeep and me. Better watch what you say. If you're not careful, we'll plow into you like a freight train with no brakes and put an end to your miserable lives. Everyone needs to show us proper respect. He slaps a hand against his forehead. *Enough. Stop it. Get this out of your head. You're here for a different purpose. There's no time for shenanigans.*

A glint of light reflects off his eye. Sterling focuses and checks out the action over by the high-tops. He finds the source of his fascination. The reflection from a mirrored pocketbook hits him squarely in the eyes once again. An Asian woman and her male companion step away from one of the tables and walk down the steps leading to the dance floor. Sterling rushes over to the vacated hi-top and pounces on a chair. He spreads his arms across the dark wooden tabletop and stakes his claim. "Oh, yeah. Mine now, suckers."

As his eyes adjust to the shadowy environs, he studies the people gyrating on the hardwood. The flash of a strobe triggers the optical illusion of dancers momentarily frozen in place. The next high-voltage spike releases another bolt of energy. With each ensuing pulse, the dancers seem caught in a time warp and strike a new pose.

Sterling's entranced by the light show. He's disappointed when a nimble waitress, her dark hair tied atop her head, flips a cardboard coaster on the table in front of him. "What are you having, honey?"

"Gimme a Mountain Dew, and I'll have a burger with fries." He knows better than to order a beer and get asked to show identification.

"Good choice." She makes a note on her pad. "How d'ya want it cooked?"

"Make it well, fries crispy. How about melting a slice of cheese on the burger?"

"Cheddar?"

He licks his lips. "Sure."

"Okay." She sticks her pad into her apron. "Got it."

The waitress hustles away and moves past the bar. His eyes follow. He turns back toward the dance floor once she disappears into the kitchen. As the song fades out, the pounding bass line from "Dreams," a tune by Fleetwood Mac, takes its place. Half a dozen people, as if entranced, jump off their seats and join the spectacle of flailing arms and looping legs on the dance floor. Sterling smiles and taps his foot in time to the music.

The peppy waitress returns with his Mountain Dew and drops it on the coaster. "Here you go, sport. Your burger's coming out." She slides a glass next to his drink.

"Thanks. Make sure you bring me ketchup and a bottle of hot sauce."

"No problem." She smiles and scampers away.

Sterling pours the fizzy liquid into his glass and takes a swallow. He loves the crisp citrus flavor and zing of the sparkly water hitting his throat as it goes down. Most of all, he's addicted to the energizing sugar rush. "There's nothing better this side of Dixie," he says aloud.

He back against the rectangular slats of the chair and smacks his lips together. Pinpoints of red, green, and blue light crisscross around him. He follows the beams to the mini lights mounted on the wooden rafters. The colors are a harsh reminder of Christmas, a holiday he despises. It's the time of year when his hatred festers and feeds his unquenchable thirst for retribution. Baby Jesus never did a thing for him.

The four young women's boisterous laughter at the next table momentarily lifts him from his doldrums and refocuses his energies. *What gives those women the right to annoy me?* He glares at them.

Sterling detests women, likes men even less. Why should he give a hoot about any of these bastards? Nobody's ever done crap for him worth mentioning. Zookeep's his only friend. For the rest of them, there's plenty of pain and misery to spread around.

A tap on his shoulder. He turns and finds a young woman in a fancy two-piece outfit smiling at him. "Hi. I'm Clara. Are you Kevin?"

"Kevin? Do I look like Kevin to you? You got the wrong guy."

She chews her bottom lip. "Oops. Sorry. I'm meeting my blind date. I saw you sitting alone. You looked the right age. I guess I'm wrong," Clara glances at her watch and frowns. "He's twenty minutes late."

The waitress comes into view. She maneuvers her tray and places a plate and the requested condiments in front of Sterling. "Enjoy." She turns away and serves a sandwich and a cup of creamed corn to a woman at a nearby table.

Sterling adds ketchup and hot sauce to the burger, sneering the whole time. Splotches of grease drip on the table as his teeth sink into the burger. Not one for practicing good table manners, he speaks with his mouth filled with food. "Looks like your guy's a no-show. You better figure out a better way to meet men."

Her face droops. "Seems like it. We hooked up on *Plenty of Fish.* Oh well. I guess I should never have trusted the internet. Guess there are too many fish in the sea. He must have found himself a fresh one."

"Never liked fishing. I don't have the patience for it. I like to hunt." Sterling bites off a chunk of his burger. "I love eating red meat. I don't imagine bringing down animals suits you much."

Clara stifles a laugh. "You're right. I don't like killing animals or catching fish. *Plenty of Fish* is a dating website."

He ignores her remark and gobbles down a handful of French fries. "Listen. Do you know if they have an event calendar around here?"

"Yeah, they do." She motions past the bar. "Outside the bathrooms. There's a bulletin board in the hallway with a calendar of events tacked to it."

Sterling doesn't share his thoughts. He drops his burger and scrambles from the table.

29

February 16, 1:00 P.M.
Georgia Perimeter College Auditorium, Dunwoody

Bradsher Hayes looks around the two hundred and fifty-seat capacity lecture hall brimming with people. He takes a whiff of the apple fragrance from the oversized potted geranium sitting at the edge of the stage.

"I'd like to thank the Atlanta Writer's Club for the invitation to speak today. You know, I'm a Georgia native. Grew up right down the road in Peachtree Corners."

A blowup of a young man wearing an old-style baseball mitt and heavy wool uniform appears on the PowerPoint pulldown screen. Emblazoned beneath the turn of the twentieth-century photo are the words *King of the Southern Diamond.*

The speaker steps out to the center of the stage and plants himself alongside the athlete's picture. "He, my friends, is Arthur Bradsher, my grandad. Everyone likes baseball. It's America's favorite pastime. Contrary to popular belief, Abner Doubleday didn't invent baseball. The game is a variation of a British sport."

"What about football?" hollers a male in the front row.

Brad brings a hand up and shields his eyes from the gleam of the spotlight. "'Love is the most important thing in the world, but baseball is pretty good, too.' Those, my fellow writers, are the words of the prolific twentieth-century philosopher, Yogi Berra."

The boisterous laughter slowly fades.

"Don't worry, my friend. College football is good too. It's next on my list. Everyone, please, settle down. We have a bunch of ground to cover."

He strides to the podium and plays with the buttons on his computer. The photo disappears. The screen fills with a list of pitching statistics.

"John Heisman coined the *King of the Southern Diamond* nickname. Believe me. You can take whatever that man said about sports as gospel. He knew baseball, football, and basketball better than any other person of his generation."

Brad squints into the first row. "You happy now? See, my friend, we didn't leave out football."

He waits for the laughter to die down. "Okay, now. Arthur Bradsher pitched for Trinity College from 1901 through 1905. Today, the school is known as Duke University. Arthur Bradsher's school pitching records are too numerous to relate right now. You can find them all on my website, *King of The Southern Diamond.com.*"

He presses on his computer keyboard. The PowerPoint switches to the original photo. "I never knew my grandfather. After hunting through numerous newspaper articles and performing extensive research, I do now. Many of you must be curious why you've never heard of him before."

The noise from the cycling air conditioner distracts the speaker for a moment. He takes a sip from his bottle of water and paces across the stage. "People are forced to make choices in their lives. My grandfather was no different. When faced with the choice to follow his dreams of professional success in baseball or marry the woman he loved, he came to his crossroad." Brad's lips contour into a frown. "A hard choice, indeed. You'll have to read my book to learn which road he chose."

He fumbles with the hand-held remote again. The projection screen fills with a modern-day photo of a lanky lefthander delivering a pitch to home plate. "You're looking at my special guest on the mound at Dodger Stadium. He worked in Los Angeles for a dozen years and was kind enough to write the forward for my book. I want to introduce you to a hometown hero and a product of Lassiter High School in Marietta. Please welcome, Travis Gentry."

Cheers and whistles of appreciation fill the auditorium. Several people stand and clap.

Travis steps out from behind the blue and white curtain. He raises his hands. His eyes travel across the sea of smiling faces. "I want to thank you all for the rousing reception. I wish the fans in Dodger Stadium would've treated me so kindly when I threw a wild pitch or gave up a home run."

The hall explodes with applause and laughter.

Brad tramps across the stage and joins his guest at the podium. "I bumped into this big guy and his fiancé at a barbeque restaurant in Alpharetta one night."

Travis throws an arm around Brad's shoulders. "Yeah, and this lunatic comes over to our table, hands me his card, and says, 'I don't have to ask if you like baseball; I know who you are.' The next second, he begins pitching this book about his grandfather. If you can't tell by now, he's one persuasive son-of-a-gun."

Brad's lips curve into a broad grin. "Well---not exactly the way you put it then."

"True, but you got me to read your manuscript. I wish I were as good a pitcher in college as your grandfather. Arthur Bradsher was an amazing talent and a couldn't-miss major leaguer."

"Such a compliment means an awful lot coming from you, even if you never pitched for the Braves." Brad plays with the remote, and a banner for the Georgia Veterans Homeless Shelter pops on the screen. "I promised Travis if he joined me here today, he could discuss his latest project. Okay, my friend, take it away."

"Thank you. I'll need my partner to help me with this. She's an amazing person who brought the plight of too many of our war veterans to my attention. Let me introduce you to my fiancé, Lisa Partainian."

She strolls to the center of the stage and waits for the perfunctory applause to fade.

"I'd like to relate a personal experience. When my mom died tragically several months ago, I learned I had two fathers. There's the one who raised me, and the biological dad I never knew existed. Of course, the realization blew my mind. I decided I wanted to find him, and with storytelling in my blood, keep a journal of my efforts. With Travis as my anchor, I found my father and discovered much more in the process. We both learned of the plight of America's patriots and the issues they face when they come home and attempt to reenter society."

She takes a step forward and looks over at Travis.

"Lisa's right," he says. "We've created an organization to help our warriors make the transition. We have fourteen residents living in our group home in Acworth and have plans for more. I'm here today, not only to talk about Brad's terrific book but to ask for your help. It's common knowledge most writers don't have a lot of money. So, we're looking for you to contribute a few hours of your time to our heroes. If you want to give back, please see Lisa or me in the café once the meeting concludes. Thank you all for listening."

The picture on the screen disappears. A black-and-white photo of three rows of young men, all with their hair shiny and slicked-back, takes its place. Displayed on each of their dark sweaters is the large white letter "T." Beneath the picture is the caption: "Trinity Baseball Team Champions."

Brad leans forward. "All right then, how about them Trinity Blue and Whites? Bunch of good-looking guys, right? There's the team picture from 1904 when they won the Southern Intercollegiate Athletic Association championship."

He shuffles over to the screen and points out a young man in the bottom row. "My grandad was team captain. He recorded thirteen of the team's fourteen victories and pitched twenty-five straight no-hit, no-run innings. He lost but one game the whole year, not too shabby a feat."

Travis and Lisa take their cue and exit stage right. They tiptoe down the steps, hoof it up the side aisle of the grey-carpeted auditorium, and exit through the wooden double doors.

••• ••• •••

February 20, 7:30 P.M.
VFW Post, Marietta.

Leo's wheelchair rolls across the stage. He squeezes the handbrake and settles next to his daughter.

Lisa checks the switch on the bottom of the microphone. Lowering the height of the stand, she clears her throat. "We thank everyone for coming to our gala this evening and for their generous contributions. Your gifts will aid the Georgia Veteran's Homeless Shelter in Acworth, as well as establishing a fund for a new suicide prevention hotline."

She holds out a check. "I have great news to share. I'm holding a donation made by Gunther Liebolt Studios for five-thousand dollars." She points to Benjamin, who's seated at a table at the side of the stage. "You are so generous. Thank you. This money will help tremendously."

Benjamin waves as those in attendance applaud.

Lisa curtseys. "I'd like you all to meet my dad. He's a decorated Vietnam vet with two tours under his belt. He's earned a Bronze and Silver Star for valor and is a recipient of two Purple Hearts. Please put your hands together for Leo Miller." She plucks the microphone from the holder and hands it to him.

"Thank you, Lisa. Hello everybody. I'm not too good at this, so if I fumble over my words, blame my daughter. She made me come up here."

He stares blankly at Travis, who smiles at him from the center table.

Leo takes a deep breath and fights off his nervousness. "Here's a special treat for you all. We're auctioning off a week's stay in my three-bedroom home in Prescott, Arizona. The house is roomy, has a hot tub, and there's a stream in the backyard."

Lisa steps off the stage and walks to her fiancé's table. She grabs a rolled-up length of paper.

"If you're not familiar with Prescot," Leo continues, "it has a reputation for having the best air quality in America, unmatched by any other city.

You'll also have lakes all around you and hiking trails galore. You'll find the best Southwestern barbeque at the local cantinas. And, to top it off, your visit will also include the use of my 2011 Race Red Ford Mustang. Make sure you leave the tank filled with gas."

Lisa steps on the stage and unrolls the poster-size photo of the property.

"Nice, huh?" Leo points to the picture. "This is a silent auction. Use the notepads on your tables. The bidding will begin at five hundred dollars."

He motions toward Travis. "Please bring your offer to my daughter's fiancé. Thank you, everybody."

He hands Lisa the microphone and rolls his wheelchair to the edge of the stage. Bunzie and Byron step onto the platform and lower Leo to the brown linoleum floor.

She waits until they finish. "We have a special treat for you all tonight. I want to introduce you to a funny man. He's a former U.S. airman who served two tours in Iraq. He's agreed to provide us with laughter. Please welcome Bunzie Martinez."

Her guest steps onto the stage and takes the microphone. "Thank you for the introduction, Lisa." He turns toward the tables. "Thank you, everybody. On my way over here, I saw a tractor-trailer pulled off to the side of the road surrounded by a dozen cops. It turns out the truck was filled with a load of stolen Viagra. The police arrested those responsible. It turns out they were a group of hardened criminals. I heard the District Attorney was worried. He didn't know if the charges would stand up."

The audience reacts with polite laughter and a smattering of applause. Bunzie eats up the attention and dives straight ahead.

"You know, I almost couldn't make it here tonight. My PTSD was acting up. Yes. That's right. Earlier this week, I had a big problem sleeping, so I went to see my shrink. 'Doc, you've got to help me,' I said. 'I'm haunted by these strange nightmares. Two nights ago, I woke in the middle of the night with heart palpitations and the cold sweats. I had a vivid memory. In my dream, I thought I was a teepee. And Doc, last night, same problem, but when I woke up, I realized this time, I was a wigwam. Strange, right? I'm so confused. What's wrong with me?'"

A loud female voice from a table in the rear interrupts. "Where do I begin? I read all about you online."

Bunzie stares at her. "You're funny. Don't you want to hear what the doctor said?"

"Sure. Why not?" the heckler answers.

"Good. My shrink stared at me and told me she knew what was wrong with me."

The noisy critic jibes him again. "You mean aside from telling unfunny jokes?"

Bunzie pokes back. "Didn't your parents tell you not to act rotten to people with mental issues? Well, that's why I'm going to ignore you."

He turns away from her and waves a hand to the people at the nearest tables. "Would you like to know what my doctor said?"

Two people voice their agreement.

"Okay, then. The shrink said my problem was simple." He pauses for several seconds. "She told me I needed to relax. I'm two tents."

"Good God," the back-of-the-room pest shouts. "You're sick. You might as well camp out in the woods on top of a totem pole."

The room explodes with laughter.

Bunzie keeps a straight face. "Seriously, folks. I've never visited Leo's house in Prescott, but I hear you better bring a plunger along. Tree roots have grown right through the pipes, and the toilets won't flush." He wrinkles his nose. "What a stinky situation. I'm kidding, of course. The house is beautiful. You'll have a great time, so bid high. I know I will."

He tries not to laugh. "Another thing. Make sure you don't turn on the lights after midnight. The roaches will think it signals the start of the fifty-yard dash. That's when you better watch out. They want food and aren't willing to share. No, no. There isn't a roach problem. I made that up. Only mice, but they eat cheese, so you don't have to worry." Bunzie bares his top teeth and mimics chewing.

The audience is feeling his routine. Their laughter and good humor fill the former skating rink and current part-time Bingo hall.

"I'm not from around here. I guess you can tell by my accent. I'm from Louisiana, the Big Easy. I bet you're dying to know how New Orleans got its nickname. There are several versions."

He nods. "Yes, that's right. It's God's honest truth Jazz musicians could find plenty of work at the clubs around Bourbon Street. Some people say the name came because it was so easy to get paid. But I believe it came from a newspaper reporter who compared New Orleans to New York City. People are too uptight in the Big Apple. We live with a lot less stress in the deep south, so that's how the name the Big Easy was born. Now you know."

The female troublemaker stands and smacks the table. "What about Hotlanta? I don't care about New Orleans."

Bunzie points to her. "If you have to ask me about Atlanta, you haven't lived for long beneath the Kudzu and Magnolia trees." He fakes wiping sweat from his brow. "But it's a fair question — the nightlife here in Atlanta is terrific. Last Friday night, I went to a club in the Virginia Highlands. The place was so crowded; you couldn't move. People packed the dance floor tighter than canned sardines soaked in mustard sauce. When the air conditioner stopped working, the bouncers kicked everyone out. They made us all stand in the parking lot. You'll never guess what happened next?"

"No, I don't wanna guess. What happened, fruitcake? asks Bunzie's nemesis. "I can't wait to hear this one."

"Well, I'm glad you asked." Bunzie grabs his collar. "A production company had TV cameras working and used us as extras in a documentary for Animal Planet. I overheard the sound engineer say they were calling it "A Night of Partying with the Orangutans of the Virginia Highlands.""

"You make no sense," the female firebrand shouts.

"I know I don't, but neither did the chimpanzees with the headsets smoking fat cigars. The video director was so busy stuffing bananas and Pumpkin seeds into his mouth; he forgot to give us our cues. Worse yet, when he yelled cut, he spat food all over us."

The audience howls.

Bunzie's critic dismisses his punchline with a wave of her hand. "Oh yeah, I can see why they wanted you in their show. You're as hairy as an orangutan and about as smart as a baboon."

"You're right. My mom went ape when she gave birth to me. But, boy, did she get even. How do you think I got the name Bunzie? My mother, God rest her soul, dumped out a bunch of Scrabble tiles and came up with the name. I consider myself lucky. Where would I be if she used one of the blanks?"

His critic puffs out her cheeks, falls on her chair, and lays her head on the table. Several people in the audience hoot, others applaud.

"Thanks for listening." The comedian takes a bow. "Enough monkey business for tonight."

As he comes off the stage, Leo's there to meet him. "Not bad, buddy. You had them cracking up. You're not half bad."

"Yeah, I know it. I'm still a work in progress. Thanks."

Leo notices the troublesome female making a beeline toward them. He taps the comic on the hip. "Don't look now, brother. We got trouble on the way to River City."

Bunzie spins around and smiles. "No big deal. She's trouble only occasionally. Let me introduce you to Sara. She's my new girlfriend and part of my act."

Leo grips the rails of his wheelchair and laughs hysterically. "You're a sick man, but I love you."

30

February 22, 9:15 A.M.
LA Fitness, Highway 92, Roswell

Lisa gooses up the level on the elliptical machine and continues to pump the pedals. She grunts and eases forward in a rhythmic and controlled motion. Rivulets of perspiration drip from her forehead while grey splotches of moisture accumulate and stain the white Spandex top covering her breasts and stomach area. She focuses on the display at the bottom of the machine's TV screen. It shows 255 calories burned thus far.

Frenetic dance music pumps through her portable headphones, courtesy of the MP3 player strapped to her arm. Lisa's filled with newfound vigor, her energy level boosted by the delight of the future birthing of a new human being. Her head keeps time to the beat of the Miami Sound Machine's rhythm section, and she joins Gloria Estefan with the vocal line to "Conga." Oblivious to the fact she's loud and more than a bit flat, Lisa doesn't pay attention to the people staring or the woman in the red outfit working the piece of equipment next to her, who smiles and shakes her head.

Lights flash on Lisa's elliptical machine. "Oh, yeah. That's the way we do it," she says aloud, happy to achieve her fitness goal for the day. "That's three miles and 350 calories burned, not at all shabby."

She gathers her towel and cell phone and hops down from the machine. Now it's time to shower and slip on a new outfit. Lisa doesn't want to be late. Suzie's meeting her at the East Cobb Roseman's Deli in an hour. They've got some important matters to discuss.

••• ••• •••

Lisa adds cream and stirs her coffee. She lays her spoon down and points to the artfully designed cutout of a mermaid and display of seashells on the wall above the hostess station. "I get a kick out of the funky decorations in this place. If I'm not mistaken, I think it's a scene from *Splash*."

Suzie swivels around. "Interesting. I hate to inform you, but she's the character from *The Little Mermaid*. Didn't you know that? Look over to your right, on the other side of the soda machine, you got Sweeny Todd, and over there by the windows, there's Cinderella."

"Wow. How dumb am I? I've eaten here half a dozen times without realizing who these characters are. Now I know." A huge grin puffs up her cheeks. "Listen. I received great news from Doctor Feinberg, my OB-GYN. The amniocentesis results came back. There are no complications, and the baby is healthy and developing nicely. I'm so happy. My due date is June 20th."

Suzie pats Lisa on the wrist. "Fantastic. I knew your test results would be fine. Look at those cheeks of yours. They're so rosy. You're glowing. It looks like having a baby agrees with you."

"You think so? My hormones are acting up. I have to use a load of blush to cover the blemishes on my face." She pats her stomach and angles a finger along her crotch. "My belly bump shows, and I have a line in my skin that runs down to my hootchie-coochie."

"Badges of honor, girl. You look fabulous. Stop complaining. I wish I had your figure."

"You want my backache too?" Lisa grumbles. "I'll give it to you for no charge. I'm trying to watch the carbs, but it's hard when you need to eat for two people. I'm hitting the gym three days a week to compensate."

Suzie takes a small bite of her blueberry bagel. "They make these fresh here. It's tasty. Want a bite?"

"Please, don't tempt me. I'm watching what I eat." Lisa digs her spoon into the bowl of granola. "Let's go over our plans for this weekend."

Suzie's eyes signal her excitement. "Yes. I can't wait. We're going to have a party you won't forget. Tonight, at my house, eight o'clock. You better not be late to your party."

"Check, eight o'clock. Do you think I'd miss my own bridal shower? We're celebrating my last two days of freedom."

"I think it's up in the air. I heard your fiancé might not let you out of the house. Rumor has it he's a lion in bed." Suzie casts a wink.

"You're sick. Travis isn't like that. Anyway, he and a half dozen of his buddies are having a bachelor party at Scottie's Retreat in Woodstock."

"Scottie's? You know the place is an infamous meet market, don't you? It's filled with Cougars on the prowl. They'll try to steal your man in a minute."

Lisa looks baffled. "I thought Scottie's is a restaurant and bar. I didn't know they had big cats in there." She chuckles at her retort and shovels a spoonful of cereal into her mouth.

"Oh, that's rich. I guess you've never been there. The Retreat is a disco filled with divorcees and single women hungry for action. The dance floor is their favorite fishing hole. They bait their hooks with sexy outfits and leave nothing at all to the imagination. Catch and release is the ongoing policy; bring in a fresh fish, take him home, then throw him back in. I'd be careful if I were you. Inside Scottie's, anything is possible."

"I'm not worried. Travis is used to dealing with pressure." She zips a hand along her body. "Do you think he could give all this up?"

Suzie drums her fingers on the table. "I hope you're right, sweetie." She waves to their waitress, who's busy chatting with a cook in front of the pickup area. "I need to get my check. I have a dental appointment in Dunwoody at eleven-thirty."

"Yeah. I have to go too. I'm meeting Travis in Acworth at noon. Don't forget the rehearsal dinner tomorrow night at Pacella Bakery and Trattoria in Buckhead. Their food is delicious. Wait until you sample the desserts. I've ordered a Venetian table. You'll have to put your diet on hold for a few days. You need to try a little of everything."

"I'm quite familiar with the restaurant. It's a terrific choice. My husband sells to them. I guess this will be my weekend to cheat. I won't dare step on the scale again until Wednesday at the earliest." Suzie hands

Lisa a ten-dollar bill. "Please be a doll and pay for me. I gotta run." She takes the last bite of her bagel. Her chair scrapes against the floor as she stands and grabs her designer handbag. "Remember, the Noyes residence at eight. Take care. I'll see you tonight."

Lisa raises a hand and wags her fingers. "Not if I see you first. Later, girl. Your house, eight o'clock sharp."

••• ••• •••

1323 Old Rockbridge Road, Avondale Estates

Lisa applies the brakes and rolls to a stop in front of the bronze pedestal mailbox. Her eyes stay glued to the horseback rider who's outfitted in nineteenth-century garb and cast in aluminum on the side of the high-end piece of overstated luxury. "Whoa, fancy, schmancy," she says, double-checking the street address.

She pulls to the curb and parks the hybrid. Amazed by the garish house at the crest of the hill, Lisa gawks. Her high heels don't allow much room for error, so she removes them and negotiates her way along the concrete path. When she arrives at the top, she steps into her shoes and rings the bell.

The door swings open. "Welcome to my humble abode." Suzie genuflects.

"My goodness. Your home is huge." Lisa gapes at the structural design of the interlacing bricks of brown and beige comprising the gaudy Tudor-styled home's outer wall. "It must've cost you a small fortune."

"Oh, no. Buzz bought the estate from one of our customers. He got a special deal. The owner sold his restaurant and was planning to move to Italy. I forgot you were never here. We have plenty of room."

"I bet you do."

Suzie glances at her watch. "You're early. No one's here yet."

"An old habit of mine. I hate being late. I think it's a sign of disrespect." She takes a step back and points to the wooden triangular gable under the pitched roof. "Wow. Your house is exquisite." Lisa marvels at the surroundings and manicured grounds. "The landscaper did a terrific job.

He trimmed the bushes so precisely." She takes in a breath. "Smells so fresh, and the grass, what an aromatic scent. You had it cut today?"

"I did. The workers left a few hours ago. They do a nice job for us." Suzie takes Lisa's hand. "Come in. I'll give you the grand tour."

A gold-framed portrait of the hostess and her husband in formal dress is the first thing Lisa notices. Screwed to the bottom of the frame is a rectangular plaque inscribed with raised black letters: The Castle of Suzanne and Buzz Noyes.

The houseguest removes her jacket as she analyzes the painting. "Nice picture. You two make a lovely couple."

"Everybody tells me the same thing when they first see it." Suzie stretches out her arm. "Here. Give me your jacket. I'll hang it for you."

Lisa steps over the cream-colored shag rug and stares at the skylight set into the center of the cathedral ceiling. "Buzz must sell an awful lot of cake. How many rooms do you have?"

"Too many. Would you believe we have five bathrooms? Every Wednesday, we have the maid service come in. The house is impossible to take care of myself. Come on. Let me show you around."

Several vases overflowing with pink and gold roses, white and peach carnations, and red and white chrysanthemums add pleasant elegance and a sugarcoating of sweet-smelling fragrance to the sunlit brilliance of the living and dining rooms.

The flowery splendor of the surroundings and Lisa's stark realization this shindig is her bachelorette party brings on a tidal wave of glistening tears. She reaches into her bag and finds a tissue. "I'm sorry, Suzie. It's hard to believe my mother's not here to share my joy." She tries on a brave face. "Can you believe it? In two more days, I'll be married. I should be floating on air. Instead, I'm depressed and feel I'm walking on eggshells. I apologize."

"There's no need. Travis Gentry is your dream come true. When the two of you broke up during college, I was dumbstruck. Right now, you should be overjoyed. He's your Prince Charming, but you are no Sleeping Beauty or damsel in distress. You're a strong independent woman, and he's lucky to have you. Travis is your perfect match. Come on, girl, wipe those eyes, and cheer up. You're here to celebrate."

••• ••• •••

Lisa smacks her lips. "Too bad, I can only take a small sip. This drink is delicious; it tastes so fruity. What did you say it is again?"

Maggie takes the glass from her. "Amaretto Bourbon Punch. It's an old family recipe made with citrus and maraschino cherry juice."

"Ah, hah. No wonder your relatives have reputations as raging alcoholics." Lisa fidgets on the couch, trying to make herself more comfortable. Any sign of her earlier anxiety or depression has dissolved. She's her jovial self once again. "You know I'm kidding you, right? I love you. Your relatives aren't drunks, sex addicts, maybe."

"Don't you start with me again." Maggie displays mock anger as she drops to the floor and parks herself on a stack of fluffy pillows.

A set of red-tipped fingernails flash as a hand reaches up and passes a joint.

Lisa passes it off to Suzie without taking a hit. "I can't smoke this. It isn't good for the baby. Hey. How about putting on some music. Do you have any Carrie Underwood? I love the song "Blown Away.""

Suzie's eyes sparkle. "Yeah. She's terrific. I was a dedicated *American Idol* fan from the get-go. I voted for Carrie every week. I have all her albums."

"Thanks. I'm going to use the little girl's room first. Be right back."

"Don't use the one in the kitchen. There's a problem with the toilet. You can use the one in the hall by the front door."

"Sure." Lisa rises from the couch and hurries from the room.

Suzie grabs her phone from the coffee table and dials. "Okay. Wait two minutes before you come to the front door."

She disconnects and makes sure Lisa isn't within earshot. "Okay, girls. Get ready for blast-off. Don't give it away. They'll be here in two minutes."

Loud murmurs of delight and anxious giggles fill the living room.

••• ••• •••

Lisa checks her face in the vanity mirror, and satisfied, opens the bathroom door. She takes a step toward the living room but stops, surprised by the triple ding-dong of the overhead chime.

Suzie waves toward the front door. "Would you be a doll and get that, sweetie?"

"Of course." Lisa reverses direction and swings open the front door. Two uniformed police officers stare at her from the bottom step.

"Good evening, ma'am," says the taller of the two. "We've received a complaint from one of your neighbors." The officer peers around Lisa and into the house. "I see you're having a party?"

"Uh, yes, a bridal shower."

He flips open a pad. "How nice, but you need to think of others. The people next door are trying to get some sleep, and you're keeping them awake. They want us to cite you for disturbing the peace."

"You can't be serious. It's only eight-thirty. What time do the neighbors go to bed? And besides, I don't think we're noisy."

The second officer adjusts the brim of his hat. "You're entitled to your opinion, ma'am. Don't try to tell us how to do our job? We need to speak to the homeowners. What are their names?"

"Uh. Suzie and Buzz Noyes own the home." The reality of what she's said hits her. *Oh, my God. This is unreal. These cops are here for a noise complaint and must think I'm a wise ass.*

Lisa slaps on her sweetest smile. "Noyes is the last name of the people who live here. I know it sounds weird, but Buzz is the husband's nickname. It has been since he was a kid. I don't know his given name."

Both policemen remain mute. Each removes their hat.

The shorter one takes a step toward Lisa. "We need to come in and look around. Please move out of the way and let us do our job, ma'am."

Dumbfounded, she shuffles backward. *Oh, no. The girls are smoking a joint in the living room. What do I do?*

Before Lisa has a chance to decide, both men rush past. She trots after them but pauses in the hall by the garish portrait of the homeowners. She notices the music. It's not Carrie Underwood's voice pumping through the living room speakers. "Love to Love You Baby," a sultry dance tune recorded by the disco queen, Donna Summer, fills the house with irresistible dance music.

The cops operate in tandem. They take their time unbuttoning their shirts as they flex their muscular bodies provocatively and surround the guest of honor with an assortment of flailing arms, twisting legs, and rotating groins.

Lisa's face turns bright red. "You two, don't fool me. You aren't the police. You're a pair of prancing perverts."

Both men pull off their shirts. They unhook their gun belts and let them drop to the floor. Ripping off their tear-away pants, the dancers move ever closer to the guest of honor.

Lisa's loosening up. She whirls to the beat of the music and sings along. "Suzie, get over here. Don't leave me alone with these guys. I can't believe I fell for the oldest trick in the book."

The rest of the female guests are on their feet, rotating toward her and the two "undercovered" cops.

31

Saturday, February 23, 5:45 A.M.
Abbotts Bridge Road and Peachtree Industrial Boulevard, Duluth

A-Frame Barricades with yellow crime scene tape attached cordon off the driveways to the Fast Express at the intersection's northwest corner. Revolving blue police lights cast ghostly shadows throughout the dimly lit crossroads and add to the mystery for anyone passing. Standing in the center of the road, a uniformed officer waves a flashlight and directs traffic into the left lane and away from the congested gas station.

"Detective, over here," shouts the female police officer camped at the edge of where the parking lot gives way to a grassy area at the entrance of an apartment complex. "Look at this." She waves a white-gloved hand and points to a patch of dirt. "I found a Bucks knife."

Collins steps away from the black Ford Explorer. He peers at the bloody knife. "Thanks, Officer Parker. Good job. It looks like you've found one of the murder weapons. Would you put it into an evidence bag? Please handle with care."

"Of course, sir."

••• ••• •••

The blond female field reporter exits from the Action News truck's passenger seat and attempts to walk past the two cops standing watch outside the restricted area. Her videographer sets up his tripod and runs his camera.

The brawny African American officer holds out his hand and points to the police tape with CRIME SCENE DO NOT CROSS, printed ad infinitum across it. "Hey, can't you read? Do not cross goes for everyone. You're not special. Get back."

She reads the name on his ID badge. "Hi, Officer Johnson. I'm Janet Crawford from Action Eleven News. What can you tell me? How many victims are there? Have they arrested a suspect?"

"I don't have any details for you, ma'am. Detective Collins is in charge. You'll have to ask him. FBI's on the way. That's all I know."

"Thank you." She swivels toward her cameraman. "Okay, cut. Let's see if we can score an interview with this detective."

While Janet tries to figure out how to achieve her objective, a black SUV with official government plates and a van from Channel Seven News pulls up simultaneously and parks at the fringe of the lot.

The front doors of the SUV swing open. The agents hop out and stride toward the chest-high yellow tape. "Officer Johnson, I'm Cobb," says the taller of the two men. "This is Special Agent Simmons. Where's Collins?"

The uniformed cop points to the grassy area on their left. "Over there, in the brown suit."

"Ah-hah, thanks. We appreciate your help." Cobb nods as Johnson lifts the tape and allows him and his partner access.

Collins straightens up as he notices the agents approaching. He readies himself for the inevitable song and dance to come.

"What do we have?" Simmons asks.

"We got three bodies." The detective points to the small one-story building with the red marquee hung over the double doors. People are visible inside through the large plate-glass windows. Outside, three blue-suited firemen mill around their hook and ladder, munching on sandwiches. A fourth leans against the air compressor while he speaks with a uniformed cop at the far corner of the lot.

"Looks like a robbery gone wrong," Collins says, flipping open his notepad. "We have three vics, all with arms and legs duct taped. There are two males, one's Caucasian, and the second is African American. Both suffered fatal gunshot wounds to their upper torsos. The third vic is female, also deceased. In her case, the cause of death is a knife wound to the throat. It looks like a serrated blade did the damage. We have what we presume is the murder weapon. A fireman found the bodies in the bathroom. Forensics is presently going over the crime scene."

The detective points to the black Ford Explorer. "We found a backpack in the front seat. There's a wallet from Jernkowski's New Year's victim. We also found two watches, gold chains, and a graduation ring from the University of North Carolina. He left a driver's license from another vic and a box of .38 caliber cartridges in the glove compartment."

Simmons scratches his chin. "Looks like he had to get out of here fast."

"Yeah, when the fireman entered the store, the suspect ran right past them. They're giving us statements right now. Jernkowski has changed his appearance. He's shaved his head and beard, but it's him."

"Where is he now?" Cobb asks. "Why isn't he in custody?"

Why's the sky blue?" Collins points to the female policewoman. "Officer Parker's the one who found the suspect's knife. It has fresh blood on it. It appears he dropped it when he made his escape through there." He points past the bushes and grassy areas around them. "I sent two officers to canvass the Medford Arms apartment complex behind us."

••• ••• •••

Johns Creek
Six Miles from the Crime Scene

Sterling directs the red Chevy Malibu north on State Bridge Road. He runs a hand over his bald head and pivots toward the empty passenger seat. "We lucked out, didn't we, buddy? Those scumbag firefighters almost got in the way. Good thing we got out of there quick. It's too bad I left the backpack in the truck and dropped the damn knife when we cut through the bushes. At least we scored a few hundred bucks from the stiffs."

"Good thing, mate. We needed a new supply of bees and honey," his cockney persona answers. "Without any scratch, we'd be three-day-old brown bread for sure."

"Not true, Zookeep. Without any money, we ain't dead. We'd find a way, always have. We got this Chevy, didn't we? Trust in me." He leans forward and grapples with the buttons on the radio. "Damn, can't find a good station." Sterling doesn't give up. He fiddles with the digital tuner. Willie Nelson's nasally tones break through the static, delivering a favorite song, "Pancho and Lefty."

"Which one are you, Zookeep? Lefty? I guess it doesn't matter much. You and me are like Siamese twins, attached at the hip. Strange how things work."

He catches a glimpse of a police cruiser traveling in the left lane and doesn't allow himself to flinch. The well-practiced lawbreaker knows what cops look for and keeps his eyes focused straight ahead. His fingers toy with the pistol tucked between his thighs.

The black-and-white passes and lays some distance between them. Sterling breathes easier and releases the grip on the weapon. "Got us three bullets left. Glad we didn't have to use them up. We'll need them tomorrow. Don't you forget, Zookeep. We have a special wedding invite."

His facial expression takes a more severe turn. "Wouldn't do any such thing, mate. I'm looking to even the blooming Bobby Moore."

"You got that right. Tomorrow, the two of us will get to even the score."

••• ••• •••

Medford Arms Apartment Complex

The Special Agents silently observe while the blue and white ambulance bounces over the broken chunks of asphalt and maneuvers toward the parking lot exit. The revolving red light reflects off the apartment windows as the driver switches on the emergency siren and cuts past a double-parked delivery truck.

"All that trauma can't be too good for their patient," Simmons remarks. "Can you believe how badly management maintains this place?"

Cobb shudders. "Ain't my business. These early morning calls are getting to me, Jack." He reaches into his trousers and comes out with a handkerchief. "I think I may be coming down with something." The agent wipes his nose and inspects the discharge. "Jernkowski pistol-whipped the bastard something fierce. We've got no wallet and no identification. It's too bad the vic lost consciousness and couldn't even tell us his name. His face looks like it went through a meatgrinder."

Simmons retracts his pen and slips his notepad back into his jacket. "Yeah. The paramedic said he might have brain damage, and it'll take a half gross of stitches to close his facial lacerations. A plastic surgeon will need to rebuild his nose. Jernkowski's scarred the poor guy for life."

Cobb rubs an eyelid. "This one's damn lucky. We got three dead inside the gas station. He could've been number four."

His partner adjusts his shoulder holster. "I guess our sicko must be slipping."

"You're not funny, Jack. We've been chasing Jernkowski for four months now, and he's usually not this careless. The lowlife left behind a box of shells. I bet the asshole's running low on ammunition, and the only reason this man's still alive."

"Makes sense. I hope Collins and his people find the vic's apartment. We need the plate number and description of his car. How can we put out a BOLO? Right now, we don't have squat."

••• ••• •••

6:45 A.M.

Collins raps on the apartment door.

"Who is it?" asks the apartment resident, her voice high-pitched and unsteady.

The detective holds his badge up to the peephole. "Police business, ma'am."

"Police? What do you want?"

"Sorry to wake you, but one of your neighbors was robbed and beaten. We're trying to identify him. Would you open the door, please?"

He nods to the female officer standing by his side. They listen to the clack of lock tumblers and the scraping sound of metal on wood.

The door opens to reveal a young Asian woman clutching the collar of a striped red-and-white bathrobe. In her left hand, she balances a coffee mug. "A neighbor? What are you talking about?"

"I'm Detective Collins. This is Officer Parker. Please, your name, ma'am?"

"Nancy Tanaka. I don't understand. Why are you here?"

"We need to identify a victim of a robbery. The incident took place in your parking lot. We don't have a lot of facts and can use your help."

She sips her coffee. "Do you have a picture?"

"Yes, we do, several. The victim's wallet and cell phone are missing. We believe they were taken during a car-jacking." Collins frowns. "The photos are bloody, miss. His nose is busted up, and his front teeth smashed. We know the victim is Caucasian or Spanish, late twenties, early thirties. He has short brown hair, about six feet tall."

Nancy takes a step forward. "You can show me the pictures. I'm a nurse. I have a strong constitution and deal with injuries and illness all day long."

"Okay, but they're pretty rough, so be prepared." Collins lowers his shoulders and wags a finger. "Go ahead, Parker."

The female officer holds out her phone and slowly scrolls through half a dozen photos.

The young woman's face flushes. She moans and shrinks back against the edge of the door frame. The ceramic mug drops from her hand and shatters, spilling the steamy caramel liquid over the parquet floor. "Dear God. It's Ned. He lives in apartment 212, right above me."

"Are you hurt, Miss Tanaka?" Collins asks.

"No, I'm okay. Let me get something and clean this up." She shuffles into the kitchen. The thwack, thwack of her flip-flops, raises a smile on Parker's face.

The detective slides over a wastebasket and picks up a piece of the broken stoneware. Officer Parker bends to helps her boss. Nancy's back with a roll of paper towels. She tears off a length of it and blots up the coffee spill.

Collins rubs his hands together. "What can you tell me about the victim?"

"We're friends. The two of us hung out together a few times." Miss Tanaka drops the balled-up material into the garbage pail. "I can tell it's him by the guitar tattoo on his forearm. This is unbelievable. How'd it happen, detective?"

"We have a decent idea, but at this point, it's mostly conjecture. Please, can you tell me Ned's last name? And do you know what type of car he owns?"

"His last name's O'Brien. He has a red Chevy, a Malibu, I think."

"Thanks, Miss Tanaka." The detective pulls his phone from his jacket and hits speed-dial. "Hello. Give me Lieutenant Gillis, please."

As he waits for the squad commander to answer, his eyes stray to the young woman. She swipes at the last of the spilled liquid and throws the paper towel into the wastebasket.

His boss's voice breaks through the dead air. "Who's this?"

"Collins, here. Our victim's name is Ned O'Brien. He owns a red Chevy. It's a Malibu, we think." He listens for the response. "Yes, that's right, Ray. Okay, great. Thank you."

The detective slips the phone into his jacket. "The lieutenant's checking the DMV database. He'll get the plate number, and dispatch will put it out over the air."

"Terrific, sir." Parker drops the last piece of broken pottery into the trash.

"Miss Tanaka, we're ready to go." Collins offers his hand. "Will you be okay?"

"Yes. I'm fine." Her knee creaks as she stands. "What about Ned's parents? I know they live in Tucker. Will you contact them?"

He pulls out his pad. "Of course. What apartment is the manager in?"

"Reggie takes care of the buildings. He's in 306." She raises a hand and aims a finger at the adjacent building. "First floor."

The detective jots down the information. "Thank you for your help." His attention shifts to the uniformed officer. "Let's go, Parker. We'll get the key and find the vic's phonebook."

"You got it, boss."

••• ••• •••

2:45 P.M.

Kroger's, States Bridge Road off Jones Bridge

A red Chevy Malibu straddles the solid white lines at the center of the supermarket's parking lot. The passenger door is ajar. Three police cruisers and a black Ford Explorer SUV Interceptor box in the unoccupied vehicle.

Three of Alpharetta's finest, two with pistols drawn, approach the stolen car from behind. The third uniformed officer, a female, carries a shotgun in the ready position, finger poised over the trigger.

She hangs back ten feet. "Sergeant Holmes, I'm in position."

The senior officer points at the passenger side door. "Carson, go around. I need you to stay alert." Holmes secures his weapon and dons white cotton gloves.

Carson's body tenses as he yanks on the handle of the driver's side door. Nothing but discarded chocolate bar wrappers lay scattered over the front bucket seats. The sergeant looks over the seatback. A polystyrene foam coffee cup and the white packaging from a sausage McMuffin lay crumpled on the carpet. He reaches beneath the map pocket on the front door and activates the trunk release. He stretches across the front seat. "Look in the trunk. I'll check the glove box."

Carson holsters his pistol. He pulls a pair of gloves from his pocket. "Sarge, there's an umbrella and a Braves bag filled with workout gear." He lifts the bag and drops it on the concrete. "What about you? Did you find anything?"

"Hold on a sec." Holmes examines a wallet. He reads the name on the driver's license. "Ned O'Brian. I found the car owner's license. There's also a gym card, a store receipt from Macy's, and a couple of photos. If O'Brien had any credit cards or cash, they're long gone."

The sergeant pushes himself up from the seat and turns toward the SUV. He waves to the driver. "Griffin, call dispatch. Tell them the vehicle's clean. Our perp's in the wind."

32

Saturday, 3:50 P.M.
Delta Terminal, Atlanta

The young taxi driver reaches for his fare's suitcase while a super-sized green bus, followed by several cars and three passenger vans, rumble past.

Hobie's long locks flutter with the rush of winter air and the explosion of rancid-smelling exhaust fumes. With the back of his hand, he swipes at his nose in a reflex action and shivers. "Yecch. Stuff stinks. Damn greenhouse gases are wrecking this planet."

The driver's expression doesn't change.

Hobie deflects an intended helping hand and shields his guitar case with a hip. "I'll hold on to this one, dude."

"That's fine, sir," the cabbie says, speaking in heavily accented English. He nods and walks toward the tail end of his vehicle.

His passenger pulls open the back door and slides the hard case across the carpet. He climbs in and pushes his instrument against the far door.

"Where to?" asks the driver as he scrambles inside and presses a button on the taximeter.

Hobie reaches into his jean's pocket. "Take me to 3143 Sandy Hills Road, in Marietta."

"I got it. Where are you coming from?"

"L.A., but where I'm going is much more exciting."

The driver pulls away from the curb and peeks at Hobie in the rearview mirror. "I've never been to California. They say it's going to fall into the ocean one day."

"Ahh. Don't listen to any of that. People have been saying the same thing for years. We have an earthquake every once in a while, but we deal with it." He scrutinizes the driver's permit glued to the dashboard above the glove box. "Where are you from, Sayed? You don't mind me asking, do you?"

"No, not at all. I'm from Pakistan. I was born in Peshawar. You heard of such a place?"

Hobie takes a few seconds before he answers. "Hmm. Can't say I have."

Sayed watches his passenger's eyes through the mirror. "Okay. What about the Khyber Pass? That's a famous trade route bordering Afghanistan. There was a big battle there in the middle of the eighteenth century. The Valley of Peshawar is where the tough Pakistanis come from."

"Yeah, okay. I remember something about the battle from history class. I thought the Persians won that one."

"Yes, they did, but my people fought hard and died bravely."

Hobie fights off a smile. "Uh, huh. Interesting."

The driver takes a quick peek into the rearview mirror. "You know many Kabul refugees came through the pass when the United States first occupied Afghanistan. They settled in my city. Peshawar became overcrowded, and life got hard. My father saved up enough money, and we came to the states in 2006."

"You've been living in Atlanta ever since?"

"Oh, no. First Chicago for two years. I've been in Atlanta since 2008. I love it here. You're lucky. You were born here in America."

"I agree. Best country in the world. We have our problems, but you can follow your dreams and do whatever you want in life as long as you have the drive."

"Funny, you say that. I do this job because I like to drive."

Hobie falls back against the cushions and smiles. "I'm sure you do."

••• ••• •••

Lisa fights to maintain her balance as Molly frolics between her legs. She avoids crashing into the arm of a chair and strides across the almond-colored cork floor. Taking a gander at her guest through the peephole, the mistress of the house unlocks the front door.

A massive smile accents Hobie's three-day growth of beard. "Don't you be shy, girl." He drops his suitcase and guitar case and throws out his arms. "Come to your uncle. Where's my hug?"

Lisa blocks Molly with her leg and steps out on the porch. She drags the door closed behind her and embraces the old Snakeskin Prophet. "I don't want the cat to get out. How was your flight."

"Good, but my arms are tired."

Lisa shakes her head. "Oh, cut it out. That's an old one."

Hobie stops flapping his arms. "Yeah, I know, but I couldn't help myself. He drops his hands to his side. "It's great to see you again. How's Travis, and where's my man, Leo?"

"Travis is good. Come inside. You're all my dad's been able to talk about for the last week. He's so excited."

She keeps an eye out for the cat as she pushes open the door. "Dad, Hobie's here."

"Get over here, corporal," Leo shouts, rolling his wheelchair into the hallway.

Hobie leans over and hugs his old buddy. "I heard about your injury, man. How are you doing otherwise?"

"Better than you. At least I shaved."

Lisa turns her head toward the living room. "Let's get out of the hall."

Her dad backs his wheelchair over the Turkish rug and parks himself next to the couch. "Sit over here, you long-haired hippie freak. Let's talk."

Molly trots after them and jumps into Leo's lap. She kneads his chest with her front paws, closes her eyes, and makes herself comfortable.

Hobie chuckles. "Boy, the cat's got poor taste. Seriously, aside from your leg thing, how the hell have you been, my brother? Can you believe we haven't seen each other for forty years? God, how time melts away. It seems like last Wednesday when our squad was out humping the boonies."

Leo pats him on the back. "Yeah, I agree. It's great to see you. My kids told me all about their trip to California. I'm happy you did so well with your music. I remember you with your guitar and big mouth entertaining us back at basecamp. I thought you sang like a three-legged frog in heat, but I guess somebody must've liked your music. I followed your career until you jumped the shark after your third album and sold out."

"Yeah, right." Hobie grips the front rail of the wheelchair. "Do you remember the nickname you gave me back then?"

"Limp dick?"

"Very funny. Don't tell me you've forgotten. You used to call me bullfrog. Coming from the likes of you, I always thought the name was a compliment. Hey, I hear you didn't do badly for yourself. Lisa told me you owned your own construction company."

Leo puffs out his chest. "Yep, damn successful one, too."

"Jeez, I'm surprised. You always had a talent for blowing things up. Strange how that works."

Lisa raises her hand. "Enough! Will you two stop; It sounds like you've been married for forty years."

"Come on, girl." Leo swallows hard. "We're having a little fun. We love each other, for crying out loud."

"Travis, get in here. These two jokers opened a few screws and can't find their Philips heads to tighten them." She harrumphs. "Can you believe this? They haven't seen each other in four decades, and all they can do is rank on each other."

Her dad swivels his wheelchair and faces her. "Relax, Lisa. We don't mean anything by it. Neither of us is serious. We're brothers. It's the only way we know how to show our love. Lighten up."

"What's happening here?" Travis asks as he tosses a squeaky rubber mouse on the floor. Molly leaps for it and grapples with the toy rodent. "Don't upset yourself, babe. You know how these people are."

Leo rolls his chair forward. "What does 'these people' mean? What are you insinuating?"

Travis cracks up. "You're way too easy, Pop. Can't you tell when I'm putting you on? You and your buddy need to cut yourselves some slack. Let's get ready. We have an hour-and-a-half until the rehearsal dinner."

Lisa gestures toward the door nearest her fiancé's back. "Hobie, your room is all set, right through there. Just follow Travis. You have crisp sheets on the bed and towels in your bathroom. Grab your stuff and get situated."

"Cool. Listen. Should I bring my guitar along tonight?"

"Hmm. What do you think, hon?"

Travis offers a thumbs-up. "Might not be a bad idea. A little entertainment can't hurt."

••• ••• •••

6:15 P.M.
Pacella Bakery and Trattoria

The four-inch slingback heels click-clack as Suzie slinks across the dining room's marble floor. Dean Martin's honeyed strains breeze through the in-ceiling speakers as the statuesque blond whizzes past a wall anointed with depictions of Popes, Bishops, and Cardinals.

She wrinkles her nose at the spicy aroma of Italian delicacies overpowering the sweet scent of her perfume. Voices hush, and heads turn to catch a glimpse of the lithe beauty. An anxious waiter drops a dish.

Her golden locks and bright lipstick glisten in the overhead lighting. She pays no mind to her flock of new admirers and strolls beneath the sculpted wooden archway and into the private party room.

Lisa greets her maid of honor. "Oh, Suzie. You look terrific." She wraps her fingers around her arm. "No cops coming to this one, I presume?"

A sardonic smile settles on her friend's face. "Not this time. If you're lucky, a firefighter or two might show up, but don't tell any of the boys. It'll get them jealous." The demure beauty presses a finger against her lips. "Shhh. Keep the secret."

"You're crazy. You know, I haven't seen your husband since high school. Where is the master baker?"

"Stop talking dirty." Suzie giggles. "You're bad."

Lisa frowns. "Hey. I didn't mean it that way."

"Oh, don't be such a prude. I'm joking. Buzz is in the front of the store with Mario, Pacella's big boss. They're discussing business. We bake half of the restaurant's cheesecakes, their Italian Chocolate Mousse, and Frosted Rum Cake."

"Whoa! Sounds like an awful lot of sugar."

"It is. We supply the restaurant with chocolate eclairs and a whole variety of cookies too."

"That's what I would call a sweet business." Lisa taps her friend's shoulder. "Get it, sweet business?"

"Oh, please." Suzie wears an exasperated smirk. "I'll let your dopey pun pass. I think Buzz is taking an order from Mario. He should be right in."

Lisa looks past the half-dozen unoccupied tables and points to one on the far side of the room. A row of photos, publicizing the Southern Mediterranean countryside's beauty, hangs on the wall above it. A man outfitted in a brown leather vest and matching cowboy hat sits chatting with Travis and Leo. The Westerner's long silver locks extend down the middle of his back. "I'd like you to meet our friend from California. He'll be playing a few songs at the dinner tonight and tomorrow at the reception."

"I wish I could grow my hair that long," Suzie whispers. "The old cowboy looks like a leftover from the sixties. He probably hasn't paid a visit to a hairdresser since then."

"Oh, stop it. Hobie's much more than that. He and Leo are buddies. They served together in Vietnam."

"Uh, huh." Suzie looks unimpressed.

"Hobie was famous back in the day. He was Viper and sang with The Snakeskin Prophets."

"Never heard of them."

"They were popular in the mid-seventies, won a couple of Grammy Awards, and sold a bunch of records." Lisa nudges her. "Come on. Let's go over. I'll introduce you."

Before they have a chance to move, Suzie's husband strolls into the room and hands his wife a folded-up piece of paper. "Here. Put this in your bag. I took a nice order."

"What am I, your secretary?" She smiles and opens her black leather purse. "Buzz, you remember, Lisa, don't you?"

"Of course, and congratulations. Buzz leans close to Lisa and whispers. "A little birdie told me you were the one who opened the door when the cops paid a visit to our house last night."

"Suzie, what's wrong with you? How could you tell your husband? I thought whatever happens at a bridal shower stays at the bridal shower, like Las Vegas?" She gives Buzz a peck on the cheek. "Neither of you better say a word to Travis."

"You can count on me." He waves a hand. "Don't worry. I'm not about to spill the beans. Your secret's safe with me."

Lisa prods Suzie with an elbow. "The same goes for you."

Her friend throws up her hands and waggles her fingers. "Come on, girl. Don't act like such a dork. It's all in good fun, but no problem. Like the Go-Go's song says, my lips are sealed. She motions toward the lone occupied table. "How about introducing us to your dad and the mysterious songsmith?"

Lisa peers at the clock on the wall. "Sure. We have fifteen minutes before the rest of the guests start to arrive."

••• ••• •••

Suzie sways in front of her seat at the main table. "Your attention, your attention, please." She balances a microphone in her left hand and hoists a glass filled with champagne with her right. Her eyes move from table to table. "Thank you for coming tonight. Please raise your glasses. Let's make a toast to Lisa and Travis. May their union be filled with health, happiness, and good times."

She takes a sip of bubbly. "I'd like to introduce the bride-to-be, Lisa Partainian, soon to become Lisa Gentry."

Whistles, applause, and a few shouts follow.

Lisa takes the microphone. "I appreciate all our family and friends who are here tonight. I'm having a great time." She points to her brother. He sports a full brown beard speckled with flecks of blonde and grey. "You may not know this, but Jared's my baby brother. Since he's been in Lima, he's decided to sport the Che Guevara look."

Jared raises both hands and waves. His girlfriend clutches his arm and laughs along with the two-and-a-half dozen guests.

"I'd also like to introduce Rosita Peres, my brother's girlfriend." Lisa extends a hand in her direction.

People at the tables applaud. The sudden center of attention's naturally rosy cheeks turns a bright red.

Jared rises and drops to one knee. "Rosita, I'm in love with you and want us to spend the rest of our lives together." He digs into his pocket and pulls out a small box. Flipping it open, he displays the diamond ring. "Will you marry me?"

She sighs. "*Madre mia.* Of course, I will, my sweet." Her words carry a Peruvian musical inflection. She reaches into her bag and comes out with a tissue. "*Te quiero mucho mi amor.* I love you so much."

Lisa uses a napkin and dabs at her eyes. She lifts the mike. "How romantic. And the craziness has only just begun. Everybody, I'd like to introduce you to our friend and funny man, Bunzie Martinez."

The budding comedian reaches for the microphone. "Thank you for the introduction. Lisa, you made a mistake. People say I'm funny-looking. You know, Jared's proposal reminded me of some sage advice my father gave me years ago. 'My son,' he said, 'when you find the girl of your dreams, remember there are three rings that are the keys to a successful marriage. The first is the engagement ring, the second, the wedding ring, and believe it or not, the third is suffering.'"

The place breaks up.

Bunzie smiles at the reaction. "How much more happiness can we witness today, people? And speaking of witness, on the way over, I got hung up in a traffic jam. Tow trucks finally showed up and removed a pair of wrecked cars from the middle of the intersection. I rolled down my window while I waited and listened to the two people involved in the collision, who were trying to explain what happened to the responding officer."

The comedian waves a hand. "It was crazy. Both drivers claimed the accident wasn't their fault. One of them, a young man, said he arrived at the intersection first, so his car had the right-of-way. The second driver, an older man with a broad Italian accent, claimed that traffic needs to proceed according to state law in clockwise order. 'If you knew this, how did the wreck happen,' the cop asked. The older man shook his head. 'What did you expect me to do? My clock hasn't worked in a month. I closed my eyes, prayed, and stepped on the gas.'"

Bunzie laughs harder at his punchline than does his audience. "Only kidding, folks. Seriously, though, I have a buddy who's a police officer in the Ninth Ward in New Orleans. He told me something fascinating. Thieves went wild one night and stole all the toilet seats from the stationhouse. The detectives figured those responsible must have been wearing gloves because they couldn't find any fingerprints. It's no wonder the police are stumped. And worse yet, they have nothing to go on."

This joke, the guests appreciate. They laugh and applaud.

"Speaking of waste, I'd like you all to put your hands together for our buddy, a Vietnam vet, and a talented musician and singer, Hobie Blake, better known as Viper. His group, The Snakeskin Prophets, had a bunch of hits back in the Stone Age when Neanderthals first invented music by banging dinosaur teeth together. You ladies better be careful. Don't let this guy wrap his arms around you. There's a rumor circulating his tongue might be poisonous." Bunzie places the microphone back on its stand. "Viper, come on up here and serenade us."

33

February 24, 6:20 P.M.
11th Bomber Squadron Restaurant, Banquet Room

Lisa clears away the watery veil clouding her eyes and flutters past the portable cocktail bar angled into the corner of the room. She gives a slight nod to the attendant, partially hidden by the collection of bottles in front of him. He returns her greeting with a smile as he pours orange-tinted liquid from a silver shaker into a trio of hurricane glasses. On the dark wooden wall behind him dangle depictions of Franklin D. Roosevelt, Winston Churchill, and Charles De Gaulle, a reminder of who had the grit and resourcefulness to defeat the Axis Powers in WWII.

A strobe flashes as a female photographer snaps away. Lisa climbs the dais steps, gathers the train of her winter-white wedding dress, and falls into a wooden wingback chair. "Travis, I'm so happy. Today is the best day of my life. It seems unreal." She leans over and removes a speck of dust from the lapel of his black pinstripe suit.

He grabs the edge of the white cotton tablecloth and guides his chair closer, careful to avoid the basket of red and pink silk roses decorating the place setting. "Oh, no. I'm the lucky one. You're the yin to my yang, the Robert Plant to my Jimmy Page." He reaches into the midst of the cloud-like blooms of baby's breath and plucks a red rose from the cheery arrangement. "Here, doll, for you."

"Thanks." Lisa drops the odorless flower on the table. "I have to say those are interesting analogies. Where'd you come up with them?"

"Let's see now…."

The restaurant manager tramps into the banquet room and climbs the two steps to the dais. "Miss Partainian, Mister Gentry, it's time. The pastor's here." He motions to a waiter supporting a tray of drinks. The server nods, lays his cache of beverages on an empty table, and follows his boss into the main room.

Several more bursts from the strobe throw intermittent sprays of brightness across the banquet room. Travis glances at his watch. "Nice. Twenty minutes late." He reaches out a hand. "Are you ready, my lady?"

Lisa swipes at her eyes again. "I could use a drink…of water." She raises her glass and takes a sip. "Ah, much better."

Travis gives her a playful nudge. "A new chapter in our book of life is about to begin?"

She takes his hand. "I have plans for a new project. This scene will take place in my sequel. I think I'll call the new book 'Pleasant Surprises,' wiseguy."

"Sounds good. Why that title?"

"Easy. After my mom died, many surprises came my way. You and I reconnected. We're getting married, and we have a baby's on the way. What about all the friends we've made and the veterans we've helped. Our lives are like snowballs gaining momentum as they surge downhill. I know this is the start of great things." Lisa lifts the red rose from the table and angles the stem behind her ear. The strobe flashes as the photographer captures the moment.

Travis gives his fiancé a wink. "This picture will be a good one. You look like a sexy Flamenco dancer. You'll fit right in when we visit Spain."

"Oh, yes. I can't wait. I've never been to Europe. Our honeymoon should be exciting."

Travis lays a hand on the small of Lisa's back and brings her to him. "You're right. It will. But it's you who rocks my world. Your attitude and outlook inspire me. You've shown me the word "quit" doesn't exist. To you, any obstacle is simply a temporary restraint. That's one of the qualities I admire in you."

She squeezes his hand. "Stop it. Whatever I am is because of you. It's the faith you have in me that keeps me strong. With you at my side,

I'm confident and unafraid." Lisa pats her stomach and plants a kiss on his cheek. "I guess we should make a move. We're going to add a new member to our family. Let's make this whole shebang official."

••• ••• •••

Jernkowski shifts the green Chevy Blazer into reverse and backs into a parking spot reserved for the disabled. "I guess a man's got to know his limitations." He climbs down from the truck and slams the door. "You know my man Dirty Harry said that, Zookeep? We're both like him. Neither of us takes any shit. You know I'm right. I've watched all of Clint Eastwood's movies at least twice. He's one bad mutha, like you and me."

He eyes a couple walking past and opens the top three buttons of the denim jacket. His hand reaches into the waistband of his jeans. The handgrip of his pistol is frosty to the touch and reassuring. He adjusts its position and creaks his neck from side to side, listening for the pop. "Ah. There it is. Yes, much better."

The muscles in his face contort. His demeanor takes a more cautionary turn. "You're a strange bloke," he says, his voice coming in the accented cockney cadence. "Dirty Arry's a made-up ero, mate. Don't be a twit. You know all this fluff is Hollywood hocus pocus, created to sell tickets. Forget this mumbo-jumbo. You've got to pay attention. It's time to take care of this Bag for Life and her Pot and Pan. They're about to get a muzzle full of our Lady from Bristol."

Jernkowski pulls at the brim of his Georgia Tech baseball cap. "I know. We need to be as wily as foxes on the hunt." His steely grey eyes refocus. They stare past the antique artillery piece and concentrate on the entrance to the restaurant.

If someone were there to see him, his body English would affirm the confidence and double helping of resolve he carries inside. "I know, Zookeep." Sterling pats the bulge beneath his store-bought Levi's blue jean jacket. "We got our medicine distributor right here. The Partainian brat and her gorilla boyfriend are about ready to pick up their prescriptions from our little homemade drug store."

He bops his head to the music he alone can decipher as he bounds toward the front door and a date with destiny.

••• ••• •••

Travis has spared no expense and hired a faux flower specialist to design a floral masterpiece that, in his opinion, rivals the combined works of Georgia O'Keeffe, Claude Monet, and Vincent Van Gogh.

The craftsman earned his money by creating a multidimensional array of dazzling colors brightening the wooden archway overlooking the three steps leading to the sacred altar. Fifty guests surround the raised platform—most lounge on folding chairs. The photographer continues to take random shots of the crowd as she backs down the center aisle.

On a piano bench parked next to the platform, Hobie plucks at his guitar strings, adding romantic overtones and tuneful sensitivity to the celebration.

Leo's wheelchair sits next to the musician, a huge smile pasted to his face as he watches his daughter and her partner mount the steps. Bunzie and Byron sit behind them on fold-up chairs.

"This reminds me of my confirmation," Bunzie whispers. "But at mine, my mother hired a hooker to dress as Mother Superior…"

Byron pokes the jokester with an elbow. "Cut it out. Now's not the time. Shhh. Pay attention."

Leo overhears their exchange but doesn't comment.

Bunzie waves a hand. "Okay, okay! He fixes his eyes on the marital couple as they find their places at the altar and bow their heads. Hobie lays his hand on the strings running over the guitar's sound hole, then leans the instrument on the stand next to him.

The crowd quiets as the pastor raises his hands. "May God bless this union. In a world filled with uncertainty, two extraordinary people have found each other. May their love grow and be blessed by the Lord on high."

He nods to Lisa. She reaches for a carafe filled with red wine and pours the liquid into a tall glass at the center of the small round table. Travis lifts the second beaker and adds white wine.

The minister cradles the glass and lifts it above his head. "Let this mingling of spirits signify the merging of these two people's hopes and dreams for a life filled with happiness. May their relationship be fruitful, filled with love, and built to stand the test of time." The holy man brings the glass to his chest and swirls the liquid. "Each of you, please take a drink of this symbolic blend."

Lisa reaches for the symbol of abundance. "Thank you, Reverend Charles." She tastes a drop and passes it to her partner.

Travis takes a swallow. He hands the wine to the pastor.

"Now, the rings, please." Charles smiles and places the drink on the table.

The groom slips the thin gold band on his bride's finger.

She whimpers and slides her matching token of love and faithfulness past the knuckle of her man's left ring finger. "I wish mom could be here."

Travis rubs her hand. "I'm sure she's watching."

Reverend Charles raises his arms. "I now pronounce you husband and wife. You may kiss the bride."

••• ••• •••

Black stanchion ropes block off either side of the center aisle connecting the main room to the banquet hall. The Zookeep killer has inserted himself into the crowd of curious onlookers and hunches down behind an older man in a tan tweed sports jacket. Sterling's fingers massage the grip of the .38 Special in his belt. He swivels his head to the left, then right. *Good. No one notices me. These idiots are all too busy staring at the Partainian dame and her overgrown clown.*

With his heartbeat pounding in his ears, the stalker digs a hand inside his belt and clutches his weapon. A shiver travels up his spine. *Hey! What the hell? The guy in the wheelchair, I know his face. He's the jerk who gave me a hard time on the porch at the veteran's shelter.* He notices Bunzie. *And, will you look at that! There's the other twitch who was with him.*

Sterling hates everyone, especially those two. The only person in this world he doesn't despise is the Zookeep. As far as he's concerned, everyone else deserves to die. But now's not the time to go messing around. Whittling down the odds will come later. He turns up his collar and pulls his cap lower to screen his eyes and protect his identity.

His fingers lock the hammer on his pistol. The sound is almost imperceptible, but to the keyed-up wedding crasher, it's as loud as the clang of a church bell on Sunday morn. His beady eyes flit from side to side, checking, taking note of the people around him.

The photographer backs down the aisle, snapping candid shots of the bridal couple. The strobe flashes as she clicks away.

Sterling cackles. "Nice day for a wedding."

A woman on his right smiles and nods her agreement.

He taps the forefinger of his right hand against the trigger housing of his Lady from Bristol. He's prepared to exact vengeance.

••• ••• •••

Bunzie rolls Leo's wheelchair toward the entrance of the banquet room. They are second in the procession, following behind the bride and groom.

The aspiring jester is careful to avoid catching Lisa's Chantilly lace train in the big wheels of the cumbersome transport. His focus on this vital detail alters his peripheral vision and limits his awareness of the crowd of people lining the aisle. He leans forward and whispers into his passenger's ear. "Some shindig, huh?"

Leo beams and rolls his head back. "You're right. This is great. I'm so happy for the two of them. My daughter couldn't have found a better man."

Bunzie nods. "Your son-in-law is one lucky guy himself. Lisa's a great lady."

The delighted dad throws an arm around his pal's neck. "Yeah, I'm truly blessed." His eyes follow the showcased couple as they stroll down the aisle, soaking up congratulatory hugs and kisses.

The photographer lowers her camera and steps around Lisa and Travis. She points her finger at Leo. "Please, Mister Miller. Let me get some photos."

"Sure thing." He nods and raises a hand. "Hold up a sec."

The silver spokes of the big wheels stop rolling. The father of the bride straightens up and accommodates the professional shutterbug with a smile. Bunzie tries a photo-bomb and shoves his face next to his friend's head.

The blonde cameraperson waves for him to move aside. "Yeah, yeah. I know you're hilarious, wiseguy." Please, out of the way."

That is the instant when both Lisa and her dad recognize the man in the denim jacket and Georgia Tech baseball cap who steps to the outer fringe of the crowd. The rays from an overhead spotlight highlight Sterling Jernkowski and the pistol he brandishes.

Waves of panic run through Lisa's body. She shrinks back.

Leo's left hand reaches for his carry-pouch. "Get out of the way!" he shouts, gritting his teeth and digging for his .357 Magnum. The index finger on his right hand presses the motorized chair's toggle control. The chariot races forward.

Bunzie rushes at the bewildered photographer. He jerks her arm and drags her out of the path of the large metal wheels.

Leo raises the pistol to eye level and squeezes the trigger while the stunned assailant readjusts his aim and fires off two rounds. Leo's upper body recoils as one of Sterling's bullets strikes his left shoulder. He bounces off the black cushion at the rear of his wheelchair and drops to the floor.

Lisa shrieks. Travis guides her to the floor and covers her with his body.

Bunzie yowls and falls backward. Blood spurts from his lower left quadricep, three inches above the knee. He grabs at the wound with both hands.

The reports from the gunshots generate chaos. Shouts ring out. The acrid odor of ignited gunpowder and the scent of fear hangs in the air.

People scream and dive for cover. Others, looking to flee the firestorm, rush headlong from the room.

Leo's aim is picture-perfect. His single projectile bores into Sterling's forehead, exploding through the back of his skull, and shattering a plate-glass window. Pieces of glass sail through the adjacent hallway as the slug embeds itself in the wooden door jamb of a utility closet.

Several tiny slivers prick the face of a waiter and send his silver tray clattering to the floor. Half-a-dozen plates filled with Caprese salads tumble and shatter as they hit the deck

A young woman on the way to the bathroom has her arm gashed by a jagged piece of glass. Teetering forward, she bounces off the sandbag wall and collapses.

Blood spatter spills out from Sterling's wound and stains the faces and clothing of those unfortunate enough to be standing in the vicinity. The mortally wounded killer staggers backward. As his body collapses, his head collides with a free-standing ashtray and bounces off the three-foot-high piece of tempered steel.

Two people grab their phones and take videos. Half a dozen calls go out to 911.

Ken, the former combat medic, pulls off his belt and ties it around Bunzie's injured thigh.

"Are you okay?" Travis asks, helping his bride from the floor.

Lisa battles with her emotions. "I'm not hurt. Oh, dear Lord. I can't believe this." She gasps when she realizes the extent of her father's injury. "Please. Travis, you've got to help him."

Her husband rushes over to his father-in-law. Byron is already tending to Leo. He leans him forward and presses a cloth napkin over the entry wound. "Quick, Travis," he shouts. "Get his back."

The groom slips out of his suit jacket and rips off a sleeve. He folds the fabric and presses it against the exit wound on Leo's rear shoulder. "Hang in there, dad. Help is on the way."

The restaurant manager rushes in with a handful of dish towels and crouches next to the overturned wheelchair. "Here. These are clean. I got them from the laundry." He hands a cloth to Travis and another to Byron, then drops the balance on the floor.

Lisa's cheeks are lined with tears as she kneels next to her father. Suzie hustles over and offers a handful of tissues. "Calm down. It'll be okay."

The bride unfolds one and wipes her eyes. She cradles her father's hand. "Are you okay, dad?"

Leo grimaces. "It hurts like hell. What about you?"

"I'm fine. I'm worried about you."

"Don't be. I'll survive." He moans softly. "How's my buddy doing?"

She turns toward the far side of the room. Bunzie's sitting up, his back supported by one of the chairs. Two men from the veteran's shelter are helping him.

"How is he?" Lisa hollers, her voice husky and unsettled.

The wails of the approaching sirens echo throughout the property. Ken finishes tightening the tourniquet on Bunzie's leg and delivers a thumbs-up. "Don't worry. This dude is tough." He sits back and glances at his bloody hands. "Would you throw me one of those towels?"

"Of course." She picks two off the top of the pile and hurries across the room.

••• ••• •••

Two paramedics push their way through the crowd and into the main room. They glance around for a moment before one rushes to help Bunzie. The second throws a chair out of the way and stoops next to Sterling. Her fingers find his carotid artery.

"Help my dad," Lisa screams, her face contorted by grief.

The paramedic ignores her remark, intent on her mission of mercy. She zips open her medical bag and finds a pair of latex gloves. "Sorry, miss. Head trauma takes priority."

"My father should take priority. Please, help him." Her voice trembles with emotion.

The request turns moot as four of Atlanta's finest and the second pair of EMS workers wend their way through the horde of people. The paramedics make a beeline for Leo.

With three stripes on his sleeve and Bailey inscribed on his nametag, a burly policeman leads the group of uniformed officers into the main room. He inspects the array of overturned chairs, the injured, and the dozens of bewildered faces.

He presses the button on his walkie-talkie. "Dispatch, this is Unit Thirty-One, Alpha. Code twenty-one. On-scene at 11th Bomber Squadron. Request Code Ten. I need a detective unit, my twenty, ASAP. We have multiple casualties. Do you copy? Over."

A business-like female voice erupts from the speaker of the portable unit. "Roger, Thirty-one, Alpha. I copy. Code Ten. Over."

Lisa points to Sterling. "Sergeant. You're looking at the Zookeep killer."

Bailey takes a step toward the paramedic and her comatose patient. He twists the volume knob on his radio. "Central, be advised. We have negative active shooters. Inform SWAT to return to base. I repeat, negative active shooters. Signal SWAT. Code Four. Discontinue code Nineteen. Inform Swat, return to base. Over."

The female voice barks through the speaker. "Affirmative, Thirty-one, Alpha. Code four. Will advise SWAT of status asap. Over."

The paramedic working on Sterling looks up at Bailey. Her dark eyes telegraph the message even before she utters a word. She peels off the blood-encrusted gloves. "It's no good. He's gone."

The sergeant stoops and retrieves Sterling's pistol. "No sweat. You did your best. Look on the bright side. A lot of people will be breathing a lot easier tonight. A serious killer is off the street."

Bailey lifts the wireless two-way. "Central, this is Thirty-One Alpha. I have a sit-rep. Over."

"Roger, that. Go ahead, Thirty-One Alpha. Over."

"Be advised, Command, Code Twenty. Supervisor request. We have a Signal Forty-Eight, suspect DRT from a GSW. Advise GBI to respond. We also have two vics with non-critical GSWs and two additional with superficial injuries from debris. We need an additional paramedic crew. Over."

"Roger, Thirty-one, Alpha. Signal Forty-Eight. One DRT. Code Twenty. Will advise GBI and EMS. Out."

Bailey clips his radio to the side of his belt and motions to a female officer. "Pratt, you and Peters make sure no one leaves the restaurant.

Carson, help me set up some tables." He waves a hand, pointing to the area against the wall. "The Detective Squad should be here any minute. We have a lot of people we'll need to interview."

34

8:38 P.M.
Emanuel Slossen Memorial Hospital on Johnson Ferry

"Paging Doctor Reynolds. Paging Nurse Pratt." The female voice with a distinct nasally tone resonates through the overhead public address system. Except for the newlyweds, the dozen people in the waiting area pay no attention to the announcements. "Code Blue, Triage room 4, STAT."

Travis strokes a hand through his hair. "Jeez! When are they going to tell us anything?"

His bride scrambles from the chair. "I've lost my patience. I'm going to find out what's happening." She gathers their coats. "Come on. Let's talk to someone in admitting. We've already been here for half an hour."

Travis chugs the rest of his Dasani water and stands. He stretches out his arms and flips the plastic bottle into the trash can between the pair of elevators. "Yeah. Okay. I'm with you. When do you think the police will release the other guests from the restaurant?"

"Let's worry about that later." Lisa grabs his hand. "We need to find out about my dad." She points to an enclosed booth at the far end of the hall.

An aide in green scrubs rolls an empty gurney past them in the hall. As they approach the main entrance, an orderly pushes a man in a wheelchair through the automatic doors and helps him outside into a waiting cab.

Travis taps his knuckles on the tempered-glass partition at the reception station.

A blonde female, barely out of her teens, lifts her hands from the computer keyboard and smiles. "Hello. Can I help you?"

Lisa notices the nametag clipped to her breast pocket. "Yes. I hope so, Rochelle. My father and his friend came in by ambulance, both victims of gunshot wounds. The police are keeping everyone out. We haven't heard a word about their condition, and we're concerned. Do you think you might find out their status?"

"Of course." The perky blonde bounces from her chair and gawks at Lisa's attire. "You're wearing a wedding dress?"

"Yes. I am." She tugs on Travis's arm. "This is my groom."

Rochelle removes her glasses and lays them next to the computer. "I guess congratulations are in order. If you give me a minute, I'll get someone out here to relieve me." She looks at her watch. "It's about time for my break." Lifting the wired receiver, she flicks a button on the base of the large telephone keypad. "Brenda, would you come out here? It's time for my dinner break, and I need to use the restroom, stat."

The young woman replaces the handset and tightens her eyes. "I didn't want to explain. It's easier to get her to relieve me if I say I need to go." She points to the snack machines across the hall. "You can wait over there. I'll see what I can find out for you. I know the police are in there with them."

Lisa raises a finger and taps her chin. "Maybe, they're taking statements."

"I don't know." The receptionist shrugs. "Am I correct in thinking the shooting happened at your wedding?"

"Yes, at my wedding. Incredible, huh? This day I'll never forget."

The young woman lays a hand on the glass divider. "Who could?"

"We'll meet you over there." Travis points to the concession area. "If you can do anything to help, we'd appreciate it."

A dark-tinted glass door slides open within the restricted area. A young black woman with orange cornrows and bright red bangs barges into the cramped workspace. Rochelle's relief balances a stack of bulging file folders in her arms. Her mouth opens and closes as she cracks her gum.

"Okay. I'm here. I have to finish these damn reports before I go home at midnight. I'll need to use your computer."

She drops her bundles of forms on a side table and falls into the black swivel chair. "Go ahead, Shelley. I got you."

••• ••• •••

8:58 P.M.

The patter of voices and squeal of rubber soles brushing across industrial vinyl floor tiles echo in the corridor.

Travis closes the *Sports Illustrated* and drops the magazine on the table. "Look, babe. Here comes our new friend."

Lisa sets her issue of *Cosmopolitan* on the next chair. Her eyes follow the approaching pair of staff members. "I hope they have some good news for us."

"We'll find out in a few seconds. Let's think positive."

The newlyweds stand in unison.

"Hi again, y'all." Rochelle turns toward her companion. "This is Doctor Goldsmith. He's the chief attending in the E.R. tonight."

The doctor removes his black-rimmed glasses. "Yes, hello. How do you do? I'm sorry for the delay in notifying you of your father's condition, but it was hectic in the E.R. earlier."

Lisa seizes the doctor's hand. "Please, tell me. How is he?"

"Mister Miller is on his way to surgery. We've controlled the bleeding, cleaned his wounds, and though he declined at first, agreed to receive morphine to neutralize the pain. The bullet fractured his scapula and infused bone fragments into his subacromial space. We're administering a regimen of antibiotics to fight any infection."

Lisa drops into a chair. "Will he be okay?"

Doctor Goldsmith's body stiffens. His shoulders go back. "Your father will undergo a relatively simple procedure. Without any unforeseen complications, his prognosis is good. At this point, we can't be certain if there's any nerve damage associated with the trauma. Time will tell."

She slides forward in the chair. "How long will my dad be in surgery?"

"Hmm." The doctor hesitates. "Not my department, but I estimate about three-and-a-half hours, plus he'll spend an hour or so in recovery."

"Uh, huh. I understand."

"What about his friend?" Travis asks.

"Mister Martinez? He's already in the O.R. I can't comment on specifics or treatment due to HIPAA laws, but his condition is stable. I can tell you he wouldn't stop with the jokes while he was in the E.R."

"Oh, my." Lisa taps her cheek with a trio of fingers. "Sounds like our Bunzie."

Doctor Goldsmith resets his glasses on the bridge of his nose. "He's a corker, alright. There's nothing you can do for either of them right now. I suggest you go home and come back around one-thirty. Once your father's awake, an orderly will transport him from recovery to the I.C.U., on the third floor."

••• ••• •••

February 25, 1:37 A.M.

Clad in jeans and a navy-blue coat, Lisa pauses at the crossroads of intersecting corridors and surveys the grey and yellow directional sign hanging directly above her. She releases her husband's hand and points a finger past the grey arrow and into the brightly lit passageway. "The ICU is this way."

As they pass the cafeteria, Travis presses his face against the glass and peers into the darkened dining hall. "Too bad the place isn't open. I could use a coffee."

"I'm good." Lisa pulls him along. "Come on. The doctor said Leo should be awake by now. I want to see him."

"So do I." He lets go of her hand and reaches into the interior pocket of his black leather jacket. He pulls out a pack of Lifesavers and drops a red candy on the tip of his tongue. Want one, hon?"

"No, thanks. Let's move."

He shoves the roll back into his pocket and hurries after her. "Hey. Wait up, baby."

As they turn left into the ICU, Detective Collins strolls out from the waiting area. "Hey. How are you doing?"

Lisa shuffles back a step and leans on Travis.

The dark circles beneath the detective's eyes bear witness to his sleep-deprived employment profile. "Sorry. I didn't mean to shock you. I've been here since midnight. Sergeant Bailey briefed me at the restaurant. Both of you should count your lucky stars."

Lisa sighs. "You're right. I thank God. My father saved our lives. Boy, I tell you, this is some night."

Collins thrusts his hands into the pockets of his frumpled trench coat. "I asked at the nurses' station. Your dad's getting transferred to room 304. He should be brought in from Recovery soon."

Her eyes follow the movement of a nurse as she pushes a patient in a wheelchair past them. "Oh, good. I can't wait to see him."

The detective pulls a small blue-covered notepad and a ballpoint pen from his coat. "As far as I'm concerned, Leo Miller's a hero and deserves a medal. Who knows how many more people Jernkowski would have killed if your dad hadn't stopped him? I do need to ask him a few follow-up questions."

"Please, give him a chance to get his head together. I'm sure he'll be groggy." Her request sounds more like a directive.

"Of course." The detective flips open the pad. "Were you aware your dad carried a pistol?"

Travis frowns. "No, the subject never came up. Why? Is there a problem?"

"Actually, no. Leo has a carry permit."

Lisa's eyes widen. "He does? How do you know that?"

"Do you remember I spoke to you when you were in Prescott?"

"Yeah. So?"

"Well, I checked the state database. Since Georgia and Arizona share a reciprocity agreement on firearms, no harm, no foul."

"Oh, my goodness." She brings a hand to her chest. "Whoa. You gave me heart palpitations there for a minute."

"Sorry, not my intention. I'm just stating the facts." The detective glimpses his notes. "Aside from your father and Mr. Martinez, additional injuries at the restaurant were kept to a minimum. The two people who suffered lacerations from flying glass were both treated and released."

Lisa motions toward the circular counter and array of computer screens at the epicenter of the I.C.U. "Travis, let's go talk to the nurses, see what's happening with my dad."

Collins closes his pad and shoves it back into his pocket. "Go ahead. I'll wait out here."

••• ••• •••

7:30 A.M.
Intensive Care Unit, Room 304

Travis rests the capped Styrofoam cup and a small white bag on the wood-grained Formica tabletop bordering Leo's bedside. "Got you a jelly donut, hon. The coffee's the way you like it, two sugars, extra cream."

Lisa ignores the stringent odor of the hospital disinfectant filling the room and reaches for the cup. "Thanks, doll. You're the best." She takes a small sip and frowns. "Ugh, taste's bitter."

Leo's right hand carefully works the remote control at the side of the bed. A persistent low-frequency hum from the overhead air vents drowns out the drone of the TV commercial and the beeping of the heart monitor. "Hard to get comfortable with this IV and blood pressure monitor hooked into me." He moans as he flexes his upper body forward, then settles back against the bed. "How's Bunzie doing?"

Travis sidesteps to the foot of the bed. "He's doing well. Bunzie told me this hospital experience inspired him to create some new material. His girlfriend's jotted it down. She read some of it to me. Sounds wacky."

Leo chuckles. "I have to give him credit. His brain never stops working. He's one crazy son-of-a-b."

Lisa bites into her donut. "You hit the nail right on the head."

A plump, light-skinned black man with permed, platinum blonde hair gooses open the door and deposits a filled food tray on the table. He lowers the height of the rolling cart and positions it over his patient's upper thighs.

The orderly taps the grey badge clipped to the breast pocket of his green scrubs. "I'm Darius. If you need anything, let me know. Enjoy your breakfast."

"Thanks, brother." Leo gives a slight head nod as the attendant walks toward the door.

Lisa lifts the circular tray cover and notes the ominous skies as she lays the silver lid on the windowsill. "Looks like a cloud's on the way."

She steps forward and examines the tray. "Let's see what we have. Want some oatmeal?"

Her father licks his lips. "Whatever it is, I'm starving. The last thing I had was a cheeseburger around noon yesterday. You'll need to feed me. I don't want to take a chance on pulling out any of the tubes."

"No problem." She stirs a portion of raisins into the bowl. "Here it comes. Open wide." Lisa guides the spoon through her dad's partially open lips. She wrinkles her nose and stares at the tray. "Umm. You can smell the bacon. Looks nice and crisp. Want a piece?"

"Naw. Bacon's not my thing." Leo licks his lips. "How about a slice of toast, and would you put some jelly on it?"

Travis reaches for the tray. "Let me give you a hand, babe." He breaks open the grape jelly packet and digs out a portion with a piece of plastic cutlery.

"Fine with me, butterbean." Lisa feeds her dad another spoonful of the warm mixture. "I knew there had to be a reason why I married you." She lifts a strip of bacon and chews it. "Umm, good. It's nice and crisp."

••• ••• •••

February 27, 8:00 A.M.
Room 304, Two Days Post-Surgery

"Time to check your vitals, Leo."

The patient's eyelids flutter before his gaze fixes on the short-haired redhead in blue scrubs standing beside his bed.

"I'm glad you're here, Tanya. Something's not right."

"What's the problem?" she asks, pulling on a pair of Latex gloves and attaching a pulse oximeter to his forefinger.

"I'm feeling off. I'm nauseous and pretty sure I have a fever. My chest feels tight whenever I take a deep breath."

The nurse slides a thermometer between Leo's lips and checks the readings on the cardiac monitor at the head of the bed. "Hmm. Blood pressure is one hundred over forty-eight. Your pulse rate is ninety-five."

Leo convulses. "I'm cold. Could I get another blanket?"

"Sure thing." Tanya hurries to the closet and gathers a tan blanket from the top shelf. She unfolds it and throws it over him. "Hope this helps." She removes the thermometer from his mouth and frowns. "102.4. I'm going to page Doctor Patel and have him look in on you. I'll be right back." She unclips the pulse oximeter from his finger and stows it in a compartment on the side of her cart. "I'll see you in a few minutes."

35

1:45 P.M.
Sandy Hills Road, Marietta

The sizzling riffs decrypted by Jimmy Page's magical hands fill the computer room with Led Zeppelin's distinctive take on psychedelic rock.

Hearing her familiar ringtone, Lisa coaxes Molly from her lap and reaches across the tabletop for her smartphone. "Hello."

"Hi. Is this Mrs. Gentry?" asks the female voice.

"Yes. This is Lisa. Who's this?"

"This is Nancy McCloud. I'm the chief social worker at Emmanuel Slossen Hospital. I coordinate your father's care."

"Uh, hello. Is anything wrong?"

"Well, …there's been a change in Mr. Miller's condition."

"What do you mean, change?" Lisa says, her voice filled with puzzlement.

"It's hospital policy not to divulge a patient's situation over the phone, Mrs. Gentry. You should come to my office as soon as possible. We need to talk. I'm in the Administrative wing on the first floor, room 112B. I'm here today until six."

Lisa takes a deep breath and tries to gather her wits. "Please, tell me. Has something happened? You're scaring me."

"I'm sorry. All I can say is your father has suffered a setback. We'll discuss it when you get here. If I were you, I would make it sooner than later."

"Yes. Thank you. I'll be there by three." Lisa disconnects the call and pulls up her phone's contact list. She scrolls and presses the entry for her husband.

••• ••• •••

2:50 P.M.
Victoria Slossen Memorial Hospital

The black Mercedes skirts past the emergency room entrance and takes a sharp left into the underground lot. The driver's electronically controlled window opens. Travis grabs a ticket from the automated machine and guides the sedan inside. Driving around to the second level, he noses into a spot fronted by a thick concrete column.

He shifts gears and kills the engine. "Okay, babe. Please, don't forget. You need to take it easy. You're carrying precious cargo."

Lisa closes the top button on her beige coat and fetches her pocketbook. "I promise I'll be careful." She taps her belly lightly and opens the door. "I know. I need to take care of the little person inside me."

Travis hustles around the back of the car and offers his hand as she steps out. "I love you more than life itself. You and the baby are both a part of me. I don't want anything to go wrong."

"You shouldn't worry so much. I'll be fine."

The couple pays extra care as they negotiate the white-lined blacktop and walk to the hospital's main entrance.

Lisa wraps her arm around Travis. "Baby, I'm concerned about my father. The conversation with the social worker didn't fill me with much confidence. Mrs. McCloud said Leo suffered a setback."

"Look. We don't know anything yet. Let's hope for the best and not assume the worst."

As the automatic doors slide open, a slight frown accentuates the laugh lines at the corners of Lisa's mouth. "You're right, hon, but the truth is still the truth."

••• ••• •••

Room 112B, Nancy McCloud's Office

Lisa's face blanches. "This is horrible. How could his blood be filled with bacteria?" Her eyes search the social worker's face for any type of reassurance. "In layman's terms, what does this mean?"

Mrs. McCloud holds out a printed sheet of paper. "Here's a fact sheet for you and Mr. Gentry to look over. Your father's immune system is compromised, and he can no longer eliminate the pathogens present in his body. The chemicals released to combat infection have entered his bloodstream and overcompensated, causing an adverse reaction."

Lisa glances at Travis. "I understand the concept. What are you doing to help him?"

"We're doing everything we can," Mrs. McCloud answers, snatching a pen from her desk and doodling on a pad. "The lab results show an abnormally low platelet count and an excess of acidity in his blood. Kidney and liver functions are irregular. Dr. Patel is sure your father is suffering from severe sepsis. He's ordered a CT scan to confirm the diagnosis,

Lisa rummages through her bag. She pulls out a crumpled tissue and wipes her eyes.

Travis shifts in his chair. "What actions are you taking to combat his illness?"

Mrs. McCloud drops her pen and reads from a sheet of paper. "Mr. Miller is receiving broad-spectrum antibiotics, IV fluids, and he's hooked up to a ventilator to assist with breathing. The doctor prescribed phenylephrine to increase his blood pressure, but unfortunately, his organs have begun to shut down. I'm sorry to say his condition is rapidly deteriorating."

"Please. Don't tell me this." The tissue drops to the floor. "You need to do anything you can to help him."

"We are, Mrs. Gentry. We're doing everything humanly possible. Doctor Patel is in his office right now. We should go upstairs and speak with him. He can answer any of your questions."

••• ••• •••

4:30 P.M., I.C.U.

Dr. Patel, Nurse Tanya, and a male P.A. hover over the bedridden patient. An oxygen mask covers Leo's nose and mouth. His breathing is shallow and labored, the skin tone ashen white. The gauge on the cardiac monitor shows a blood pressure reading of 85/45 and plummeting. His pulse rate is 135, and it's continuing to climb.

"Please," Lisa shouts from inside the doorway. "There must be something more you can do. You can't let him die."

Two females dressed in blue scrubs dash into the room.

"Lookout, please. You're in my way," the larger of the two shouts as she brushes against Travis's hip.

"Oops. Sorry, miss." He swivels out of her path, avoiding a major collision.

The nurse doesn't reply. She and her counterpart move to Leo's bedside.

Doctor Patel spins around and points his finger at Travis. "Please. You and your wife must leave the room. Let us work." His voice surges with intensity. "Right now! Please, go. You're in our way. The patient's gone into septic shock. Please wait inside the visitor lounge by the elevator."

••• ••• •••

5:15 P.M.

Lisa rests her head against Travis's chest and sobs. He folds his left arm around her shoulders and gently lifts her chin with the fingers on his right hand. "Honey, please. You need to take it easy. The baby feels every wave of emotion."

She sniffles and wipes her eyes. "I know, but it's so hard to control myself. My father's dying. I've had such a brief time with him. It seems so unfair."

Travis stares into her eyes. "I'm with you every step of the way. Please, take a deep breath."

He fills his lungs and exhales. "Come on. Do it with me."

Lisa balls up her fists and follows his example. Her body trembles as she gulps in the fresh air.

"That's right," he says, dropping his hand. "Try again. In and out. In and out."

The sound of shuffling feet and the rush of air interrupt the couple's impromptu exercise session. Doctor Patel enters the waiting room. His stoic facial expression conveys the news he's there to deliver.

He lowers his body into a chair next to Lisa. "I'm sorry to tell you this, but we've lost Mr. Miller. Our staff made every effort to save him, but his illness was too severe. He did not survive."

Lisa digs her fingers into Travis's forearm. "How could this happen, Doctor Patel? He was under your care."

The physician leans forward and clasps his hands. "We're not miracle workers, Mrs. Gentry. Your father's preexisting conditions were mitigating factors. Mr. Miller had diabetes and suffered from stage four kidney disease. Unfortunately, his immune system couldn't fight off the post-surgical infection. In the end, an insufficient supply of blood to his tissues resulted in ischemia and end-stage organ dysfunction, leading to his death. I'm so sorry."

Lisa twists around and burrows her head into her husband's chest.

Travis rubs a hand over her back as he considers the doctor's explanation. "I realize the only things guaranteed in life are death and taxes. I do understand the seriousness of Leo's illness and appreciate the efforts of you and your staff. My wife is distraught. She also lost her mother recently."

"My deepest sympathies," the doctor replies. "If you'd like to speak to a chaplain, please tell the head nurse. She'll arrange it." He stands and pushes the door open. "Again, I'm so sorry about your father."

Epilogue

September 25, 10:12 A.M.
The Eternal Flame Memorial Cemetery

Lisa shoves the baby's bottle into the diaper bag and examines the notepad on the seat next to her. She catches her husband's eye in the rear-view mirror. "Travis, this is the entrance to Tranquility Gardens. Leo's in section 163, plot 14A. I guess you can park right here. It's not far."

Her husband nods and brings the pebble-grey SUV to a stop. He boosts the gear shift into park and shuts the engine.

Lisa lifts the baby from the safety seat and gently lays his bonnet-covered head on her shoulder. "Would you be a doll and get the carriage for me, honey?"

The infant squirms inside his periwinkle-blue blanket and lets out a massive burp. His mom wipes his mouth with a washcloth and nestles him in the crook of her arm. "I think your son takes after you."

Travis chuckles. His finger pokes at the dashboard instrument panel. "Oh, you're funny. Give me a minute. I'll come around and get you."

The electronic hum of the motorized rear liftgate melds with the chirps of the cardinals, red-breasted robins, and distinctive warbles of an American redstart. Travis lifts his head and searches amongst the branches. The sight of the birds flitting about beneath the canopy of cedars and magnolias lifts his spirits. The constant head-bobs of the yellow-bellied sapsuckers pecking in the upper reaches of a tall white pine brings a tiny smile to his face. He grunts and collects the stroller from the back of the truck. Opening its legs, he sets the wheels on the ground. "All ready," he says, unlocking his wife's door. "You can give me the baby."

Lisa lifts their fifteen-pound hope for the brightest of futures and hands him to her husband. Travis plants a kiss on their son's cheek. He lays the baby inside the stroller and fastens the safety straps. The infant objects with soft whimpers but hushes and settles back to sleep.

Retrieving the diaper bag from the back seat, Travis hoists it on his shoulder. "This is such a peaceful spot, hon. Your dad would be happy to know he has all these tall trees and feathered friends to keep him company."

"I'm sure he does." She unlocks the wheels of her son's carriage and tucks in the sides of the blanket. "Both he and my mom aren't gone. I feel them around us every day. Their spirits are part of our lives."

Lisa pauses at the memorial garden filled with star-shaped asters, bluestem goldenrod, and an assortment of colorful mums. "Look how beautiful." She breathes deeply, drawing in the musky scent. "Smells so light and breezy."

Travis skims his fingertips along his love's jawline. "Since when did you become a fragrance aficionado?"

She leans over and checks the baby. Satisfied, Lisa takes her husband's hand. "My nose is ultra-sensitive ever since the art of the diaper change became such an integral part of my life." They both laugh softly and share a tender kiss.

"I love you, honey," he says. "Please, you need to give me a little credit. I change the baby some of the time."

"I know you do, and I appreciate your help." Lisa waves a hand toward the second row of granite headstones beyond the flower garden. "He's right over there. Come on." She wraps her fingers around the handle grips, and guides the stroller to the edge of the manicured grass.

Travis rests the diaper bag on the ground and unzips it. He lifts out a plastic bag. "Here, doll."

"You carry the baby," she says, locking the wheels on the carriage and taking the package. "It's time for little Leo to meet his grandfather."

The baby fusses, then settles down. Travis cradles the infant as the family strolls past a half dozen markers.

"This is it," Lisa says, pausing in front of the miniature American flag embedded in the dirt next to the grave. The chiseled dedication on the tombstone reads:

Loving Father, Vietnam Veteran, American Hero
LEO A. MILLER
Born: April 23, 1951
Died: February 27, 2013
The World Is A Better Place Because Of His Sacrifice

Misty-eyed, Lisa contemplates the engraving. "Yep, the world sure is, Dad." She reaches into the plastic bag and removes a multi-colored plaque. "I'm sure Leo would be happy to know my book will be out before Christmas." She leans the plastic-coated replica of the front cover against the headstone.

The centerpiece of the eight-and-a-half by eleven print is a lagoon filled with tranquil blue waters. A dozen sailboats float in the distance. Cloudless skies surround the brilliant golden orb of nature's light. Fields of southern magnolias dot the banks. In the foreground appears a side view of a hatless soldier in dress greens. He grips the handles of a baby carriage; its precious cargo is fast asleep.

The black print across the head of the page is the title of the work, *Lullaby for Leo.* At the bottom appears the author's name: Lisa Partainian Gentry.

Travis settles beside his wife. "Your father would love the title. And I think the cover's fantastic. He'd be bursting with pride. I know I am."

She reaches for the baby. "You've helped me so much."

"I didn't do anything. It was you who did the research and work. I was strictly along for the ride."

Lisa lays her head on his shoulder. "Oh, no, honey. With you at my side, I feel I can climb mountains. You make me a better person. I know it sounds like a cliché, but your inner strength lifts me."

The baby kicks at his blanket and brings his hands to his face.

"It's too bad little Leo will never know his grandfather." She gently rocks the baby. "My biggest regret is not having more time with Leo." She stares at Travis. "If not for him, our little family wouldn't be here today. He saved our lives."

"Yes. Your father was a great man."

The baby smacks his lips together and sucks on one of his fists.

"Leo's looking for his bottle." Lisa takes a final look at the gravestone and the memento resting on it. "We should go."

"Okay, honey." Travis stoops and picks up three stones. He lays them on the top of his father-in-law's tombstone and drops his head. "Thank you for giving us our lives, Leo. We owe you everything."

Acknowledgments

I have the following people to thank for providing
inspiration and encouragement:

Marie, my partner in all things.
My children, Scott, Alan, and Lisa.
Our writing group: Brad, Ed, Harry, Ken, and Sharon.
A big shoutout to Harriet Louden. You have moved on,
but your spirit hasn't faded.
Thank you to my brother, Glenn, and his wife, Leslie.
To my parents, Jeanette and Larry, who taught me to care about
others and share in the joys of life.

Born and bred in Brooklyn, Michael attended the Fashion Institute of Technology in Manhattan before pursuing his first love, to sing in a rock and roll band.

Uncle Sam had an alternative plan and decided the author would be more valuable as a member of the Eleventh Armored Cavalry Regiment in Vietnam. After fulfilling his military obligation, he returned home and traveled the country searching for the soul of his generation.

Today, his mission continues; only now, his laptop serves as his mode of transportation. He hopes you'll stick out a thumb and ride along.

Made in the USA
Columbia, SC
09 October 2021